# Soft Lies and Hard Truths

by

Dalia Dupris

This is a work of fiction. Names, characters, places, and incidents are either the product of the author's imagination or are used fictitiously, and any resemblance to actual persons living or dead, business establishments, events, or locales, is entirely coincidental.

**Soft Lies and Hard Truths**

Cover Art by *The Wild Rose Press, Inc.*

The Wild Rose Press, Inc.
PO Box 708
Adams Basin, NY 14410-0708
Visit us at www.thewildrosepress.com

Publishing History
First Edition, 2024
Trade Paperback ISBN 978-1-5092-5351-7
Digital ISBN 978-1-5092-5352-4


Published in the United States of America

"I have a suite at the inn. Come home with me."

Her eyes narrow as she shakes her head. "I couldn't inconvenience you." She runs a finger through her hair. "I don't want to be a nuisance. I'll figure something out, even if I don't know what it is yet." Her voice trembles even though she sounds determined.

"You could never be a nuisance. I'm staying in a cottage. It's big enough for two people." I quickly decide not to mention that it's the honeymoon cottage; I don't want her to think I'm trying to make a move on her when she's vulnerable. "I promise you that the place is spacious." Faint, crescent shaped shadows under her eyes confirm her sleepless night. "Say yes."

"Okay. I'll do it." Her head falls back against the seat. "I'll stay for one night. I need time away from the situation at my father's house. A good night's rest won't hurt either."

"No problem." Leah in the honeymoon cottage; that's what I call temptation. It's going to be one long night and a true test of my willpower. She doesn't suspect that she stole my heart almost twenty years ago and there's never been anyone else. Is this the time to come clean and let her know that my interest in her isn't platonic?

# Praise

Book 1 in the series, ORANGE BLOSSOMS-LOVE BLOOMS, is a two time EMMA award winner: Best Debut author and Best Commercial Fiction.

Book 2 in the California Heart Series is ANYTHING BUT LOVE

SOFT LIES & HARD TRUTHS is the much anticipated third and final book in the California Heart series.

"Dalia Dupris' talent and skill elevate the traditional romance novel to new heights. Orange Blossoms-Love Blooms is a romance for readers who want more than hugs, kisses and happy endings."

La Rhonda Crosby Johnson, Author

"A Whirl With My Mocha-Chocolate Swirl is a delicious story with a delectable setting. I wish I could visit this town, particularly the ice cream shop. I love the characters, especially Raymond and Rebecca. I can't wait for a sequel."

Susan B. James, Author

## Dedication

This book is dedicated to all the brave men and women in my family who have served our country through military service and personal sacrifice. Thank you.

Other Wild Rose Press Titles by Dalia Dupris:


Orange Blossoms-Love Blooms
A Whirl with My Mocha-Chocolate Swirl
Twice as Sweet
Anything But Love

# Chapter 1

*Leah*

"Everyone looks so lovely," Mrs. Layton, mother of the bride, announces before making her way along the bridal party table, stopping to chat with each of us before moving on to the next person.

"Leah Ann." Drawing out my name, she grasps my hand while her dark eyes peer at me with genuine concern. Twisting her lip, and, with a pained expression, she pats my hand and leans closer so that we are nose-to-nose, which is *way* too close for my comfort zone. Worse yet, she smells wonderful.

I know that fragrance—Fleur de Lis, which was also my mother's favorite fragrance.

How I wish she were here now so I could share how I really feel about this day and the colossal amount of energy it's taking for me *not* to run screaming from the reception as fast as I can. But that's not possible. My first-generation Irish American mother, who loved St. Patrick's Day as much as July 4th, is gone and I'm struggling to grasp that reality as much as I am seeing Raymond Colton—the man I have loved for years—walk down the aisle with someone other than me.

Straightening my back and swallowing my feelings, I plaster a smile on my face and focus on Mrs. Layton. No use embarrassing myself further by bursting out in tears—what a show *that* would give people in Sunnyville. Then they'd *really* have something to talk about for years to come. Life in small towns…the place where gossip never dies.

Mrs. Layton squeezes my hand. "I told Rebecca that, even though you two were best friends in middle school and have grown close again, this might be asking too much of you." Leaning toward me, she lowers her voice. "Is it?"

Her expression is one that I've seen a million times today—it has pity written all over it.

"Oh, no," I lie. Smiling brightly, I free my fingers from her grip. Chuckling, I wave my hand nonchalantly. "I'm good. Rebecca looks beautiful. That dress is really stunning on her, don't you think?"

"Yes, it is." Obviously thrown-off by my unexpected over-the-top gushing, she stands up straight and looks at me as if I might be a little unhinged. "And it was sweet of the bridesmaids to help her select it."

"That was the fun part." I force myself not to cringe. It'd been pure torture seeing her try on sample-size-eight gown after gown, each of them fitting more perfectly than the previous one. "After all, as her two best friends, Cindy and I wouldn't dream of missing out on helping her select the dress that will commemorate her special day and will be immortalized in pictures for the rest of her life." I'm laying it on thick, but I can't seem to stop myself. If I state how I really feel, I may start sobbing.

Was it only ninety minutes ago that Miguel and I, following behind Cindy and Sam, had marched down the aisle, preceding the stunning bride and ruggedly handsome groom as they made their way to the decorated altar? I could have sworn that at least *four hours* had lapsed. This is definitely, unquestionably, and without a doubt, one of the longest and worst days of my life. It's not as if I couldn't see the surreptitious glances in my direction as Miguel and I passed by each row of seats. Never taking their appraising gaze from me, the curious onlookers stared at me as they mumbled to the person they were sitting beside. Half the time, I could hear them.

"She's in love with the groom" or "That's the one he didn't pick." Worst of all was "She was so in love with him that she bought herself an engagement ring." Inevitably, someone would gasp before shaking their head at my folly, or worse yet, perceived stupidity and desperation.

"Well, I'm glad to see you are doing well… considering everything." A line creases her forehead and she looks flustered, as if the wrong sentence had slipped out.

Smoothing a hand over her shimmering gray semi-formal dress, she adds, "I'm sorry your mother couldn't be with us."

Sadness alters her features and I'm reminded that I'm not the only one who misses my mother. Mrs. Layton and my mother, both single parents, had been close friends who'd often exchanged cookie recipes and Christmas ornaments.

"Me, too." I'm fond of Mrs. Layton, but, right now, I'm too close to crying to continue this conversation. Losing my mother was brutal, and then learning that the man I loved didn't love me back fractured my already aching heart.

Miguel, sitting beside me, places a comforting

hand on my shoulder.

That's all the prompting I need. "Will you excuse us, Mrs. Layton? I love this song and" I nudge him. "Miguel has been asking me to dance."

"Huh?" Miguel, clearly confused, frowns at me. "You want to dance? But I thought you said—"

"That if they played *this* song," I bob my head enthusiastically and silently pray that Miguel will go along with the ruse, "I *would* dance with you because, after all, this is *our* song."

"Oh, lovely. I didn't realize you two were—" Puzzled, Mrs. Layton's gaze darts from Miguel to me.

"A couple." Miguel gives me one of his warm smiles and helps me up from my chair.

I'm so grateful that I could kiss him.

"We didn't want to steal any attention from Rebecca and Raymond, right, babe?"

"Right." Now it's my turn to be surprised as he slips a firm arm around my waist and pulls me close. Wow, he's really gotten into the spirit of this little deception. Why hadn't I thought of this sooner? If the people at the wedding see me as part of a couple, maybe they'll stop looking at me with that "We feel sorry for you" expression. Maybe I can even go back to just being Leah Ann, kindergarten teacher, and *not* the loser who's a bridesmaid at her ex-boyfriend's wedding.

"Well, you two do make a nice couple." Mrs. Layton, her face awash with relief, gestures toward the dance floor. "Don't let me stop you. Enjoy yourselves."

"Our song?" Miguel raises a brow as we head toward the half-empty dance floor, but there's amusement in his voice. "I didn't know we had one, but

I'm always ready to oblige." He swirls me around in a circle before pulling me against him.

"Very impressive." Breathless, I release a much-needed giggle as he continues his salsa-style dance moves. "Sorry for grabbing you like that." Stumbling, I attempt to keep up with his smooth maneuvers.

"Are you kidding me?" He swings me out then in again. "I enjoyed it." Giving me a quick wink, he adds, "You can shove me around any time you want."

Eyeing him suspiciously, I rest my palms against his chest. "Sounds a little kinky to me."

"Well, a man can only hope." Taking my hands in his, he pulls me close again. His dark chocolate brown eyes with impossibly long black eyelashes are no longer twinkling with mirth.

If I didn't know better, I could believe he was serious. "You can stop pretending now."

Miguel was a late arrival to town, which is how we refer to anyone who wasn't born in Sunnyville. When he moved from his parents' home in Santa Lorena in middle school, he was just a pudgy, shy pre-teen, but as my eyes slowly roam over his even brown skin and athletic physique, I realize that he has really changed. How had I never noticed?

"She's gone. You did a great job. Feel free to release me."

"Are you sure?" His voice is low and almost sexy when he whispers the way he is now. Okay, well, not *almost*—it *is* sexy. He nonchalantly shrugs, before continuing, "Maybe we should let everyone else think we are a couple, too—I mean, if it would make you feel more comfortable. I know today hasn't been easy for you."

"I like the way you think, and I like how much you're putting into your role as the attentive boyfriend. The way you're looking at me now could convince anyone that you really care about me." I wink at him conspiratorially.

"Always willing to help. It's part of my military training to be of assistance whenever possible." His body is warm as he continues to swirl his hips and I'm beginning to think that we may be going overboard with our ploy.

"Ahem." Pulling away from him, I stand still as the music abruptly comes to a halt. Feeling flushed and more than a little warm, I look at him with newfound appreciation. "You're the best guy friend a girl could wish for. I mean, how many men would go along with pretending to care, so I won't look desperate and pitiful?"

"You could never look pitiful, not even if you tried. And a woman who looks like you is never desperate for male attention."

He leads me off the dance floor and I'm glad to be out of the spotlight. Not many other people had decided to join us on the dance floor, which might be a good thing. Now they could shift their focus away from me being alone to the possibility of me being part of a couple.

"Aren't you the flatterer."

Trust Miguel to say something kind in an effort to lift my spirits. But, right now, my stomach feels as unsettled as my nerves and this off-the-shoulder yellow chiffon dress has me looking washed out and frumpy.

"Please." I roll my eyes. "You've done enough by getting me out of that conversation with Rebecca's mother." No need to add that I'd been blinking back tears.

As a slow song starts, Rebecca and Raymond make their way to the floor and begin dancing in perfect step with one another's movements. Soon, other couples join them. Jenny, my number one female best friend and the wedding photographer, has her long blue braids tied back in a yellow ribbon as she makes her way around the room, snapping photographs of the guests. She has a way of making people feel at ease in front of the camera, so that her pictures reveal their best selves.

Moments later, she makes her way to Miguel and I where we are standing off to the side, watching the festivities.

"Hey, you two, mind if I snap a few pictures?"

Shaking my head, I hold my hands up, partially blocking my face. "No thanks. We've taken enough pictures for the day." Jenny has already taken dozens of shots of us with the bridal party.

"I hear you." Jenny flashes me a grin. "I always take extra. You never know which photo will give you the best shot." She raises the camera while adjusting the lens. "Plus, you two look mighty fine together."

"I think we do, too." Miguel, still playing the part of the attentive boyfriend, lifts my chin with his finger before wrapping an arm around my waist. "Why not?"

Loudly sighing in resignation, I absently lace my fingers through my untamable curls. I will not win this particular battle. Jenny is tenacious and serious about capturing the perfect image. If she needs a particular photo, she won't give up until she captures it. "Okay, since you two don't know how to take no for an answer." I lean into the warmth of his touch, deciding to take comfort where I can get it tonight. Besides, Miguel is doing a stellar job of pretending to be my love interest. If he wants to pose, once again, for the camera, I could at least return the favor and comply.

Plus, a quick scan of the room reveals that people are no longer assessing me with undisguised pity. The image of me having someone of my own, false as it may be, is apparently a relief for my local community.

My shoulders tense. Had my disastrous love life made others feel awkward? What a strangely unsettling thought. *Get a life, folks.*

Glancing into Miguel's eyes, I bat my lashes and place a hand on his arm. "You're right. Let's make certain Raymond and Rebecca have loads of pictures."

"This one's for me, Leah." Only Miguel can call me Leah.

As a child, my classmates frequently teased me about my *boy's* name. In response, I'd eventually insisted on being called by both my first *and* middle names. Miguel had moved to Sunnyville in later years, so he'd known nothing about using both my names, so he called me Leah. There was something about the way he pronounced it, even back then, that made me give him a pass. *Leah*, it was—but for him only.

"That's great." Jenny directs us to pose first one way and then another. Side-by-side. Front-to-back. Smiling and then serious. "I'd like to get one of you facing each other."

"For God's sake." Shifting my position, I directly face Miguel, who appears to be enjoying our impromptu photo session, while I'm growing increasingly weary of the charade. As soon as Jenny is finished, I'm going to help myself to more champagne.

"She's almost done." Miguel intently studies my face, while Jenny changes her camera lens. "I know this day is rough on you, but you don't want that tension to come across in the pictures. Let me help you out." He takes advantage of this pause in the picture-taking to give my shoulders a two-minute massage. "Better?"

"Hmmm. Much better." I hadn't realized that my discomfort was evident, at least to Miguel, who somehow always knows how to make me feel both seen and cared for. "Thank you. I don't know what I did to deserve such a good friend."

"You deserve the best of everything and don't ever forget that." Pausing, he looks around the room. "Relax, this reception won't last forever."

But it does.

There's the customary toast by Cindy, the maid-of-honor, and Sammy, the best man, the ritual cake cutting, and the traditional garter toss. I don't bother to join the fray of hopeful females eagerly raising their arms, stumbling and jostling against one another as Rebecca turns her back to them and tosses her bouquet over her shoulder.

Picking up a champagne bottle, I slowly pour myself another glass. "This is good stuff," I murmur more to myself than anyone else. All the other members of the bridal party have left our designated table to mingle with other guests and family members. Any tension I was previously experiencing fades as I enjoy the bubbly liquid trickling down my throat. Exhaling deeply, I am more relaxed than I have been in the last couple of weeks, maybe even longer. What a relief to know that I'm finally done with the whole *love* thing.

Draining my glass, I make my way to a sliding

glass door that leads to an open veranda and join the other guests as they wait for the couple to appear and make their exit in the waiting white stretch limousine.

"You okay?" Miguel appears from out of nowhere, grasping my arm as I stumble over the cobbled patio.

"Of course." I glance up at him. "Where did you come from?" He wasn't here a minute ago. After the pictures, he had disappeared.

"Don't you know? I've been here all along."

His brows come together, forming one thick line above his eyes. He runs a finger along my cheek. What's that look? Is it annoyance or frustration?

"I know you've been here, silly." Feeling unsteady on my feet, I lean against him. "I mean for the last few minutes. I was sitting up there." I point at the table I've just vacated. "I didn't see you. I thought you'd left."

"Not yet. I wouldn't leave without saying goodbye." His jaw tightens as he studies my face. "I think you would know that by now." He shifts his focus away from me. "Never mind. Here they come."

Following his gaze, I spot Rebecca and Raymond walking through the open door. They have changed into more casual, all white attire. Rebecca is wearing a strapless white summer dress and Raymond looks as if he's won the lottery. Earlier, I hugged both Rebecca and Raymond and congratulated them on their nuptials. They deserve their own happily-ever-after, even if Raymond's rejection of me had felt like a puncture wound to *my* heart. It's bleeding right now, as I toss rice in their direction as they run, heads bowed, toward the limo.

"That's some ride," Miguel says with one last wave. "I guess we are no longer on duty."

"You're right." Some part of me is grateful that the ceremony and the reception are finally over. Pretending that I haven't been brokenhearted for the past few months has left me drained, and the over-indulgence of champagne has kicked my developing headache up a notch. "Thanks for pretending to care."

"Whoa." His voice is stern. The one word is almost a growl. "That's not fair. You know I care."

The limousine drives off, and we join the guests making their way back to the main reception hall.

"Oh, I know you do. You and Jenny are my best friends." Between the champagne and my headache, finding the right words isn't easy. "*Pretending* that you care." Satisfied that I've made myself clear, I flash him my brightest smile.

"Okay. I know what you mean," His voice is flat, very matter-of-fact. "Are you ready to leave now?"

"Yes." I relax my shoulders, eager to leave and get out of this unflattering dress. It looked great on svelte Cindy, but the A-line dress was not created for women who had lots of curves. "I've had enough for one day. I just have to grab my purse from the back room."

"I'll wait here. When you come back, I'll walk you to your car."

"That's not necessary." Straightening my back, I lift my chin and wave. "You are officially off duty, Mr. Montoya." I give him a quick salute. "You are free to go on your way."

"It was my pleasure." His lips curve upwards. "This was fun."

"Yep." About as much fun as having your private parts waxed. "So much fun." If he notices the sarcasm in my voice, he doesn't comment. The truth is that I'm barely holding it together.

Before he can say another word, I head to the back room and retrieve my beige handbag from a shelf in the closet. My throat aches and I swallow, trying to suppress the longing that's bringing tears to my eyes. I can feel the waterworks coming, so I rush out the door as quickly as I can, hoping to avoid any embarrassment. I don't need to fall apart the minute the wedding is over.

But… there it is. As soon as I'm in my car, a whole tidal wave of tears comes rushing out, drenching my cheeks and smearing my eyeliner. I might as well give in and let it all out. My head rests against the steering wheel while I sob loudly, glad that I parked in the far corner of the lot.

Hearing a light tapping on the car window, I pause, not wanting to look up. Who could it be? Who found me here? Why didn't I drive home *first* before losing it? Oh, that's right, because home is sad, too. Memories of my mother are *everywhere*. The aneurysm that took her from me was only six months ago and I haven't been able to force myself to clear out her closets and donate her clothes.

The tapping persists.

How embarrassing.

Glancing up beneath partially opened eyes, I see Miguel, hand on the car door handle, looking very concerned.

"Miguel." Sniffling, I purse my lips and wish I could disappear. "What are you doing here?" My nose is running, my hair has toppled over my head, and my mascara is probably streaming down my cheeks in long, squiggly lines. I slide down lower in my seat, grabbing the box of tissue from the passenger seat and turning away from his shocked expression, I loudly blow my nose.

"Doing what I should have done earlier." His voice is as determined as the set of his jaw as he struts over to the passenger door and grabs the handle. "Open it. I'm getting in."

Chapter 2

*Miguel*

Grasping the handle, I attempt to pull open the passenger door. "Leah, please unlock the door." I've never seen her like this. Before today, I would have said that Leah's defining characteristic, the one trait that comes to mind when I think of her, is her cheery disposition and optimism. Of course, I always knew there was something deeper there, but I had never seen her upset—until now.

"Go away." She blows her nose again before swiping at her eyes with a fresh tissue.

It just smears more makeup across her high cheekbones. I would laugh, but I'm sure she wouldn't appreciate it.

"Not going to happen." I shake the door handle.

"Pardon?" Large hazel eyes stare back at me in disbelief.

"You heard right. I'm not going anywhere." I swivel around and look out at the parking lot before turning back and piercing her with a look that I hope she can read as me being determined. "In case you haven't noticed, guests have left the wedding and are now walking to their cars." I point at her and then at myself. "We are beginning to attract attention."

She stops blowing her nose long enough to sit up

and look out the car window. "I'm fine, really." She sniffles and waves her hand as if shooing me away.

"Let me put it this way." I glance over my shoulder before continuing, "Marion Hightower, is walking over here and… she's a fast walker. Unless you want to have a chat with her, I suggest you open this door *now*."

"All right." Leah, a petulant expression on her face, pushes the button to release the lock on the passenger door. "Happy now?" She snarls at me, as I get in the car.

"Not yet." Finally, I'm seeing something besides the smiling face Leah displays to the world. I've always known she couldn't possibly be happy *all* the time, especially not with the day—or even the year—she's just experienced. This day feels like a breakthrough. "You can't take yourself home." There's no way I'm allowing her to drive in her present condition.

"I can drive myself." Pursing her lips, she grasps the steering wheel.

"In about two minutes, Marion will be here. I suggest we trade places now, if you don't want her to see you looking—"

"You don't have to say it." With surprising agility, she slithers between the front bucket seats and crawls into the backseat, where she immediately throws a blanket over her head.

Seconds before Marion approaches the car, I slide over to the driver's side and shove the seat back so my knees aren't tucked under my chin.

"Oh, Miguel." Marion, our high school cafeteria lady, tilts her head to the side, clearly puzzled. "Well, my goodness, I could have sworn this was Leah Ann's car." Brows furrowed, she stares at me suspiciously before peering into the back window. "Oh my." She brings a hand to her chest before lowering her face closer to the window. "Is that *her*?" Marion glares at me as if I'm an axe murderer.

"Yes, it is." Time to troubleshoot. No use in giving the Sunnyville rumor mill a fresh story to chat about over tea and scones at Yolanda's Tea Room. "She's exhausted. Fell asleep the minute we got in the car."

"*Really*?" She folds her hands across her waist, clearly not certain if she should believe me or not. "Well, bless her heart. I'm not surprised she's tuckered out from everything."

"Exactly." Reassured that Marion is no longer eyeing me suspiciously, I adjust the seat belt and release the emergency break. "Seeing how she was so tired, I suggested she take a nap in the back and allow me to take her home."

"What a gentleman." She nods with approval before piercing me with a perplexed expression. "I saw your car near the back patio, right next to Sammy's blue convertible. Are you planning to keep it there all night?"

"I'll get it later." How could I forget Marion's keen observation of absolutely everything? The woman could have been a detective, but she's our resident artist and notices everything and everyone. Capturing those details is probably what contributes to the life-like quality of her paintings.

"Well, I won't keep you any longer." She steps away from the car. "Have a great evening."

Now that I've reassured Marion that I'm not up to anything nefarious, I drive out of the lot, occasionally nodding at the people who look at me curiously, probably wondering why I'm driving Leah's car and why she's not in it with me.

"Okay, you can sit up now." Peering in the rearview mirror, I see that Leah is still hunkered down beneath the blanket. "The coast is clear. I'm going to stop driving, so you can sit upfront." I drive a few yards further before pulling over to park along the side of the road.

"Are you awake back there?"

When she still doesn't respond, I face the back seat and lower the blanket. Her hands are tucked beneath her head and her thick lashes rest on her flushed cheeks. She's fast asleep. Seeing her like this—soft, vulnerable, completely relaxed—it's hard for me to turn away. The sweet girl with the honey-colored hair and the hazel eyes, who I'd had a crush on and who'd helped me with my seventh-grade algebra when I'd first moved here, has always occupied a special place in my heart.

Luckily for me, Raymond never stopped loving Rebecca, even after she left Sunnyville to attend college in New York.

Unluckily for me, Leah still loves Raymond. Sometimes life is cruel.

*Eyes on the road.* I have to remind myself to keep my eyes on the road and *not* on Leah as she lies curled up in a ball in the back seat. She looks peaceful. She may have fooled other people, but I could see beneath the cheerful façade—something about the distant look in her eyes, a kind of sadness that the casual observer wouldn't notice. But I've always noticed *everything* about Leah from the moment I'd landed in her algebra class and she'd saved my numerically-challenged self from failing.

Smiling at the memory, I continue driving through the quiet town square while occasionally glancing in the rearview mirror. She stirs and moans softly. Normally not much of a drinker, she'd had more than I'd expect during the reception. I'd never known her to have more than one or two glasses.

As I pull up to her house, I mentally kick myself for not thinking of driving her home sooner. There was no way she should have been behind the wheel of the car in the first place. I'd made the mistake of letting her out of my sight for five minutes—ten tops—when I'd made my way across the dance floor to speak to my friend Rico who was DJing for the evening. When I'd returned to the table, she'd been gone. Something in my chest had tightened as I'd scanned the room, trying to figure where she could have disappeared to so quickly. Luckily, she hadn't made it beyond the parking lot.

Since she's still asleep, I put the car in Park before turning off the engine. Pulling out my cell phone, I type a text to my best friend, Sammy. As Raymond's closest friend, he was, naturally, the best man at the wedding. I was surprised to be in the wedding at all. I know I was not Raymond's first choice—not when he'd initially thought I'd had a thing for Rebecca, which I never did. My friendship with Rebecca had flourished since I had returned from serving four years in the Marines, but it'd never been anything romantic. It had taken Raymond a while to acknowledge that truth. She'd had to have been the one who'd insisted on having me in the wedding. Eventually, Raymond had chilled out enough to know I hadn't been about to make a move on his woman. After that, we were cool, especially since we were both tight with Sammy. Plus, Sunnyville is a small town, so it's hard to not bump into the same people frequently, and it's easier to become friends than to stay enemies.

Knowing that I'm going to need a ride home, I text Sammy.

*—Hey, man. Still at the reception?—*

Because Sammy is an editor at *The Sunnyville Tribune*, I know he always has his phone on vibrate. The man wouldn't want to risk missing any details of a breaking news story.

Sure enough, within minutes, he texts me back.

*—You know it. Cindy has me loading the gifts into the car. What's up? We'll probably be the last ones to leave. I saw your car in the lot, but no you???—*

Not wanting to go into much detail, I keep it simple.

*—I drove Leah home. My car door isn't locked. The keys are in the glove compartment. Could you do me a big favor, and—no rush—but when you get a chance, could you pick me up?—*

Sunnyville isn't the kind of community where you feel the need to always lock car or home doors, which isn't smart, but I didn't want my keys jingling while I walked down the aisle in the ceremony, so I left them in my truck.

Glancing down, I see that Sammy has responded.

*—Way to go! Score one for Miguel. It's about damn time, bro!—*

Shaking my head in disbelief, I clearly see Sammy's writer mind has created a whole story with a happy ending. However, he's *way* off base and, knowing Sammy, if I don't correct him, he'll be composing a feature story about Leah and I being the next couple to tie the knot.

—*You got it wrong. Can you pick me up? If not, I'll take a ride share.*—

Was it a mistake to ask Sammy? Now, he'll ask a hundred questions about my evening, but I won't have a juicy story to give him. With a sigh, I look back at Sleeping Beauty.

—*Don't do that. I'll text you when I'm on my way. I'm proud of you man. Later.*—

I'll have plenty of time to clarify the situation when Sammy arrives, but, for now, I need to focus on waking Leah and getting her inside the house.

Unbuckling my seatbelt, I face the back seat and take a few more moments to enjoy the view. How does someone manage to still look beautiful with makeup smeared across her cheeks and her hair fanned out in disarray around a heart-shaped face? Crazy as it sounds, I could just sit here and gaze at her for hours.

"Leah." I keep my voice low, not wanting to startle her. I almost add "Are you awake?" but I've always found it irritating when people wake me to ask if I'm sleeping.

When she doesn't respond, I raise my voice, "Leah. We're at your house."

"Hmmm." Rolling over, she provides me with an excellent view of her backside. The bottom of her dress wraps around her full thighs, revealing golden skin that appears to glow under the streetlight.

My hand is shaky as I scrape it across my jaw. A surge of desire infuses me with a jolt of heat, warming me to my core. I'm not sure which view I like better— front or back, both sides are appealing. The woman looks soft and round, with curves in all the right places and, just for a minute, I'm frozen with desire, but then I remember my military training—all those years of mastering control in difficult situations. Didn't know I'd have to utilize that strict discipline here, but the other thing I learned in the military is that you never know where life can lead.

Reaching out to gently shake her shoulder, I try again. "Leah, we have to get out of the car."

"Sleep," she mumbles while pulling the cover over her face.

Well, my first strategy isn't effective, so I swivel back around, take the key out of the ignition, exit the car, then open the back door. At this point, I'm no longer concerned that she's going to suddenly wake with a jolt. Obviously, she's a heavy sleeper.

I slide one hand behind her back and one under her knees before lifting her out of the car. God, she smells good. What is that fragrance? Something floral, perhaps jasmine. Why am I not surprised that she feels as soft in my arms as she looks? As a personal trainer, I've lifted weights that weigh more than she does and with ease.

I make my way to her doorstep, only to realize that her clutch is still in the car, and I don't have a key to get in the house. I can't set her down and leave her here while I return to the car, but it could be awkward to bring her back to the car, open the door and try to hold onto her bag and keep a grip on her at the same time.

"Open." Her eyes flash open and shut, before she smiles and resumes snuggling against my chest and falling back to sleep.

"What?" Okay, not sure, what that one word meant, but she's clearly gone back to sleep. As I stand on the doorstep, I know I can't stay here forever deciding what my next move will be. Then it dawns on me what she'd said.

This is Sunnyville after all, a city whose worst crime last year was when Bobby Smith stole twelve dollars' worth of candy bars from the Bet Your Dollar Store.

Placing one foot on the upper step, I balance this luscious package of pure temptation on my knee while keeping a firm grip on her back, and manage to grasp the door knob, giving it a twist to the right.

Nothing happens.

I exhale deeply and try Plan B, which is turning the knob to the left. All right! I'm in.

The first thing I do is search for a light switch. The last thing I want is to trip and have both of us go sprawling across the floor.

But how to do that in the dark? Then, I see a flicker of light coming from a back room and cautiously make my way toward it. Thankfully, the nightlight is in the hall outside of the open door to her bedroom. I strain to make out the bed, then carefully place her on it. Picking up the throw blanket that's at the foot of the bed, I arrange it across her shoulders.

"Raymond."

Just as I'm closing her bedroom door, the word echoes across the room. My gut twists in knots, constricting the flow of blood until I feel actual pain, and I know with one hundred percent certainty that wanting Leah to ever have feelings for me is like expecting gold to fall from the sky. It's a lost cause and will never happen. I can't win this battle because she doesn't even know that I'm on the field.

Chapter 3

*Leah*

Lifting my head from the pillow is no easy task. I swear it feels like it's doubled in size overnight. *Note to self: do not overindulge in alcohol. Ever. Again.* I force myself to sit still, hoping to stop the heavy pounding in my skull. Great. I have a giant throbbing head and a dry, parched throat.

Walking gingerly, I am heading to the bathroom when the doorbell rings. Loudly and repeatedly. Who could it be at this time of morning?

Holding my head to steady it, because, at this point, it feels like a bobblehead, I walk to the door and open it. It's Jenny, looking bright-eyed and perky, as if she's been awake for hours.

"Rough night, huh?" Her voice is matter-of-fact as she steps into the living room. Twisting her lip and raising her brows, she continues, "You don't look so great."

"Thanks. I don't feel so great either." Pointing to my head, I say, "I have an enormous headache."

"I believe it would be accurate to call it a hangover." She plops onto the sofa then props her feet on the blue ottoman.

"Well, make yourself at home, why don't you?" I focus on her eggplant-colored toenails and several toe rings.

"I always do." She chuckles, then picks up one of the fashion magazines I have on the coffee table and leafs through it. "By the way, this was left in your car, which was left unlocked. I swear the people in this boondock town just *beg* people to commit crimes." She displays my clutch. "Growing up in Los Angeles, I knew better than to leave my valuables out in the open."

Jenny and her girlfriend, Lisa, had come to Sunnyville for a beachside vacation at one of our numerous resort cabins. At the end of a week, Lisa had returned to Los Angeles alone. Jenny said the slower pace was something she didn't know she needed, but now that she'd found it, she was here to stay. Even if she talks about the town as if we are backward and totally out of touch with the rest of the world, she loves it here. Otherwise, why wouldn't she return to Los Angeles?

"Yeah, yeah." I wave a hand dismissively. "Did you come to chastise me for being irresponsible?"

With a pensive expression on her face, she places a finger to her lips and pauses before replying, "Why no, I didn't, but it *is* fun. Plus, it never makes a difference anyway. You are very good at ignoring pretty much everything I say."

"Not everything." Taking the purse from her hand, I walk over and set it on the table in the dinette. Jenny's background in psychology and interest in all things mystical means she always has a lot to say, and even if I don't fully comprehend everything, I do listen.

"Okay, not to be critical or anything, because I know that your inner spirit is beautiful, but, right now, your outward appearance needs some, uh, attention." She points a slender finger in my direction. "For one, you still have yesterday's clothes on and… have you looked at yourself? It's one o'clock and, if I'm not mistaken, you look like someone who just woke up." She holds her hands up. "I'm just saying—"

"If *that's* not critical, I don't know what is, but I love you anyway. I can trust you to always give it to me straight." The headache is slowly beginning to subside as I make my way to the kitchen and get a glass of water. "To answer your question, no, I haven't seen what I look like, but I know how I feel and it's not good. I was just about to take a shower and get dressed when you began your persistent ringing of my doorbell." After downing two glasses of water, my throat no longer feels like a desert storm is blowing through it.

"By all means, don't let me stop you from tidying up your appearance." She rolls her eyes before picking up the remote control and clicking on the television. "I'll be here when you get out."

Now that I'm in the bathroom and facing the mirror, I can attest to the fact that Jenny was not exaggerating. With the way I look right now, I would easily frighten small children and animals.

Slipping off the bright yellow bridesmaid dress, I know that it will never see the light of day again, at least not on me anyway. However, I will drop it off at Sally's Hidden Treasure's Secondhand Store. Maybe some teenager will want to wear it for her prom. This dress would be perfect for a sixteen-year-old, but, at thirty, I would have preferred something with less bounce and flounce, but it was the bride's choice not mine.

Stepping into the shower, I squash the thought of anything having to do with Raymond and Rebecca. The last thing I want to envision is the thought of them on their honeymoon.

In the not-too-distant past, I had harbored the inane belief that Raymond had feelings for me. We had dated for several months before Rebecca decided to return home from living in New York. Six years the woman had been gone and the minute she returned, my relationship with Raymond begin to slide into an abyss—

Okay, while this was *not* thinking of them on their honeymoon, it was still thinking of them. I need to move on, not just on the outside, but on the inside as well.

Just as I'm drying off, there's a light tap on the door.

"Can I have a few moments of privacy please?"

Jenny is not known for her patience, except when she's taking pictures; that's when she'll take all the time she needs to set up everything perfectly and get the photograph she envisions.

"Hey, I'm starving out here and your cabinets and refrigerator are pretty bare," she announces. "My stomach is grumbling."

"Sorry to disappoint you!" I yell through the door. Taking a paper towel and wiping off the mirror, I scrutinize my face. Even though my eyes are bloodshot, I'm not looking as if I totally overindulged last night.

"You know, Yolanda's serves breakfast all day." She lets out an enthusiastic yelp.

For someone who's super slender—i.e.,

supermodel size—she has an abundance of enthusiasm at even the thought of a delicious meal. If I ate half as much as Jenny ate, I'd go up a dress size in a week. Another example of how unfair life can be. "Give me five minutes and I'll be out of here. Now, step away from the door so I can at least pretend like I'm having some privacy in my bathroom." Pulling my hair back into a top ponytail, I decide to forego any makeup. Rebecca had had a professional makeup artist arrive early at her house yesterday and work her wizardry on our bare faces. I barely recognized myself, what with all of the eyeliner, lip liner, and what I called the compression body liner—otherwise known as the super snug slimmer trimmer. I could barely breathe because of the flesh-toned undergarment that molded my body into one smooth, unlined, and unrecognizable letter S shape.

Appreciatively rubbing my soft, round belly, all I can say is that it feels good to be able to breathe freely without a rubber band-type garment cinching my waist and rib cage. Besides, I liked being a full-figured woman. Smiling, I recall how my mother referred to my body type as Rubenesque and I came to appreciate her saying that as a compliment.

Seems I'm feeling better this morning, I'm also proud of myself for being a team player. I did my part for my one-time best friend and smiled as she wed the man I loved; I had donned the aforementioned hideous bridesmaid dress and matching yellow satin pumps and, now that the wedding is over, I can breathe again, both literally and figuratively.

Wrapping one of my pink, oversized towels around my body, I step out of the bathroom into the living room and am completely thrown off-guard when I see Miguel standing by the front door.

"Miguel," I stammer, wondering when he got here and where Jenny is. When I lift my hand to rub the back of my head, the towel slips down a quarter of an inch in the front, revealing a peek of cleavage. "Oops." I smile. Thank God, it's only Miguel.

"Sorry to pop in unannounced." He looks as awkward as I do as he shuffles his feet and looks anywhere but at me. "I was heading out for my Sunday morning jog and decided to check on you." As a personal trainer and fitness teacher at the local recreation center, Miguel is always exercising. Today, he's wearing black jogging shorts and a tank top that reveals his perfectly formed biceps. "Jenny let me in. She said she was hungry and couldn't wait for you to get ready." He runs a hand across the back of his neck and clears his throat. "She said she'd eat slowly, so she'll be there when you join her."

"You are so thoughtful. Always." Stepping aside, I usher him in. "We both know that a hungry Jenny is an irritable Jenny. However, I'm glad you're here." I sit on the couch and pat the cushion next to me. "Have a seat. I want to talk to you."

"Umm…" Ignoring the place I'd patted, he sits down on the other end of the sofa. "Did you want to get… dressed first?"

"What?" Shaking my head and feeling a flush move up my chest to my neck, I abruptly stand. "Oh, I'm sorry. Am I making you uncomfortable?"

"Me? No, of course not. I was thinking that *you* might be cold or something." Clearing his throat, he continues in a firm voice, "Plus, I didn't want you to catch a chill, seeing as you hardly have any clothes on."

"Right. Good point." Now that he puts it that way, I'm suddenly self-conscious as I scurry to my room. Even though I see Miguel as the brother I never had, he's right—I *do* only have a towel on, but it's not like I knew he was in the house. Besides, it would have been nice if Jenny had given me a heads-up, I think as I walk into my bedroom.

Pulling out drawers, I take out a pair of panties and a bra, before pulling on a white V-necked T-shirt and a pair of light blue denim jeans.

"Better?" Moments later, when I've returned to the living room, I feel warm inside valuing how Miguel is consistently concerned about my comfort.

"Yes, much." He eyes me approvingly. "Thank you."

"You are sweet to be so concerned." Sitting beside him, I give him a quick hug. "You're my guardian angel, always watching out for me. Thank you for getting me home last night."

"No thanks are necessary. It was my pleasure." A dimple in his cheek only shows when he's smiling, like he is right now.

"Was it really?" Babysitting me couldn't have been the best way for him to end the day. "I definitely had too much champagne and shouldn't even have *thought* about driving myself home." Abruptly standing, I head for the kitchen. "Can I at least fix you a cup of coffee or tea?"

"Coffee would be fine." His voice no longer sounds strained.

I get that; sometimes the thought of something warm to drink is all it takes to lift my mood.

"The last thing I recall is talking to you when you were standing outside my car." From now on, I'll refrain from any futile attempts to drown my sorrows with alcohol. I measure coffee before adding it to the filter and looking at him quizzically. "I'm guessing you drove me home?" I scrounge around in the refrigerator as the coffee brews. Apparently, Jenny overlooked the brown paper bag in the back that contains two honey raisin blueberry muffins.

"Yes, I did." Miguel has joined me in the kitchen and is struggling to keep a straight face as he takes a seat at the island.

"What's so funny?" Placing the muffins on a glass plate, I set them in the microwave to warm.

"You really don't remember?" He chuckles, no longer concealing his mirth.

Apprehension kicks in as I hand him his coffee. After offering him the sugar and creamer, I fold my arms across my waist. Did I do something to embarrass myself? "Just tell me what I did."

He silently peers at me over the rim of his mug. "All right, I've tortured you enough." He takes a sip of coffee before nodding his head. "Good coffee, Leah."

"Thanks, now get to the point." I scowl while removing the warm muffins from the microwave. "Either tell me how I embarrassed myself or I'll take my coffee back and not let you have one of these delicious muffins."

"Okay. I do want one of those, so I better fill you in." He snatches a muffin from the plate and bites into it. Closing his eyes, he moans appreciatively. "This is good. You make it?"

"I wish. Muffins aren't my specialty." Pulling up a

chair next to him, I say, "Stop stalling. You're making me nervous."

"Sorry." He pats my hands and, if he weren't such a good friend, I'd almost think I felt something, but that's not possible. Miguel is not my type. Too traditionally good looking, unlike Raymond, who has a rugged, gruff type of charm that wouldn't be appealing to some women. Miguel is a female magnet and he doesn't even know it. If I ever dated him—which I never would—I'd constantly have to be on the alert that some stunning woman would be plotting to steal him away from me. Even when we are hanging out together, women ignore me as if I'm invisible while they aggressively flirt or suggest he take their cell phone numbers. Nope, a man as drop-dead gorgeous as Miguel can have any woman he desires. It makes sense; they would match and have equally stunningly attractive children together.

"Mrs. Hightower walked up to the car, and you were… uh, having a hard time." He takes another bite of his muffin.

"Hard time? How?" As soon as I ask the question, it all comes rushing back.

Holding out a hand, I block him from adding more embarrassing, pitiful details that he had the misfortune of witnessing. Now *I'm* the one whose avoiding eye contact. "I remember now. I was crying in the car, wasn't I?"

"Yes, and I thought you probably wouldn't want her to see you like that."

"Good deduction." The muffin suddenly tastes like sawdust, and I set it back on the plate. "She does tend to know *everyone's* business. Although, in Sunnyville, who doesn't? So, what happened next?"

"You really don't remember?" He drains his mug of coffee before helping himself to a second cup.

"Of course not." I wring my hands. "*That's* why I'm asking you."

"No need to be embarrassed. It was my suggestion that you get in the back seat and pretend that you were asleep and, before I knew it, you were really out. I guess all the wedding stuff was exhausting, huh?"

"It was." The farce of pretending to be okay when I wasn't *had* taken an emotional toll, leaving me feeling as if I had to keep a smile on my face, pretending that I was over Raymond, when I wasn't. Leaning forward, I clutch his arm. "I also don't remember coming home." I never used to believe people when they got drunk and stated they couldn't remember what happened the night before. Now, I know they weren't lying. Blackouts are real.

"I hope you don't mind, but I carried you inside." He looks at me sheepishly. "I couldn't wake you up and, believe me, I tried."

"Are you kidding me?" I shriek, knowing how much I weigh and he's asking me if *I* don't mind? Incredible, he's the one who could have gotten hurt, even if he *is* a personal trainer and physical education instructor. "You could have hurt yourself." And I would have felt guilty and been totally mortified.

His face clouds with confusion as his jaw tightens. "What are you talking about? I couldn't hurt myself from picking you up. It's not like you weigh that much."

"Oh, Miguel." A huge grin spreads across my face as I wrap my arms around his neck and kiss his cheek.

"You're the best." I kiss the other cheek. "I love you."

"I love you, too." His breath is warm against my ear.

"Enough mushy stuff." Releasing my hold, I lean back on my stool. "You're the best brother a girl could have."

"Only... we aren't related, so, you know we aren't really—"

"No, don't say it." I squeeze his upper arm. "My family was already small to begin with and now, with my mother gone, it's even smaller. So don't you *dare* say we aren't family, because we are, if not by blood, then by heart." My throat aches as I struggle to catch my breath before adding, "I don't know what I'd do without you, and I'm not planning to find out."

Chapter 4

*Miguel*

"I'm not going anywhere." Frustration surges in my chest. How I feel about this woman is anything but filial, especially earlier when she'd been wearing nothing but that skimpy towel that didn't leave a lot to the imagination. My imagination had run wild with thoughts of what she looked like under that towel, but, because her feelings for me are completely platonic, she can't imagine the effect she has on me. I'd rather have a platonic relationship with Leah then none at all, so I'm not going to do anything stupid that would have her questioning my loyalty. "Well, that's not completely true."

"Huh?" She stands. "What's not completely true?" A look of pure panic fills her eyes. She's been on an emotional roller coaster since the sudden loss of her mother last year and having her heart broken by Raymond, which turned out to be good for me, even if she clearly isn't over the guy. Regardless of how much she pretends like she's good, I know she isn't. Last night made that abundantly clear. "Are you going somewhere?"

"I'm going home." The words come out bitter, as if I'm saying I have to take a series of shots.

"What do you mean you're going home?" She

raises an inquisitive brow. "Do you mean back to your apartment or something else?"

"Something else." The thought of returning to Santa Lorena is not a happy one, but I've put it off long enough.

"You did your time in the military and now you've returned to Sunnyville—*this* has been your home for years."

"I moved here to live with my Aunt Esther when I was in seventh grade, so, yes, this is my home, too, but my parents live in Santa Lorena." Santa Lorena, one hundred and fifty miles from here, is lush, green, and filled with small-town charm and families that have known each other for decades. Fruit and nuts grow in abundance on family-owned farms and provide produce for grocery stores throughout California and beyond. "Therefore, Santa Lorena is my *first* home."

"I remember now, but, in my mind, it's as if you belong here." She twists a strand of hair between her fingers. "I think it's because when my mother and I moved away from Sunnyville, you were still here." She chuckles. "That year when we left, I was in ninth grade, and I imagined all my friends were continuing to have fun without me, and it made me sad. I wanted to stay in Sunnyville."

"I remember you leaving." Back then, we hadn't been what I would call friends; it was more like acquaintances. I'd been just an outsider she had once helped with algebra. "I was sorry to see you go." The crush that had taken root then had never subsided; it just continued to grow and morph into something even stronger. "Look, I know Jenny is waiting for you, so I'll get to the other reason that I came by this morning, besides seeing how you're faring. I'm going to Santa Lorena in a couple of days and thought you might want to come with me. Plus, doesn't your dad still live there?"

"Yes, he's there. I plan to visit him later in the year." Blinking rapidly, she hunches her shoulders, and it's obvious my suggestion has caught her off-guard. "Thanks for the offer, but I've still got so much work to do. Summer vacation is when I do my planning and preparation for the next school year. Plus," she pauses before sighing loudly and scanning the living room. "I haven't been able to force myself to clear out some of my mother's things. It's ridiculous. Look at all of this stuff."

"You have a point." I don't have to search for evidence of her mother's presence. It's everywhere throughout the three-bedroom, Tudor-style house she shared with her pediatrician mother. The mauve reclining chair in the living room where Mrs. James sat to read her books still has the older woman's lavender sweater draped across the back. A stack of her knitting and crocheting magazines remains stacked on the coffee table, and I wonder if Leah cancelled the subscriptions yet. The year before she died, her mother had won second place in the annual garden show and the certificate she won is on display on the fireplace mantel.

"Getting away might be good for you." With shock and some concern, I realize that Leah has not made the house her own. Everything is set up the same way her mother had arranged when Leah returned from college and living in Templeton, six years ago. "I can see you still have some work you need to do here, but, well—" I struggle to think of a way to break the news to her about the images I saw on my phone this morning.

She jerks her hands up, as if to block me from finishing my sentence. "I think I need to stay and decide what to do with my mom's stuff," her voice trembles, but she continues, "and get ready for the next kindergarten class I'll be teaching."

"I understand." Standing, I step toward her. "But you might want to look at this first." I remove my cell phone from the back pocket of my jeans and open my text messages before thrusting the phone into her hand.

"What? Maybe I can look at your texts later." Without glancing at the phone, she attempts to return it to me, but I don't take it. "Jenny is going to kill me if I don't hurry up and get myself to the coffee shop."

"Leah." This time I say her name more firmly. She needs to see this. Now.

"Okay." She looks at me impatiently before reluctantly taking the phone. "This better not take too long because I really don't have time to read someone's latest rant."

"Just read it." Folding my hands across my chest, I watch her intently as she finally looks at the pictures and reads the tweet.

"Oh my God! Who took this picture? When? How *could* they? Talk about mortifying." She's practically screaming as the words tumble out. Her skin is flushed as she paces the floor. "I can't believe this!"

"The dark side of social media." A white-hot rage had consumed me when this image popped up on my phone this morning. I knew I had to get to Leah and let her know about it before anyone else said anything. "Any idiot can take a picture and post it."

"But it's what they *wrote* that's so hurtful." Leaning against the counter, she presses two fingers against her temple.

"Any jerk can write whatever they want and take a picture these days." Removing the phone from her hand, I turn it off before replacing it in my pocket. There are two pictures. One of her at the wedding, sitting alone at the bridal party table and pouring herself a glass of champagne with the caption: JILTED LOVER DROWNS HER SORROWS. The next picture is of Leah, slumped over in her car, hair covering her face, as she rests her head against the steering wheel. The caption reads: OH THE PAIN OF REJECTION. "They can post whatever rubbish they want."

Her voice rises in anger as shame flashes in her eyes and I know that the anger is directed at herself. "It's all true and we both know it." She plops down onto the carpet. "I don't know who in town would post this." There's hurt in her eyes. "Why?"

Joining her on the floor, I wrap an arm around her shoulder. "Who knows?" I shrug. "There were a lot of people at the wedding, including a slew of teenagers. Remember that some of the summer people were helping in the kitchen and with set-up. Raymond and Rebecca had cousins and other people from out of town. Someone probably heard some gossip that you were Raymond's ex and thought it would be funny."

"You're probably right. I mean, I don't think anyone in Sunnyville could be this cruel. Plus, how many people in town are even on social media?" Waving her hands excitedly, she continues. "Not *that* many, right? I mean, this is a town where most people still subscribe to the local print newspaper." She abruptly hops up and places her hands on her hips. "I'm not going to let whoever wrote that bother me."

"Good for you." I'm glad she's determined not to let the mean-spirited pictures and words get her down. "I just thought, well, since I'm driving to Santa Lorena in two days, you might want to get away for a while."

"Absolutely not!" Her skin turns pink as she paces. "Thanks for giving me a heads-up, but I'm not going to allow a jerk who posted a couple of silly pictures to change my plans. I doubt anyone has even seen those stupid tweets." Smiling confidently, she escorts me to the door. "Thanks for watching out for me, but I've got a breakfast date I don't want to miss."

Shaking my head, I wonder about Leah's quick reversal of emotions regarding the social media post. I thought she'd be upset longer and am surprised she ultimately felt confident that no one would pay much attention to the images. Clicking on the key fob, I stride over to my sports utility vehicle, and, after securing my seat belt, release the emergency break, and start the engine.

As I slowly drive along the scenic coastline, I hope her reaction is a sign of recovery from her double losses of a parent and a love interest. Rolling down the window, I enjoy the feel of the warm summer breeze as I reflect for the hundredth time that Raymond was never right for Leah. Oh, he's a good guy all right. But I could tell he never *really* saw her. Not the way I do. It was as if he was looking *through* her. He didn't recognize the magic she performs with those kids at her school or how she always greets people with a warm smile. At the end of the school day, she'd be the library, providing free tutoring for students whose parents didn't have the money to pay for private tutors. No, Raymond never saw her like I do, which is lucky for me, otherwise he'd have never let her go. She was just a place-keeper until Rebecca returned.

Pulling over to the side of the road, I stop on Ocean Park Boulevard, glad to find a spot at this time of day. It's going to reach the mid-nineties and the beaches are already packed with families enjoying the surf and sand at the best place to cool off. There are the usual surfers balancing on crests of undulating waves before being tossed into the water, which then washes them back to the shoreline, exhilarated, and ready to catch the next one. Several sailboats bop in the distance, creating a scenic backdrop against a clear blue sky.

Stepping out of the vehicle, I begin my usual twenty-minute set of stretches so I'll be prepped for my daily five-mile run. The physical training discipline is one of the things that most attracted me to the military. As an overweight kid, I'd always felt self-conscious and insecure.

I do my last set of hamstring stretches before I ease into my jog, modulating my breathing and maintaining a steady, even pace. Growing up, the unmistakable look of disappointment in my father's eyes whenever he looked my way made me feel like a failure. As I continue jogging, I remember how much I couldn't wait to get away from Santa Lorena and him but, now, it's time to return. I've put it off long enough; my mother needs me.

The time always goes by too quickly when I'm exercising. The focus on the physical activity allows me to block out all troubling thoughts, but... not today. A heaviness settles in my chest at how messed up it is that

Leah sees me as no more than a trusted friend. For some reason, she doesn't see me as the man I am, which explains why she felt comfortable talking to me when she was wearing only a towel. Now that's what I'd call frustrating—even insulting—if I didn't know her so well. I know her comfort around me is a reflection of her trust in me. With that thought, I increase my pace until I'm no longer jogging, but running full speed ahead.

Five more minutes and I'm slowing my pace before stopping at the end of the next block. Bending over and bracing my hands above my knees, I control my heavy breathing until I can resume walking back to the car at an even pace.

After completing ten minutes of warm-down exercises, I remove the key fob from the inside pocket of my shorts and open the door. Hopping in the car, I grab the hand towel I keep in the backseat and wipe the sweat from my brow. I know I can't give up, at least, not yet. One way or another, I'm going to figure out a way to make Leah see me as more than just a good friend. At some point, I'm going to have to stop playing it safe and go ahead and spin the dice. She needs to know that the man she *should* give her love to is me, not the previous high school quarterback and prom king, Raymond Colton, who is now a happily married man. With that thought, I drive home.

"Miguel." My Aunt Esther greets me as I walk into the kitchen of her two-bedroom single-story blue-and-gray house. "After you take your shower," she scrunches her nose dramatically, "we can eat and you can tell me all about the wedding last night."

"Sounds good." I lean over to kiss her cheek, but

she leans away from me.

"Please, shower first." With a lift of her chin, she indicates the hall leading to the bathroom. "I will never understand the point of running down the street for exercise. Basketball, baseball, I understand." She pulls a chair out from the table. "But running makes no sense. Return when you don't smell so... sweaty."

Chuckling, I head to the bathroom to shower. Aunt Esther and I have this same conversation on the banality of running versus an organized team sport several times each week. If there is no team and no ball, she doesn't see the purpose, even though she admits I'm in great shape.

Pulling off my damp clothes, I step into the warm water and lather up, thinking of Leah the whole time. If only she had been open to getting away from here for a few days. She could use a break from the gossip regarding her past relationship with Raymond.

Turning off the shower, I dry off, then slip on a black T-shirt and sweats before heading back into the spotlessly clean kitchen.

"*Now* you may kiss my cheek." Smiling, she turns toward me and taps the skin along the side of her unlined face. Inhaling deeply, she adds, "Ah, that is *so* much better. After working with stinky animals all day, do you think I want to come home and smell a sweaty man?"

"Not really." I laugh while walking into the kitchen and opening one of several take-out bags. My aunt works long hours as the town's only veterinarian, and, when she gets home, she's too exhausted to cook. I've offered countless times to grocery shop and cook, but she makes it clear she doesn't want me to make a mess of her immaculate—and mostly unused—state-of-the-art kitchen. Some people might say she has OCD, but she's always been this way, so it's nothing new for me. "I'll get the paper plates."

"Great. Since today is Sunday, I stopped at the deli and picked up a roast chicken, some asparagus, and brown rice." Taking the forks and knives out of the drawer, she adds, "Oh, and corn muffins." She holds up the smallest bag.

"You know, I *could* do the cooking." I set the food and the paper plates on the clear glass table and we both take a seat.

"Please." She raises a hand as if to block me from saying anything else. "We have gone over this many times. When you have your own kitchen, you can cook as much as you like, leave pots and pans in the sink and ketchup on the counter." She smirks. "But not here." Gazing at her kitchen with a contented expression, she continues, "It's beautiful exactly the way it is—spotless."

"That it is." Shrugging, I give up. My aunt has very strong views on how things should be done. She says she cooks like her mother—my paternal grandmother. My understanding is that my abuela didn't cook very well. I never knew her. She died the year before I was born, but her children say she was not the most skilled chef, although, unlike her daughter, she, at least, tried. It's no wonder my father married my mother, who is known for making some of the most delicious food south of Los Angeles. She's been written up in various culinary magazines, and she owns and operates a bed-and-breakfast inn where they serve all-you-can-eat Sunday brunch, plus homemade pastries. It wasn't difficult to figure out how I'd gotten to be twenty pounds overweight by the time I'd been ten years old.

"How was the wedding?" She places a corn muffin on each of our plates.

"Raymond and Rebecca make a great couple." I pick up another piece of chicken before continuing. "Everything was fine."

"Was it?" Glancing up from her plate, she raises her brows and looks at me inquisitively. "Because, even at the clinic today, all everyone could talk about was your friend, Leah Ann."

"What?" I abruptly set down my glass of almond milk, causing some to spill. I briskly take the paper towel and wipe the table. "They were talking about Leah?"

"Surely you aren't surprised?" She laughs while cutting up her asparagus. "Sunnyville is a small town and there's not a whole lot to gossip about, except, of course, some of the people who rent the cabins for the summer." Rolling her eyes and scowling, she continues, "Did you know someone actually brought a pet tarantula with them on vacation and they thought it had caught a cold?" Pointing her fork at me, she adds, "The stories I could tell you."

"I'm sure." I swallow the last of my chicken before voicing my thoughts about Leah being the subject of the gossip mill. "I was hoping they would spend at least a day talking about the bride and groom, but I saw the tweets early this morning and it had already gone viral."

"Poor girl. Falling apart like that and everyone seeing it." Shaking her head, she pats my hand. "That's what I don't like about this social media thing. It lets the whole world know everyone's business. Just imagine if someone posted, 'Poor Esther Montoya, never got married or had her own children.' " Pushing back from the table, she picks up her empty plate and tosses it into the garbage can under the kitchen cabinet. Shifting to look at me, she folds her arms across her waist and focuses on me. "And people would believe it." Shaking her head in disgust, she shrugs. "They would never know I turned down three marriage proposals and that I'd rather take care of animals than children. You," she tilts her chin in my direction, "are the one exception. You have been a blessing and a delight. People don't usually know the real details, so they make-up a story. What a shame."

"I agree." I clear the rest of the cartons and plates from the table. All it takes is a few negative words to ruin someone's day. Everyone is brave when they are anonymous. "That's why I asked Leah if she wants to go with me to Santa Lorena later this week."

"That's my boy." Aunt Esther clasps her hands together before giving me a quick nod. "Make this work for you."

"No, it's not like that." *But… wasn't it?* "Her father lives in Santa Lorena and I thought she could use a break from Sunnyville." Maybe Aunt Esther is a little bit correct. I did think Leah might need an escape from the predictable gossip, but I was looking forward to being alone with her. "She turned down the offer—said she could handle it."

"Oh well." She brushes her hands against each other. "That's that, then. Good for her. Maybe not so good for you, but good for her for feeling like she can dismiss the rumors that she's still in love with Raymond." Walking over to stand by me at the sink, she gives my arm a mild squeeze. "They *are* just rumors, aren't they?"

Although I've never openly shared my feelings about Leah with my aunt, she's a smart woman who knows me well enough to figure out what's in my heart. "Honestly, I don't know."

I'm worried about Leah but decide not to contact her. I got the message—I need to step back and allow her to handle this on her own terms. It's really none of my business—though anything having to do with Leah *does* affect me. Very much. But, as much as I wish I could protect her from her broken heart and prevent her from having to deal with gossip, I know this battle is hers to handle, not mine. Plus, I have enough on my mind already. The thought of seeing my father again is something I'm not looking forward to, but since my mother's phone call two days ago saying that my father isn't well and she'd appreciate it if I'd come home, I haven't felt like I have much choice *but* to make the trip.

Later that evening, before I fall asleep, I leaf through two of my sports and fitness magazines and review the daily health data from my sports watch. Just as I turn on my side and reach over to flick off the lamp on the nightstand, my cell phone rings.

"Hello," I say gruffly, thinking this is probably Sammy calling to complain about some disagreement between him and Cindy. "This better be good. I was just about to get some sleep. Though why you call me, I don't know. What do I know about relationships?"

"Miguel." Leah's voice carries a slight quiver. She doesn't sound like her usual confident self. "It's me."

"Oh, ignore what I just said." Twisting my lip, I

know I should have allowed her to speak first before rambling on. "I thought you were someone else."

"No problem." She sighs loudly. "Did I wake you?"

"I was awake." Sitting back up in bed, I turn the light on. "What's up? Are you okay?" She's never contacted me this late in the evening and I'm wondering if someone has gone too far or said the wrong thing, and now she needs me to come and get her or beat someone up. If some fool has offended her, they'll have to contend with me.

"I'm good—kind of." She pauses before continuing, "I decided I *will* take you up on your offer to go to Santa Lorena." Clearing her throat, she adds hesitantly, "That is, if you'll have me."

Chapter 5

*Leah*

I'm cramming a few last-minute items into my small suitcase, realizing I forgot to ask Miguel how long he planned to stay in Santa Lorena. Sure, I could pack an overnight bag if we're just going to be gone for the weekend, but there's a possibility we could be out of town for a week, what with his father being ill and all.

I'm in the kitchen selecting snacks for the trip, when I hear a knock at the front door. "Come in." My head is half-way in the refrigerator where I'm consciously selecting an assortment of healthy snacks— which is probably what Miguel is accustomed to— when what I really want to munch on during the road trip are sesame bagels with cream cheese, chocolate chip cookies, and spicy-hot tortilla chips— all of which have too many carbs and limited, if any, nutritional value to be part of anyone's healthy diet plan.

A couple of minutes later, I've found the bag of purple grapes and carrot sticks in the back of the vegetable bin. Straightening my back, I see Miguel, clad in a khaki shirt and dark denim pants, standing in the kitchen, looking uncomfortable.

"Good morning." Has he changed his mind? Is he already regretting his decision to have me tag along?

He's so thoughtful and polite, he probably asked without expecting me to say yes. "Is everything all right?"

Setting the bags on the counter, I take a couple of steps toward him. "Would you rather drive alone?" I'll give him an out, even though I am now eager to escape my hometown.

"No, of course not." He grins while taking a grape out of the bag and popping it into his mouth.

"Yuck." I swipe at his hand. "Please let me wash these first, before you start munching on our snacks." Opening the shelf above the sink, I remove the colander and dump the grapes in it before rinsing them thoroughly under the cool running water.

"Why would you think I'd change my mind?" Raising one of his eyebrows, he looks at me with a hurt expression.

"I don't know." Shrugging and avoiding his probing gaze, I add, "Sometimes, people change their minds."

Within days of Rebecca's return, Raymond's feelings for me had changed. Just like *that*. One minute we were a happy couple—or so I thought, and the next—I was standing on the outside, watching my dreams unravel like a ball of loose yarn rolling down a steep hill.

"I haven't changed my mind." He grabs another grape and eats it. "I'm glad you're coming."

I exhale loudly, not realizing I'd been holding my breath until I've released it. "Good." What was I thinking? Miguel is reliable and consistent. Apparently, the whole Raymond situation has affected me more than I've realized. "Sorry, about that." I place the grapes in my canvas bag along with two bananas, a bag of granola, four water bottles, and a stack of paper napkins.

"Leah." Most people pronounce my first name with one syllable, but not Miguel. He draws out the word, making it longer, which, somehow, feels more intimate, even special. His expression is somber as he grasps my shoulders and stands so close that I can't avoid eye contact.

"Yes?" Miguel always smells so good. One day, I'll ask him what product he uses, so I can buy that same woodsy fragrance for my future man.

"You can always trust me."

His voice is somber, as if he wants to brand the words into my consciousness, and I know that he's right. He's as trustworthy as they come.

"I know." I remove his hands from my shoulders and take a step back. "That's what makes you the perfect friend." Turning from him, I head toward the living room.

"Yeah, that's great." He follows me into the living room.

There's a different timbre to his deep voice that I don't recognize, but I don't comment or try to analyze it. My ability to read men is obviously impaired—as the entire town knows. "What's with all the boxes?"

"They're for the thrift store." So far, I've got five full boxes and still have a closet to tackle.

Blowing an errant curl off my forehead, I look into one of the open boxes and see my mother's lavender floral print house dress—knee-length, round collar, short sleeves, and snaps down the front. I can see her in it, sitting at the kitchen table early on a Saturday morning, sunlight streaming through the bay window and reflecting on her silver hair. Packing has been harder than I'd expected.

Shaking my head to erase the image from my mind, I quickly fold the flaps of the box into place. "I figured that, since I was going to the thrift store to offer up my hideous bridesmaid's dress, I might as well stop procrastinating and finish packing my mother's belongings, too. She has some nice things." Of course, spontaneously deciding to go to Santa Lorena is another distraction from facing the finality of my mother's absence. But I could really use some love right now and the only other biological relative I have left is my father.

"First of all, let's get one thing clear." Miguel interrupts my thoughts. His voice is firm, and I suppress the impulse to salute him. Shaking his head slowly, he continues, "That dress was *not* hideous. You looked… beautiful."

"Really?" I can't help it, laughter bubbles up inside me. "Come on now. Don't worry about hurting my feelings. You know I looked like a slice of lemon meringue pie." It's a relief to be laughing, to focus on something besides packing up the leftover remnants of my mother's life.

"I'm telling the truth," he says emphatically. "Are you ready to get going?"

"Okay." I stop laughing. I can definitely recognize the irritation in his voice now, but why is it there? "I'm laughing at myself, not at what you're saying."

"I don't think you can hear what I'm saying." Walking over to the living room window, he stands silently, looking out at the street. The shrieks and chatter of children's voices can be heard as they play hopscotch on the sidewalk and ride their bicycles down the street to the end of the cul-de-sac.

"Yes, I do," I say in my own defense. Making my way around the boxes, I stand beside him. Placing my hand in the crook of his elbow, I rest my head on his shoulder. "I just don't happen to agree with you." I give him a hopeful look, but his eyes stay focused on what's going on outside the window. "Is that okay?"

"Of course," he says gruffly.

I can feel the stiffness of his body and the irritation in his voice.

"It's your right."

"Yep, packed and ready to go." I give his arm a nudge, hoping to lighten his abrupt mood change. I remind myself that Miguel is a veteran, and his suddenly shifting moods have nothing to do with me, most likely. While he was gone, he'd had experiences that I know nothing about. Maybe, one day, he'll share some of them.

Releasing my hold on his arm, I lift my head and look up at his face. "You feel so good to lean on. Great shoulders, by the way."

"Thank you." Smiling down at me, he meets my gaze. "Notice how I accepted *your* compliment?" He points a finger in my direction.

"Okay." I squirm under his gaze. "You're right. I've always struggled to take compliments seriously or… graciously, for that matter."

"I've noticed." He rubs his chin. "Why is that?"

"Good question." Shrugging, I press my lips together, trying to think back to a time when I'd felt confident enough to accept a compliment, but I come up with nothing. "Maybe it's because my mother was so awesome. I mean, she was in beauty pageants when she was a teenager, which is how she ended up winning multiple full scholarships for medical school. It's hard to grow up in the shadow of that kind of brilliance." She was also kind and loving, but I don't need to tell him that. He knew my mother and she had always been fond of Miguel. "Anyway, we need to get going. I'm pretty certain that you don't want to hear my life story."

Releasing my hold on his arm, I step away, ready to go to my room and retrieve my overnight bag, but he stands in front of me, blocking my path.

"You don't know what I want because I haven't told you."

Why did his voice go down a couple of octaves? Suddenly, he's a baritone.

"Maybe there are things I haven't shared with you… yet," he says. "Have you thought of that?"

"Okay, I get it. You have some deep buried secrets that I know nothing about. Fair enough. Maybe, on this trip, I'll learn more." Again, I think of his military experiences. Had he experienced combat? Maybe he suffers from residual trauma that I know nothing about. I've been so self-absorbed that I haven't provided him with an opportunity to share what he may be going through. "I know I've been focused on me lately and haven't really checked in with you, but I'm hoping that we can catch up on this trip. I do want to know what's going on with you."

"I know that the last few months have been tough for you." Reaching over, he smooths a curl from my forehead. "When the time is right, I'll share some of what has been on my mind. That's a promise."

"I'll hold you to that." It's time for me to get over my pity party and focus on someone besides myself. I do hope that Miguel feels comfortable enough to share whatever is on his mind with me. Lord knows I've leaned on him, both figuratively and literally. I've mistakenly overlooked the possibility that he may be struggling with some challenges of his own. For example, he doesn't appear very thrilled to be returning to Santa Lorena. What had he said about his troubled relationship with his father? I'm embarrassed to face the fact that I know very little about my best friend's troubles. It's time for me to do better, and this trip will provide me with the overdue opportunity to be as great a friend to him as he's been to me.

"Well, if you are ready, we can head out now." He looks more relaxed, not as stressed as he did a few minutes ago.

"If you get the snacks from the kitchen counter, I'll get my overnight bag."

While he heads to the kitchen, I retrieve my suitcase from my bed and wheel it to the front door.

"Whoa," Miguel exclaims as he heads out of the kitchen, snack pack in hand. His eyes grow huge, and he blinks a couple of times before tilting his head to the side to stare at the suitcase as if it's a foreign object I'm dragging in from outer space. "That's a large suitcase."

"No, it's not." Is he kidding? My large suitcase is under my bed and it's twice the size of what I've brought into the room. Then I remember, as a veteran, Miguel is no doubt accustomed to packing super efficiently, so, in comparison, my baggage *does* appear oversized. Plus, they probably used duffle bags, not standard luggage. "I'll have you know that this happens to be my medium-sized suitcase." I twirl it around on its four wheels.

"I'd hate to see what the large size looks like." Walking over, he leans down and studies my suitcase while running a hand along his jaw. "Mind if I ask how long you think we'll be gone?"

"That's just it." I check the zipper on the suitcase, before continuing, "I forgot to ask you, so I figured it's better to have extra clothes than not enough."

"Sure, that makes sense," he says easily, his lips tilting up at the corners. "Let's trade." He hands me the snacks before grasping the suitcase handle. "That's better."

While he loads my suitcase into the trunk, I hop into his gray sports utility vehicle. He'd bought it the week he came home from his tour of duty, so I know it's not new, but it's spotless with shiny chrome nobs and a black leather interior. There's a small brown duffle in the back seat and a pair of track shoes.

"I see you brought your running shoes." I point to the pair of well-worn brown-and-beige running shoes on the floor of the back seat. "You are the most disciplined person I know. I admire that about you." The results of his labor are evident in the way his shirt clings to his muscular arms and the flatness of his abdominal muscles. Of course, that's why he's in constant demand as a fitness instructor and a personal trainer.

He taps a round button on the consul and the car starts without the key being inserted into the ignition. "Thanks. I had to be in shape while I was in the military. My life and the life of the women and men I served with was dependent on me being able to do my job, and now it's a habit." Maneuvering the car away from the curb, he glances in my direction before scanning the area to make sure none of the children are behind us. "Adjust your seat so you're comfortable."

"I'm good," I say, before locating the lever on the side of my seat and increasing my legroom. "I'm guessing your last date was petite."

"Why would you say that?" He gives me a quick side-eye as he approaches Main Street, which will lead us directly to Highway 57, the quickest route out of Sunnyville that merges into the 101 freeway that runs parallel to the Pacific Ocean.

I shrug. "Your passenger seat was pulled up so high, obviously a tall person could not have been the last person you drove around." Now my mind is racing, trying to figure out the name of the lucky woman who has been his companion. Miguel is a good man by anyone's standards. He's shy of six feet by about an inch and has thick, wavy, black hair and chocolate brown eyes. A woman would have to be a fool not to appreciate what he has to offer. He's managed to keep his love life private, which is not easy to do in a small town. Maybe I'll find out more before the end of our trip, but I won't push. I understand how important it is to not feel like you're allowed a private personal life.

"Interesting deduction." He chuckles, clearly amused. "What if I told you it wasn't a woman?"

"Please." I look at him incredulously. "I cannot believe how many women in Sunnyville suddenly need a personal trainer." Folding my hands across my waist, I frown. Prior to Miguel's return to Sunnyville, the town's fitness center had been in danger of closing its doors, that's how few people utilized it. But once

Miguel began offering personal training and regular fitness classes, it seemed as if every other person— women in particular—suddenly became serious about working out. His classes have been such a hit, that there's now a waiting list.

"Sunnyville never had a personal trainer before, so I'm just filling a need." He dismisses my comment with a shrug before turning on the air-conditioning. Cool air rushes into the car. The weather forecaster had announced that the temperatures would reach the upper nineties, so the cool air against my skin is a welcome relief from the sweat that was already beginning to form on my forehead and thighs. Maybe I shouldn't have worn shorts, but, at the time, it seemed to make sense.

"Come on now, you cannot possibly believe it's only because they want to get fit." Tossing my hands in the air, I make a tsk-ing sound. "The beach has been there forever, but, suddenly, you've got how many women participating in your eight a.m. morning jog?" Tapping my hands on my thighs, I wait for him to respond.

"Give me a minute." He hums a tune as he mentally calculates the numbers.

"The fact that you don't know the number off the top of your head proves my point." I've spotted them in the mornings when I'm driving to work. Pleasant Elementary School is three miles from the beach, and I always prefer the scenic route. The waves rolling in and the early morning surfers are part of what drew me back to Sunnyville, along with the fact that no other place has ever felt like home. Miguel returned a month after I arrived back from Santa Cruz, where I had attended college and lived for two years afterward. I'd wanted to complete my teaching credential before I returned. By that time, my mother had retired, so she'd joined me. "Face it. *You* are the main attraction." Everyone could use a little eye candy to jump-start their days. I can't say I blame his devotees. If he wasn't one of my best friends, I'd be attracted to him, too.

"The only reason I don't know is because we have some drop-ins and two more students signed up last week."

"Aha!" I say as if I'm an attorney who just won an important court case. "There you have it." I snap my fingers. "New women are continuously registering for your classes... doesn't it make you wonder *why*?" The man is totally oblivious to the fact that a good percentage of the single female population drools when they see him walking around town in his workout shorts, his tan skin glistening golden brown from his most recent workout.

"I like to believe it's because I'm a good instructor."

It's kind of sweet that he's so oblivious. He truly does not know the effect he has on the average woman. No wonder I like him so much. Modesty is not something you see every day in men who are as good-looking as Miguel.

"By the way, men also train with me."

"Sure they do. Probably to see if they can get to know some of the women in your class." I laugh at my own assessment. "But, seriously, maybe ten percent of your students are men. Clearly, they are not the majority." Miguel is obviously a very intelligent man, but when it comes to why his business is booming, he is clueless. It's evident by his physique and the results I already see with a couple of friends that he's an excellent trainer. But the *it* factor must be considered. The man is drop-dead gorgeous, and, in a small town, where everyone knows each other since elementary school, having someone return home who's bigger and better than before, is cause for celebration and—who knows—maybe a love connection for one lucky woman.

Traffic slows down as we leave Sunnyville and approach the city of Alameda, another beach city that lures beachgoers. Our town decided to maintain its small-town charm by retaining its original architecture of one-story, stucco-and-brick storefronts, which are mostly family-owned businesses. High-rises of any type are not allowed.

Alameda, on the other hand, has extended vertically with the addition of modern condominiums, designer outlet stores, and national retail stores and restaurant chains.

"What about you?"

We are at a complete standstill as we exit the freeway. Gridlock never happens in Sunnyville. Miguel gives me a disapproving look.

"What about me?" Reaching into the clear plastic snack bag, I take out a banana. "Want one?"

"No." As cars begin moving again, he shifts his eyes back to the road. "I had a protein shake this morning before I came to get you."

"Of course you did." I don't mention the strawberry protein powder canister I have on a shelf in the back of a cupboard at home. It's been there unopened for a year. It seems too time-consuming to take the blender out of the cabinet and add frozen fruit and ice when the cereal box and milk are within easy reach. "You are so good. I could learn a thing or two from you."

"It's what I do for a living." Keeping his eyes focused on the road, he adds, "I have to follow through or what kind of fitness instructor would I be? Plus, I love it."

"That all makes sense." Taking a bite of my banana, I slump down in my seat, feeling frumpier by the minute. How many times have I vowed to start an exercise routine only to get bored and give up? "You are a walking advertisement for fitness."

"You look good yourself."

He says it so effortlessly, that I want to believe him.

"Always."

"Really, Miguel." I don't try to disguise the irritation in my voice. "I know you have to encourage your clients by acknowledging their accomplishments, but you don't have to pretend like I'm the picture of fitness."

"*Excuse* me?" His voice is as irritated as mine was, possibly more. "I'm not pretending anything. Have you looked in the mirror lately? Your body is perfect the way it is. We aren't all supposed to have the same build. How boring would that be?"

A muscle in his jaw twitches and my adrenaline surges as I watch the odometer go from sixty to seventy-five in a matter of seconds.

"Don't tell me I don't know what I'm saying. It's my business to know."

"I didn't mean to offend you." Placing my hand on

his arm, I squeeze it. "Will you please slow down?" *Note to self, do not say anything to set off Miguel when he is driving.* But what triggered this mood? I'm just stating the truth, at least as I see it. I want him to know he doesn't have to say things to try to make me feel like I'm in shape when I know that I could definitely do better. "I don't exercise." I'm not Catholic, but I do feel like I'm in one of those church booths where you confess all of your sins to a priest. "I have protein powder, too, but I never create enough time to prepare a shake."

He doesn't immediately respond, but I notice his grip on the steering wheel loosens and he resumes driving within the speed limit again. I have never seen him like this. Is he mad because I don't exercise or because of something else?

"Sorry. I don't like it when people put themselves down, *especially* you." He gives me a quick reassuring glance, the smile on his face letting me know that he's cooled down. "You probably don't realize how frequently you make statements putting yourself down."

What's Miguel talking about? I don't put myself down or, at least, not that I'm aware of. Perhaps the breakup with Raymond may have done more of a number on me than I've recognized… "I do like myself, except, maybe, I don't know—bouncing back after being dumped for someone else has bruised my ego." Feeling guilty, as if I've unknowingly committed a crime, I chuckle, attempting to lighten the mood.

"I believe you." He pats my knee.

It's a quick, light touch, but it's still soothing. I almost want to ask him to do it again. Dogs and cats are smart; they let their humans know when they need a gentle touch.

Reaching forward, he turns off the air-conditioner and opens his window. "It's just that I've been there."

"What do you mean?" I continue eating my banana, recovering from being chastised. Who was I trying to fool? The whole town has seen pictures of me falling apart and Miguel, well, he knows me better than anyone else. But can I say the same about knowing him as well? "You've been where?"

"You know, the place where you put yourself down all the time." His lips compress into a tight line. "All it takes is a dig here and there because you feel inadequate or, like, you aren't good enough."

"*You*?" I'm momentarily speechless, wondering how we got on this serious topic. One minute, I'm mentally visualizing how beautiful he looks while exercising, and the next minute, we're discussing feelings of inadequacy, "Okay, I'll admit that I am guilty as charged, but I don't do it consciously. I'm probably not even aware of it, most of the time."

"I noticed," he says simply. "That's what makes it so troubling."

"I guess I'll have to pay more attention to what I'm saying." I hope he doesn't notice the quiver in my voice. Now that he's brought my attention to how I put myself down, I suppose there's an expectation that I'll stop doing it.

I wring my hands together. That will be easier said than done, but what had he just said about himself? Surely, I misunderstood. He couldn't possibly relate to feeling like he's not being his best self. "How could *you* not feel good about yourself?" I turn the tables on him.

"Have *you* looked in the mirror lately, Mr. Montoya?"

"Yes." He taps his fingers against the steering wheel. "I do regularly."

"Come on now, you've got to love what you see." I stare at him.

"Sometimes yes and sometimes no." The jaw twitch is back. "Some days when I look in the mirror, I see the military man who served his country to the best of his ability and who makes a living attempting to help people become fit and live a healthy lifestyle. At other times, however, I see a fat kid who doesn't feel good about himself."

Before I can comment, he presses a button on the steering wheel and says, "Hey, we're almost there. Let's listen to some music."

It's not a question of if I want to listen to music; his voice, firm, direct, and clear, has abruptly ended the conversation.

And, without a word, I realize a door revealing a previously unknown dimension of my dearest friend just got cracked open, but before I can step in and explore, he's slammed the door shut—possibly throwing away the key.

## Chapter 6

*Miguel*

"What made you change your mind?" We've been listening to the music in silence for the last twenty minutes, neither of us commenting after my completely unexpected comment about my twelve-year-old self. From Leah's stunned expression, I know my last comment startled her. Heck, it startled me. Why did the disturbing memory of my former self emerge now? "A couple of days ago, you weren't interested in joining me." By changing the subject, I hope to lighten the mood—everything had been fine until I'd started getting intense. It must be the thought of being back in my parents' house again that has me on edge.

Now who looks uncomfortable? Out of the corner of my eye, I see her shoulders slump.

"I had prioritized my tasks to be completed for this weekend, but going out of town was not on my list. After months of putting off packing my mother's clothes to donate to the thrift store, I had decided it was time for me to stop procrastinating and finally take care of business. I didn't want that nasty tweet to change my plans, but you were right. You warned me that the social media hoopla could get intense before it dies down." She brings a hand up and runs it through her curly hair. "I didn't think many people would pay attention to what someone had written about… "

She pauses, and I wonder if she's searching for the right word.

"… Raymond and me."

"Right." My voice is deceptively calm, but the question that I want to blurt out is sealed inside my heart. I know Leah is not ready to tell me when she'll stop longing for someone who clearly has never appreciated her… and what if she never is? It takes a lot on my part to not tell her that she's better off without him, but I know that she's not ready to hear it. At least not yet. Plus, she needs to come to that conclusion herself or it really won't mean anything for us. I'll have to bide my time, no matter how difficult it is.

"I think it was the pictures of me at the table looking like I was the jilted ex-girlfriend. Which, come to think of it, is an accurate assessment of the situation. Of course, the second picture of me slumped over in the car, makes me look like I was totally distraught." Sitting up straight, she weaves her fingers together.

Gone is the large ring she had previously bought herself, which town folk had mistakenly thought was a not-so-subtle attempt to nudge Raymond to replace it with an engagement ring.

"Suddenly, the thought of leaving town began to seem like a good idea." She attempts to smile, but there's no light in those eyes, only the traces of a lingering sadness.

She can't fool me.

"Did someone say something to you?" Anger stirs in my chest as I think about anyone saying or doing anything to make Leah feel uncomfortable or, worse yet, ashamed. "Just tell me who it was, and I'll straighten them out when we return."

Startled, she brings a hand to her throat. "No, it was nothing like that. You don't need to 'straighten them out'—whatever that means."

"It just means I would talk to them." I steer the car off exit 49 and head toward Leah's father's home. "That's all. I'm not a Neanderthal. I wouldn't go punch them or anything violent." No, that was never me. Even when other students used to call me Fatso or Chubby, I'd never resorted to retaliating physically. Instead, I'd vowed to myself that, one day, I'd have a physique that would make my father proud, not embarrassed for having me as a son.

"It was the whispering. Wherever I went, people would actually point at me and whisper. Sometimes, loud enough for me to hear."

"The people in town mean well, but the truth is that they don't have enough to occupy their thoughts. Especially now that the wedding of the previous prom king and queen is a done deal."

"Uh huh," Leah mumbles in response.

I wish I hadn't mentioned the high school prom. Leah and her mom had already moved away from Sunnyville when she was a high school freshman.

I had secretly harbored feelings for her since middle school. Feelings I knew would subside, but no matter how many other women I've dated, my feelings for the woman sitting beside me never faltered. As a matter of fact, with no encouragement from her, what I'd felt continued to flourish, even as the years had progressed and now, here I am, like some kind of love-sick fool, soothing her because she didn't choose me— has never even *considered* me as anything more than a damn buddy.

Maybe I am a fool.

What a fine pair Leah and I are, each stuck on the wrong person and not knowing how to move forward.

"Remember the day after the wedding, when you came over and I was going to meet Jenny in town for breakfast?"

She rushes her words together as if she can't wait to get the sentence out and over with. Maybe she's eager to say what she has to say before we arrive at her father's house, which is less than ten miles away. I've been driving for a couple of hours, but the time I spend with Leah always goes by too quickly. I don't have the time to explain to her how I feel. Talk about pitiful excuses.

"Yes." I never forget the time I spend with her or what we talk about. She may not see me as more than a friend, but I always see her *not* as a pal. "You two were going to get breakfast."

"Well, people were looking at me with… pity."

Her voice rises and I hear the underlying anger. "Can you believe it? I don't want *anyone's* pity. I'll get through this. Good Lord, that's the last thing I want or need."

I like her like this, filled with resolve and determination.

"I figure, a few days away so when I come back, they'll have someone else to talk about besides me."

"Maybe someone stole a candy bar from the drug store or someone besides Jed Smith will run for mayor," I chime in, relieved to see she's ready to move forward, which means there's hope for me yet. Hope for us *both* in the future. She's not the only one who's willing to go after what she wants.

"Exactly!" Her voice brims with excitement as she warms to the prospect of taking control of her life. "Honestly, when I saw myself in those pictures, I was disgusted… with me, not the person who took them. It's time for me to get a grip and get over that man." Her voice is stronger now, as if she's come to a new resolution. "My mother always said the right man for me will come along one day, and, when he does, he will love me just as I am."

"I always liked your mother." I'm grinning and feeling like we are turning a corner, away from the past and moving toward a better place. "Your mother was a very intelligent woman."

"She was." Leah's eyes light up, as if the mere memory of her mother sparks joy. "That she was." Pausing, she hesitates, as if not sure if she should say more. "You aren't going to believe this, but she once told me that she didn't believe Raymond was the man for me. Said he was a nice guy, but not the right man for her daughter."

"Really?" I turn left onto her father's street and slow down almost to a stop because I don't want the conversation to end.

"She saw something I didn't, and she was right." She grabs a bottle of water and twists the top off before taking a long sip. "I needed to see those pictures, even if it's mortifying on some level. I needed to face how ridiculous I was being about the whole Raymond/Rebecca thing." Leaning back so that her head falls against the headrest, she closes her eyes. "That's why I'm here. I know I'm getting strong, but I figure I can still use my father's support right about now as well as a break from Sunnyville."

"You have support from more than your father." Pulling up, I stop in front of a yellow house with neatly formed hedges and three rose bushes on either side of a small patch of green grass. Turning off the ignition, I unfasten my seatbelt, and shift position so that she's looking at me when I say what I have to say next. "I'm always here for you."

"I know, and I appreciate it—appreciate you as the best brother-friend a girl could have." Leaning forward, she presses soft lips against my right cheek.

Crazy thing is, even though the contact is brief, maybe a nanosecond long, it sends a surge of adrenaline through my system, igniting my desire to have so much more. Some primal part of me wants to reach over and pull her into my arms, feel the softness of her lush body pressed against mine. Let her feel the pressure of my lips against hers and release the hunger for her that has consumed me for so many years… the hunger I haven't been able to outgrow. Make it clear, in no uncertain terms that I am *not* a brother; I'm a man with wants and needs, and those needs include Leah.

She looks at me expectantly, hazel eyes unblinking, waiting for me to respond, and I have to pull myself together and not scare her away, because I'd rather have her friendship and trust than nothing at all.

At least, that's what I tell myself… for now.

"We're here!" Clearing my throat, I inject enthusiasm I don't feel into my voice. One day, when the time is right and I know without a doubt that she has recovered from the breakup with Raymond, I'll share my genuine emotions, but, until then, I'll keep my feelings to myself. And, based on what she said earlier about being eager to move on, that might be sooner rather than later. "Was your father excited about your visit?"

"Definitely." Chewing on her bottom lip, she looks uncertain as she absently laces her fingers together, which is a sure sign that she's anxious about something. "He asked how long I was staying." She brushes her hair away from her face. "By the way, how long *are* we staying?"

Before I respond, she continues, "I told him a few days."

"I meant to mention that sooner." I wish it were only a day. I'd been avoiding thinking about how long I might be here. Not because of my mother; we're close. She always has my back—always has and always will. My father... Well, that's a whole other story. Leah being here will make it easier for me to have an excuse to make sure this trip is brief. After all, I have to drive her back to Sunnyville. I have a month vacation, but I'm not about to volunteer that information to my parents, not if I don't have to. "Maybe four days." Unfastening my seat belt, I add, "If that's too long, just let me know."

"Four days sounds good." It's as if she's looking right past me over my shoulder and out the window. "The other reason I decided to come with you was that I didn't have an opportunity to speak with my father at my mother's funeral. There was so much going on and things I had to do." Her full lips turn down at the corners. "I feel bad about only speaking to him briefly. Even though my parents divorced when I was one, I know that, at one point, they had to have loved each other or I wouldn't be here. My mother's death must have been hard on him. Neither of them remarried, so it makes me wonder, right?"

"Of course." Although, if her parents had never stopped loving each other and had never married anyone else, why hadn't they gotten back together? I'm not about to share that question with Leah because it's really none of my business. Plus, it's hard for me to relate when my parents are still in love and affectionate with each other. As a kid, I was embarrassed when I saw them kissing, holding hands in public or what I then called "all that other mushy stuff". Years later, as an adult, I realized I was fortunate to have parents whose love only grew stronger as time went by. I'm hoping to have that same kind of good fortune in my life. "Let's plan to leave on Friday."

"Okay. I better get going." She gives me a weak smile. "My dad is probably looking through the window right now, wondering what's taking me so long to come inside." She shifts in her seat so she can get a better view of her father's home, the home she lived in with both parents until they divorced.

"I'll get your suitcase out of the trunk." I open my car door.

"No." Placing a hand on my arm, she continues, "You don't have to get out of the car. If you open the trunk, I'll take my luggage inside."

"All right." If only I could kiss her goodbye, but I can't, so I need to focus. I tap the button on the console to open the trunk. "Call me if you need a ride. I'm in the valley. It's not that far." Leah's father's home is in a residential neighborhood that borders the center of a town.

"Thanks, but I don't plan on going anywhere." She

continues talking as she walks to the back of the car. "It's only four days. I'd like to spend that time with my father."

Deciding to get out of the car anyway, I lift open the trunk and, reaching in, I remove her suitcase. "Here you go." I hug her and wonder if she can hear my heartbeat pounding against my chest as I wrap my arms around her. Why does she have to always feel so good, so right in my arms?

Because she's Leah, and she belongs next to me. As far as I'm concerned, it's that simple. My challenge is figuring out how to share my feelings and praying to the powers that be, that she can share my love.

Back in the car and on the road again, I allow myself to feel optimistic. Finally, it sounds like Leah is ready to take back her life, and, maybe, when she emerges from the fog of being in love with the wrong man, she'll understand what her mother was trying to tell her all along—which is that there's someone out there who appreciates who she is without any reservations.

Before this trip is over, she'll know I've never stopped loving her, not since I'd first met her in middle school. She'd noticed when the teacher called on me during our algebra class that I unfailingly answered each question asked, incorrectly. One day, as we'd left class, she'd walked beside me and had graciously volunteered to help me with math after school. I'd been her first teaching job, and she'd been my first and only love. So, in a sense, I'd helped her identify her career path and she'd helped me know that there is such a thing as love at first sight.

As I continue coasting through downtown Santa

Lorena, I don't see any vestiges of the damage from the raging fires ignited by the dry Santa Ana winds two years ago. Several new businesses have popped up since my last visit. Annie's Pottery Barn and Joe's Snip and Clip Barber Shop are unchanged, but the Yoga 4U Studio, Sarah's Day Spa, and the Yummy Yogurt shops are new Main Street attractions.

As I navigate past the central area and through the outskirts of town, past Paradise Homes, which is a small cluster of trailer park homes, I now know where the most damage was done. Less than ten homes remain where there once had been thirty trailers.

My cell phone vibrates as I continue up the hill toward my childhood home. Glancing down, I see my mother's image appear on the screen. Smiling, I tap the section of the steering wheel that allows the call to come through my console.

"Mom." If she hadn't requested I come home, I would have stayed in Sunnyville, but my mother had made it clear as glass that she needed to talk to me in person, so here I am. She'd been unclear about what, specifically, had happened with my father, but she'd urged me to come to Santa Lorena soon. I have never been able to deny a direct request by my mother, whom I love dearly.

"Son, it's good to hear your voice." She sounds breathless, which isn't unusual. Her bed-and-breakfast inn keeps her busy with customers and overseeing the menu. Of course, she wouldn't have it any other way. Lucia's Inn is a dream she'd nursed for many years before it came to fruition, and it has turned out to be a huge success.

"You say that every time we talk, which is about

once a week." Chuckling, I'm grateful for our relationship. At least I know I've never been a disappointment to *her*.

"That's because it's true." Her voice brims with pride. "I always love speaking to my boy."

"Almost thirty is hardly a boy." Of course, we've also had this conversation before, and it always ends the same way.

"Shush." She makes a familiar dismissive sound, letting me know that she's not about to change her perception of me. "I'm doing good not calling you my baby." Her rich laughter echoes in the car. "Because you know you will *always* be my child, and a mother has the right to call her son a boy, even though I know you are a grown man who has travelled the world and is back home."

"I look forward to seeing you." This is true. I love spending time with her and eating the special dishes she makes specifically for me. "I'll probably be there within the next twenty minutes."

"That's why I was calling—to see how close you were." She mumbles something under her breath. "Look, I'm going to get off this phone. I need to pick up something I forgot to get at the store, but I'll be back before you get here. See you soon, son."

I don't want to take a chance and arrive before she returns, so I slow down and take the longer route around the incline, past Hartland Ranch and the orange groves. Thomas Hart, owner of the profitable citrus crop, and my father had been best friends ever since they'd attended Santa Lorena High School and met in a wood shop class. They'd been like brothers in many ways, and his death a couple of years ago had left a void in all of our lives. He was the closest I'd ever come to having an uncle and I haven't returned to the ranch since his funeral.

To this day, I refer to his two daughters, Elaine and Morgan, as two of my closest friends. I always make it a point to visit Elaine since she got married, had baby Twyla, and took over the running of the ranch. Morgan, on the other hand, has always been a free spirit, and I'd be lucky to see her at all, considering that she'd adopted a daughter and now works as a grant writer for an orphanage in South Africa. My mother has informed me that Morgan does visit twice a year. If I'm lucky, one of her two visits will coincide with my time in Sunnyville.

Driving up the narrow dirt road, I spot my mother's blue Mercedes parked in her designated spot on the side of the inn. I breathe more easily when I don't see my father's silver Volvo parked next to it. *The coast is clear*. It's a shame to still feel that way after all these years, but my father and I have never been able to have a warm father-and-son relationship, where he pats me on the back and tells me that he's proud of me.

A strong breeze causes the hand-carved wooden sign, with the words Lucia's Bed-and-Breakfast, to sway back and forth. Several cars are in the lot, which signals she has overnight customers or people who have stopped in for breakfast.

I park in a space in the back of the building. My throat feels dry as I remind myself not to get into any verbal altercations with my father.

I leave my duffle bag in the car for now and head toward the front door, pausing to glance admiringly at the herb garden, which is lush with aromatic fresh plants that add the rich flavors that make my mother's dishes known throughout the state. The familiar sound of chimes reverberate in the spacious wood-paneled lobby as I step inside.

Maple wood floors shine in the rays of sunlight that stream through the large windows and the sunroof. Two oversized brown leather chairs face the fireplace and, further back, is a cluster of straight-back chairs with colorful orange, green, and yellow pillows clustered around a circular table. Round, almost flat, earth-tone plant holders contain succulents clipped from the gardens bordering the back perimeter of the inn.

"Welcome," a cheery female voice calls out to me from the reception desk. A slender woman with straight black hair and a wide smile eagerly waves me over. "You check in over here."

As I approach the desk, I look more closely, wondering why she looks familiar. "I'm not checking in."

"Oh." A shadow of disappointment crosses her face. Maybe business isn't doing so well. She picks a pen up from the desk, before furtively glancing to the right. "I guess that means you're here for the restaurant." She points in the direction of the café. "It's right around that corner." She directs her attention to a sheet of paper with a long list of names. "I suppose you have a reservation."

"No, I don't." I respond absently, wondering if my mother has returned and is in the kitchen or somewhere else on the grounds. I scan the lobby before I head toward the dining room.

"Now wait just a minute." Her tone is scolding as she flips a swath of dark hair over one shoulder. "You may be starving, but you can't sashay in there like you own the place."

Something in her brown eyes flickers conspiratorially, and I'm curious about what she'll say next.

"I'm confident I can find a place for you at one of the tables." Scurrying from behind the counter, she comes to stand beside me. "Stay here for a minute. Don't worry, I'll take care of you."

"But—" I begin, holding my hands out, ready to explain before she interrupts me.

Tilting her head, she says, "Please, it would be *my* pleasure."

Before I can say another word, she's turned and, with purposeful strides, she's marching toward the dining room.

"You wait right there. Don't go anywhere. I'll be back soon."

Less than five minutes pass before my mother bursts through the dining room door. Her silver-streaked black hair is cut in a short, symmetrical style that compliments her high cheekbones, and she's wearing tailored, beige slacks and a turquoise blouse as she rushes over and embraces me. "Taylor told me some handsome stranger was out here and I knew she had to be talking about you." She kisses me on both cheeks, then rocks me in her arms before releasing me. It's this way every time she sees me.

Guilt flares as I wonder if it's because I visit so seldom. I'd like to believe it's because she's always been an affectionate and enthusiastic parent.

"I tried to tell her, but she moved so fast, I couldn't stop her." The woman was like a torpedo. One minute she was at the counter and the next she was bustling over to the restaurant, trying to figure out a way they could accommodate me. "She didn't give me a chance to explain who I was." Not wanting my mother to get the wrong idea, I add, "She's very friendly and was trying to be helpful."

"She's right about one thing; you do look good." My mother links her arm in mine and leads me to the lobby chairs.

The woman my mother called Taylor rushes over. "Miguel, is that really you?"

Raising her brows, her eyes slowly and thoroughly assess me from head to toe. It doesn't bother me, though. As a fitness instructor, I'm used to people perusing me and my level of fitness. I understand that I am the brand representative for my fitness services. Still, Taylor doesn't know anything about what I do for a living, unless my mother has shared that information.

"Damn. When did you get so fine?" She nervously glances at my mother before clearing her throat. "Excuse me, Mrs. Montoya. I meant to say, Miguel, it's so good to see you again. There's so much to catch up on." She gives me a warm smile. "When are you available?"

*So much to catch up on?* Who is she? As I study her face more closely, she does begin to look vaguely familiar, but it's been years since I'd lived here. And when I did return, I pretty much stuck close to home. "So, we know each other?" I hesitantly ask, trying not to offend this woman who's gone out of her way to be accommodating.

"You attended elementary school with Taylor." Touching my arm, my mother comes to the rescue. It's a role she's familiar with. She was always attempting to intervene and deescalate when my father was coming down hard on me for some infraction or the other.

"That's all right." Taylor's mouth lifts in a bright smile as she sweeps a hand across her forehead.

That's when I see the small pink birthmark on her wrist. "Taylor heart." The words spill out in a burst of sudden recollection. The other students gave her that nickname because of the heart-shaped birthmark on her wrist. "Fifth and sixth grade in Mrs. Thompson's class. It was such a long time ago."

"Don't remind me of my age, please. I'm trying to forget how quickly the years are going by." She says wistfully, "It's good to see you again."

My mother tugs on my arm and clears her throat. "You two will have ample time to chat about old times later." She tilts her head toward Taylor. "Taylor works here."

"I noticed that." She hasn't really changed that much, except now she's taller and her hair is longer. But she was friendly back then and it seems that hasn't changed.

"I'll get back to work." Dark eyes dart from me to my mother as she lifts her chin in the direction of the reception desk.

"Let's get some food in you. Have you eaten today?" Not waiting for a response, my mother leads me through the dining area and toward the kitchen. "I'll fix a plate for you and then we can talk in my office." She lifts lids off the pans and the aroma of her black beans, red rice, and fried plantains has my mouth watering.

"I always have room for your cooking." And it's

true. That'd been part of the problem when I'd been younger. I'd been unable to resist her cooking and had probably eaten too much of it, which explains why I'd always been the biggest—not the tallest—child in my classes throughout elementary school.

"That's my boy." She piles a stack of food on the plate before pointing to a drawer near the sink. "Get your silverware and a napkin." She indicates the industrial-sized stainless-steel refrigerator. "Grab something to drink, too."

I remove a pitcher of *horchata,* a sweet cinnamon rice beverage I'd loved as a kid. It tasted more like liquid dessert than anything else. I probably should have spent more time outside playing than hanging out in the kitchen with my mother, but, uninterested in the orange groves where my father worked as foreman or the grapevines he was growing for the small vineyard he was developing, I'd decline his offers to come work with him outside. When I'd had no option *but* to go with him, to say I was unenthusiastic was an understatement.

"The glasses are in the same place they've always been."

Just in case I've forgotten, she stands in front of a cabinet where an assortment of beveled glasses is arranged by size on several shelves.

"Right." Time to get my head back in the present. Being here opens the shaft that lets in memories, both good and bad. "Aren't you eating anything?"

"You know me." Removing a stack of papers from her desk, she sets down the plate. "I do so much tasting and munching while I'm cooking that I couldn't possibly eat a full meal."

"But you're feeling okay?" I shove a forkful of rice into my mouth and savor the rich flavors of mild red and green peppers, paprika, and a hint of cinnamon. Leah's mother's sudden death had me reflecting on my own parents' mortality in a way I never had before. Something in my gut twists at even the thought of them not being here, which I know at some point is inevitable.

My mom pulls out her desk chair and sits across from me while clasping the silver cross from Puerto Nuevo, her hometown located on the Pacific Coast of Mexico. "Thank God, yes. I am good. No health problems for me." Sighing heavily, she holds out her hands. "This place keeps me busy, but you know I love it." She pauses long enough to pick up a pen and doodle on a notepad before meeting my eyes. Maybe she's waiting for me to ask about my father.

Okay, I'll do it, now that I'm reassured that she's fine. "And Dad?" He's always been strong and stubborn, impossible to please. "What's happening with him? When we spoke on the phone, you said I needed to see him because he wasn't doing well." When she'd called, she had sounded oddly ominous. She is normally outspoken and doesn't hesitate to speak her mind, but, that day, she had been unusually vague, and I didn't know if that was because the situation was bad and she didn't want to reveal the bleak details over the phone or if she was in a hurry to get off the phone.

"It's too much for him—the orange groves at Hartland, helping out here, and the wine making. He needs to slow down." Picking up a stack of invoices, she leafs through them absently. "I'd like him to slow down." Worry lines are etched around her eyes. My mother is still beautiful, with a gaze that seems to look right through me, all the way down to my soul. She's intuitive and always senses when I'm troubled.

"Mom, nothing new about that." I cut my fried plantains in half, then close my eyes as I savor the sticky sweetness. "You've always thought he works too much, so that can't be why you wanted me to come home." I should have come home just to have this home-cooked meal.

"No." Setting the papers down, she purses her lips. "We are older, and we all should slow down. That's why I hired Taylor to help out." Wrinkling her nose, she looks directly at me. "She's a great girl, by the way. Speaking of getting older, where's your wife?" she demands, as if I've secretly gotten married and didn't tell her about it. Leaning back in her chair, she folds her arms and glares at me.

"What?" Inhaling suddenly causes a piece of the fried fruit to lodge in my throat, causing me to cough.

My mother pulls her chair closer to me, then pounds on my back. "Take a long drink."

After gulping down the rice drink, I'm finally able to swallow the fruit. "Look what you did."

"Oh, so I'm to blame for you scarfing down your food like you haven't eaten in weeks?" She makes a dismissive sound. "I always told you to chew slowly, but no. You never listen to me. I wouldn't be surprised if that happens to you all the time."

"Really, Mom?" I have to laugh at her assessment of the situation. "It was your question about my marriage that almost killed me."

"Miguel, don't be so dramatic." She folds her arms again. Red spots of anger dot her cheeks and it looks as if she could start crying any time now. And she tells *me* not to be so dramatic? "So you *are* married. I knew it." She throws her hands up.

"I am *not* married. You're the one who said that." My head is spinning from all the twists and turns of this conversation.

"Good." She leans over, takes a tissue from the box on her desk, then dabs at her wet eyes. "I want to meet the bride first." Her voice is defiant.

How did this conversation get derailed? "We were talking about Dad, not *me* getting married." Frustrated, I run a hand across the back of my neck.

"If you want to know how he's doing, you'll have to ask him yourself." Pushing her chair back from the table, she stands up. "He's out in the fields somewhere."

I forgot how my lovely mother is able to manipulate me in ways I'll never begin to understand. In another life, she could have been a crime scene investigator and tricked people into confessing to crimes they never committed.

"By the way," She walks toward the door to the kitchen, before turning around and facing me with a hint of mischief in her eyes. "Taylor is a lovely girl and I've grown quite fond of her. You could do worse." Pausing, she taps her electronic watch. "Speaking of time, *tick-tock,* you aren't getting any younger either. Your father and I would love a grandchild before we are senior citizens. As handsome as you are, I'm sure you could find a lovely Santa Lorena girl to settle down with."

"Mom—" Before I can finish my sentence, she's out the door and I wonder what I've gotten myself into by coming home. If she's thinking that I'd be interested in a local Santa Lorena woman, she's wrong. My heart is already taken by a woman who's visiting this town, not living in it, and, in a couple of days, we will both be on our way back to Sunnyville.

Clearing my plate from the desk, I shake my head and hope that my conversation with my father is a lot less frustrating than the one I just had with my mother.

Chapter 7

*Leah*

Childhood memories flood back as I roll my suitcase up the walkway leading to the front door of my father's house. The maraschino-cherry-colored red door is a new addition. Previously, the door had been a deep gray that matched the rest of the house. I liked this new burst of color. Had my father read about feng shui and how a red door was connected to good fortune? For good measure, I run my fingers across the wood. I could use a dose of good fortune.

How long has it been since I'd last visited my father, here in his small bungalow-style home? When I was in elementary school, my mother would drive me here to spend time with him on long holiday weekends and for a week during summer, spring, and winter breaks. Our visits were always awkward. I figured it was because I didn't live with him, so the beginning hours of each visit involved becoming reacquainted with one another. I can't recall exactly when or even why the visits gradually dwindled down to only once or twice yearly.

There's a comforting sense of familiarity in seeing the patches of faded green grass bordering the path to the front door. The same pink-tinged white lilac shrubs line the border along the narrow walkway. But there are other new additions besides the vivid red door, like the wind chimes swaying in the breeze which add a lyrical note as I step onto the porch. Centered on a glass-topped wicker table is a turquoise flowerpot containing an assortment of purple, red, and pink vincas and peonies. As I notice the two matching chairs, I wonder if my father sits out here and grades the papers of his history students. Smiling, I think how his decorating skills have improved.

Before I can open the door, it swings open. "Leah Ann, come on in." Leaning forward as if to embrace me is a freckle-faced, red-haired woman, who I estimate to be in her early twenties. She hesitates before dropping her arms and taking a step back. Instead, she picks up my suitcase and carries it into the living room. She indicates the couch. "Have a seat. Your dad is so excited about you coming to visit."

Blue eyes sparkle as she leads the way into the living room, and I wonder if she's one of the college students he's hired to help around the house. Students are always looking for ways to earn extra cash. Then again, he does have a spare room and he may be renting it out. There's a lot of that happening these days, and, with the community college being within walking distance, it makes sense.

"I'm at a disadvantage." The couch has changed, too. I sit back on a butterscotch-colored sofa. The touch of color wasn't limited to the outside of the house. Back in the day, all the furnishings were either brown or beige. This is much better. "You know my name, but I don't know yours." Folding my hands in my lap, I wonder why my father hasn't come out yet. Maybe he's in the bathroom.

"Oh." Long slender fingers cover her mouth, and her eyes grow wide. "Sorry about that." Giggling self-consciously, she holds out her hand for me to shake. "Melissa O'Shaughnessy. I've heard so much about you that I feel like we've already met."

"Nice to meet you, Melissa." Her hand feels moist in mine. For several seconds, I say nothing, distracted by a feeling of unease. Has something happened to my father? After my mother's unexpected death, I'm more aware than ever how quickly circumstances and people's health can change. Concern about his father prompted Miguel's return to Santa Lorena. My chest constricts as I remember the doctors informing me that my mother hadn't survived the aneurism. She'd died instantly. It'd only taken minutes. Did they send one of his students to break the news; is that why she's fidgeting in her seat?

"I'm here to see my father." The words come out harsher than intended. Standing abruptly, I glance past her toward the hallway that leads to the other rooms. "Is he here?" A quiet desperation creeps into my voice. In the past year, I've already lost two people I love; I don't think I can stand losing another one. That's why I came here—I need to be around the one remaining relative I have on the planet.

"Of course. You want to see your father." Her somber expression fuels my growing anxiety.

"Well, is he home or not?" This is my father's house, and although she seems nice enough, I came here to spend time with him, not her. Maybe try to get closer than we were before. Maybe we'll no longer have the strange awkwardness between us, now that we just have each other.

I look at her expectantly, waiting for her response. Inhaling deeply, I will myself to calm down, thinking that I'm probably making too much of his not being here. He's probably on his way now. He *does* have classes to teach and I didn't give him much notice that I would be arriving.

"Oops." She lowers her head, before continuing, "I should have told you that right away. Ed, uh... Professor Lawrence, called a while ago and said one of his students wanted to speak with him after class, so he's running late." She abruptly stands. "Would you like something to drink?"

"Yes. Water, would be fine." Relief rushes through my veins and I feel foolish for jumping to the wrong conclusion. "I was worried there for a minute." I follow her into the kitchen, then lean against the cracked tile counter.

"No need to worry." She opens the refrigerator and takes out a pitcher, setting it on the counter. "I have iced tea."

"Sounds even better." Now that I know my father is fine, I'm more relaxed. "I'm guessing you're one of his students."

"Yes." Her eyes light up as she hands me a glass. "He's the best professor I've ever had. His African American history class has taught me so much."

I follow her lead as she takes a seat at the dining room table. "I know what you mean. When I was a child, he was always teaching me about events that had happened in the early twentieth century." I pause long enough to sip my tea. "I think I inherited the teaching gene from him." Holding up a hand, I add, "Granted, I know teaching five- and six-year-olds is *not* the same as teaching college age students."

"Leah Ann." My father's voice comes from the living room.

I hear the sound of the windchimes before the door slams and he appears in the kitchen. No one would ever guess he was sixty-two. He's still lean and fit, with not a touch of gray hair in sight. Disregarding the faint lines around his eyes, he could easily be mistaken for a much younger man.

"Good to see you." His eyes dart nervously—or so it seems—from Melissa to me. He gives me a stiff hug. "You've obviously met Melissa."

"I have." I remember my favorite teacher, Mrs. Jones, who I'd had in third and fourth grade. She had a simple stylish elegance and was always patient and kind. I can never forget how much I'd looked up to her. From the look in Melissa's eyes, it seems that she feels that way about my father. I'd never had that type of relationship with one of my college professors, but it would have been nice. "She speaks highly of you."

"Well, she was a good student." His eyes warm as he looks at her. "She was always doing extra work." He makes his way to the refrigerator and pulls out a beer, unscrews the top, then takes a long drink.

"I'm afraid I took up a lot of your father's office hours," she says apologetically. "I always had so many questions."

"Good students usually do." It's obvious that he's fond of Melissa, which explains why he's probably hired her to assist him at home, assuming she's his assistant or student aide.

I cross my legs at the ankles, trying to get more comfortable on the chair. "I was telling Melissa I probably inherited the teaching gene from you." My voice is light as I try to squelch the uneasy feeling that's settled over me since I walked in the door.

"I don't know about that." He wrinkles his brows before taking another swallow of beer.

"I'll leave you two alone." Melissa furtively glances in my father's direction, before clearing her throat... "I'm sure you have a lot of catching up to do." She heads down the hall instead of to the front door. Apparently, her workday isn't finished.

"It's nice outside." My father's eyes shift toward the enclosed patio area. "Want to sit out there?" The patio contains a large jacaranda tree; its delicate fallen lavender petals create a lush covering of the grass. The two foldaway chairs of my childhood have been replaced with white wicker seats and a small wicker sofa. I'm surprised to see a barbeque pit, because I've never known him to do any outdoor grilling.

"That would be nice." Santa Lorena is a scenic town, reminiscent of a quaint village, with weather that hovers in the mid-seventies year-round, except when the heat spikes and the possibility of turbulent Santa Ana winds and untamed wildfires swirl and strike without warning, leaving a streak of devastation in their wake. That knowledge of potential impending destruction as much as my father's taciturn nature kept me from ever feeling at home in Santa Lorena.

"Great." With the beer in his hand, he opens the patio doors, motioning for me to sit across from him.

"I like what you've done with the place." I set my glass on the tabletop. "When I used to visit, everything was various shades of brown—light brown, beige-brown, deep brown, and dark, almost black brown."

"Very funny."

It's good to hear him laugh; perhaps some of the tension between us will dissipate. It's a start anyway. I used to wonder how my father could talk in front of a group of students who were virtually strangers when he seldom had anything to say to me. But still, I loved him and needed him now. "It's true. I do love brown. Maybe a little too much."

"How are you feeling?" I no longer ask this superficially. Ever since my mother died, I'm expecting an honest answer from people. She wasn't ill before the aneurism. It'd been an ordinary day and she'd been healthy. No high blood pressure or harmful habits, but, in the end, it didn't matter. It took only moments for her to be taken from me, without any warning. "You look like you are taking care of yourself." He hasn't put on a pound and is obviously keeping fit. "Is the garage still filled with exercise equipment?"

"Yes." As usual, he doesn't look at me directly. "Treadmill, elliptical, and the weights. They're still there."

"That's great." Will he ask about me now? It is usual and customary to return the question about the other person's health. I am his daughter after all, and I haven't seen him since the funeral. He'd been out of the church so quickly, we didn't have an opportunity to talk. I don't think he attended the wake. Granted, I'd been busy, but I didn't see him. I'd thought he would have wanted to say good-bye.

"What brought you here?" His eyes finally meet mine—not with the warmth he showed Melissa, but it's something.

"You." *Does he really have to ask that?* "I haven't

been to Santa Lorena in a while and we didn't get a chance to talk at the funeral. I know you loved my mother."

"Humph."

He grunts and I remember now why I dreaded visiting him. Speaking to him—I mean, having a genuine conversation with this man—feels like climbing a steep mountain while wearing twenty-five-pound weights. It's a lot of work. I always felt like I had done something wrong, and I didn't know what.

"That's true. Your mom was a wonderful, intelligent woman. We were very much in love—once." A pained expression crosses his face, as if the admission is difficult.

"I miss her." I haven't said that to anyone else, but it's true. My mother's absence has left a cavernous void in my life. Even if things had worked out with Raymond and I, I would still be mourning my mother's loss. "*You* are the only family I have left." The words tumble out, shaky and raw.

"Surely, you have a lot of people in Sunnyville you are close to." He speaks matter-of-factly, as if we are discussing the weather, not my need to connect with family, which, basically, means him.

"True." An image of Miguel's face emerges and tension eases from my neck and shoulders. "I drove up with Miguel. He came to check on his father, which reminded me that I wanted to spend some time with you." It wasn't exactly the truth. I had wanted to see him, but I'd also wanted to escape the gossip surrounding the pictures of me circulating on social media.

"Okay." He swallows the last of his beer. "You see

that I'm fine." Somber, he peers at the blistering sun. "What about that other fellow?" He snaps his fingers. "Raymond. That was his name, wasn't it?"

"Yes." Under the table, I stretch my legs before setting my glass down. "We broke up when his ex-girlfriend returned to town. To be more specific, *he* broke up with me."

"Ahhh. I see. Sorry to hear that." His eyes search the sky as if looking for answers or, at least, something appropriate to say. "I know you were dating him for a while."

"Mom didn't feel he was right for me." She'd probably been right all along. If he *had* ever loved me, he wouldn't have left me so quickly—and hadn't some part of me, deep inside, known that on some level, he hadn't been *that* into me? I was just the proxy—filling in until his *real* true love made an appearance. "When did you know that Mom was the right one for you? I know you divorced, but still… at some point in time, you both were in love."

"Your mother and I were young." He shifts his gaze from me. "Almost ten years younger than you are now. Barely out of our teens. What we felt for one another was real, but, ultimately, we wanted different things out of life." As if the sentence has drained him, he sighs with resignation before abruptly standing and terminating any further revelations about his life with my mother. "I've got some papers to grade. The second bedroom is not available for use at this time."

"What? Where will I sleep?" The needy part of me immediately feels slighted. I should have given him more advance notice of my arrival, but I hadn't expected him to rent out my old room, although I know it's common now for people to earn income by leasing out extra space in their homes. What do they say? You can never go home again. Or maybe you can go home again, but you may not have a place to rest your head. Of course, that's where his boarder is staying. "Is that where Melissa sleeps?"

"Tomorrow." His hands jerk up, effectively blocking me from asking more questions.

Again, I wonder how my father is able to stand in front of a room of students and actually fill an entire hour by lecturing when he's the master of one-word sentences when he speaks to me.

"I'll go over everything then. Melissa will put out some blankets and towels for you."

"Okay, then." I don't try to disguise the disappointment in my voice. Was it a mistake to come here? Once my father ends a conversation, that's it—the discussion is over. He's always been that way, and peppering him with more questions won't get me anywhere, so I won't even try.

"You can wash up down the hall in the second bathroom and I'll order food delivery for dinner." Opening the patio door leading to the living room, he pauses before stepping inside. "You still like Indian food?"

"Yes." I pat my empty stomach. I hadn't had a full meal all day. His remembering that I love Indian food helps relieve some of the discomfort that I can't shake. "Love it."

"I'll have Tandoor Kitchen deliver and we'll eat at six."

"Sounds good." That's right; feed me my favorite foods, but don't actually speak with me. Nothing here feels right as I watch my father leave the room, as if he can't wait to begin grading papers, create a lesson plan or doing anything *except* talk with his only child, who he hasn't seen in months.

Moments later, I'm still sitting, sweating in the sweltering sun, wondering what I was expecting from this visit. Sure, my talk with my father was a little stilted; that's nothing out of the ordinary. But what about Melissa? Who is she and why is she here?

I'm wiping a film of perspiration from my forehead when my cell phone rings and the gray cloud that's been circling my thoughts like a vulture swooping around a fresh carcass lifts. I reach into my pockets; the thought of speaking to Miguel is like being thrown a lifeline while I'm in a sinking ship. He'll likely tell me that I'm blowing the whole situation out of proportion, that I need to chill out and not worry about the student sleeping in my room while I'll be snoozing on the sofa. But it's not Miguel, but Jenny. I dismiss the tinge of disappointment that it's not Miguel on the other end of the line, but I'm always glad to speak to my second favorite person in the universe. The girl always has my back.

"So, you got there safely?" There's a hint of chastisement in her voice.

I had forgotten to call when I'd arrived. Even when I drive the two miles home from her apartment to my house, she expects a text confirming I am safely back home.

"Hello to you, too." I don't try to disguise the amusement in my voice. "Should I text you now or is it too late?"

"Very funny." The irritation has already dissipated.

"I just like knowing that you arrived safely."

"This I know." Truth is, I kind of like it, especially since my mother is gone. It's nice having someone care enough to worry about me. Jenny and Miguel are as reliable as they come.

"What's wrong?"

She's way too perceptive. At times, it's almost eerie. Maybe the assortment of colorful crystals she wears or carries with her at all times provide her with some sort of psychic powers.

"And don't say *nothing*, because I can hear it in your voice. It's a dead giveaway."

"Well." I hesitate, uncertain where to begin or even how to describe my vague feeling of something being out of kilter, so I switch topics, to something safer, like Miguel. "The drive here wasn't bad, although whenever I'm with Miguel, time always goes by quickly."

"We know he's a great guy." Her tone is dismissive, as if what I said was a foregone conclusion. "Do you ever think of letting him know how much you appreciate him?"

"You'll be proud of me."

Jenny is a strong believer in sharing the positive in life, especially when it comes to expressing emotions—something about creating positive vibrational energy.

"I told him he was the best brother I could have, considering I have no actual siblings."

"Good goddess, girl." Now the irritation has returned. Jenny, who has half a dozen siblings, feels that they can be overrated, which is easy for her to say, considering her parents had three children together. After nine years, they divorced and remarried other people and then proceeded to procreate until their combined families had enough children to create a basketball team. "I'd like to help you out here, but some things a person has to figure out for themselves. And so it is."

"Huh?" There are instances where I'm unable to decode Jenny's New Age mumbo jumbo. "You lost me there."

"Never mind." Her sigh is heavy. "Miguel is a good man. I'm sure that when you told him that he was like a brother he felt… er, something." She pauses as if she's momentarily at a loss for words, which practically never happens. "I'm not sure what."

"I meant it as a compliment." I recall how his one eyebrow had shot up and his mouth had twisted in what almost looked like a frown, which made no sense. "Now, that you mention it, he didn't seem overly pleased with the comment, which is odd, considering that you can't get closer to someone than telling them that they are like family to you."

"Interesting. I can think of several other ways you can definitely get closer." Her voice deepens as she chuckles.

"You *would* go there, wouldn't you?"

Jenny also has a whole theory about the importance of releasing sexual energy.

"It has nothing to do with that," I quickly add. Walking over to the patio door, I make sure that it's securely closed before returning to my chair and lowering my voice. "It's my father. It's so weird with him."

"In what way?" She pauses. "Would you care to elaborate?"

"That's just it; it's difficult to explain." I control

the urge to chip away at what remains of my nail polish. "He's kind of aloof."

"Ah, I see. What's his sign?" Jenny believes one's astrological signs explain all aspects of personality.

"I have no idea." I need to prevent her from insisting that she needs to know his birthday, so she can figure out how the sun and moon and probably past life experiences have made him so aloof. "Listen, there's more."

"There's always so much more than the human eye can see—as opposed to the third eye."

Her digressions frequently leave me wondering if we are speaking the same language. "There's *someone* here. With him. At the house." I chose to ignore the third eye comment. It's a concept Jenny has been struggling to help me understand for the past six months, and my brain is already in a fog about my father. I don't need to add any more confusion to my already muddled thoughts. "She appears to be in her early twenties and was one of his students."

"So now we're getting somewhere." She hums and I wonder if she's starting to chant, but then she continues. "Your father's *lover*?"

"Oh my God! No way." Laughter bubbles up in my chest and spills out so quickly, I have to cover my mouth, so Melissa and my father can't hear me. "That was a good one. She's younger than us."

"So?" Jenny's voice is somber. "Mercury *is* in retrograde. This is the time when people from our past make an appearance and relationships can either be reignited or reconfigured."

She clearly doesn't see the absurdity of her suggestion. Jenny has a master's degree in psychology and works at Sunnyville's counseling clinic when she's not being the town photographer and tarot card reader.

"It's a classic relationship dynamic. Older professor, in the throes of a midlife crisis, happens upon a nubile, very impressionable, attractive woman who either has unresolved daddy issues or a misguided sense of hero worship and they latch on to each other for dear life."

"That's absurd." Wiping damp palms on my thighs, I'm finally able to stand up straight and suppress my out-of-control mirth. Jenny's impromptu assessment has sucked any humor out of the situation. "No way. You're wrong. One hundred percent incorrect. *I* have unresolved father issues. Melissa—that's her name—can't have them, too. Not with my father she can't." The last sentence comes out louder than intended.

"I didn't mean to upset you." She uses her smooth, lower octave therapist voice that's supposed to soothe and calm untamed emotions that have run amok. And, strangely, that perfectly modulated tone does just that.

Taking in a giant gulp of air, I say, "I'm not upset in the least." Not caring anymore about my perfect manicure, I scrape at the polish on my little finger, then watch the soft pink color chips fall into my lap. "It's just that my father is, well… He's not exactly the emotionally available type."

"At least not to you." She says this matter-of-factly.

"Exactly." *Ouch.* That hurt, but I've talked about my relationship with my father frequently enough that she knows the truth. After all, this is why I'm so glad she called so I can tell her that I'm having difficulty connecting with him—again. "He lights up when he *looks* at Melissa and he looks at me like I'm a complete stranger." I swallow the lump in my throat while peeling off more polish, leaving my little fingernail exposed, while attempting to not sound whiny.

"Maybe he looks at Melissa that way because they are two people who just happen to have fallen in love."

"Not possible." The words are clipped, as if the end of the sentence was cut off with sharp scissors. Since when did I become so certain about anything? I mean, look how I misjudged what Raymond felt for me.

"It's been a *long* time since your parents divorced."

Neither of us says anything for a minute. My mind has completely shut down. This conversation has not helped me clear my head.

"Now, *my* parents, on the other hand, didn't waste any time finding new partners. Within a year, we had our own version of a blended-family-television-situation-comedy." She chuckles before continuing. "But other people may take years to love again."

"I've got to go." I am barely able to squeak out the words. The thought of my father dating a student or actually living with someone he could possibly have some type of romantic relationship with is unnerving.

After quickly disconnecting, I place the phone back in my pocket and decide not to rush back in the house even though the sun has disappeared over the horizon and the patio is now cloaked in darkness. Streetlights block out some of the stars, but I can still spot a few shining brightly, casting flickering sparks of light in what is turning out to be a cool night.

Finally, I push myself up from my wicker chair, walk to the double glass patio door, then shove it open. A silver coffee table lamp casts a warm glow throughout the living room. Either my father or Melissa has converted the sofa to a bed, complete with two pillows and a green and brown bedspread. A folded white towel and washcloth have been placed near the gray throw blanket that's been spread across the foot of the bed.

I hadn't heard the doorbell ring when the Indian food was delivered, but I see the containers neatly stacked on the kitchen counter. The scent is tempting, but I've lost my appetite and just want to sleep, so I place the food in the refrigerator before gathering the face cloth and towel and making my way to the guest bathroom, which is the one I always use on my visits. My father's room has its own bathroom so I'm expecting to see Melissa's toiletries scattered on the counter near the sink.

So much for my expectations. There's zero evidence that a woman or anybody else ever uses this bathroom. It's spotless, not a stray streak of red hair on the counters or in the sink.

Maybe Melissa is a neat freak and keeps personal items out of sight in the cabinets and drawers.

Like a mad woman or a miner searching for gold, I open every drawer and cabinet but find… nothing.

It's not until after I've taken a quick shower and made my way to my makeshift bed that I've come up with a plausible explanation. College students frequently keep all of their toiletries in a plastic carrying container they take to and from the bathroom. That's what I did when I lived in Kendrick Hall, my freshman dormitory, and even later when I shared a two-bedroom apartment with three other girls and didn't want my roommates to help themselves to my favorite shampoo.

I head to the couch, but no matter which way I toss and turn or readjust my position, the hard metal springs press against my skin, and I wish I had brought flannel instead of cotton baby-doll pajamas. The mattress—and I use that term loosely—on the sofa bed feels oddly like a box spring.

It takes a while, but finally, I fall asleep. What seems like a short time later, I wake to the distinct sound of voices. Groaning, I scrunch lower on the sofa and yank the thin blanket over my head, wishing I had thought to pack earplugs. Squeezing my eyes shut tighter, I futilely attempt to block out the disruptive conversation.

The front door opens and closes several times before I finally give up on getting anywhere near the amount of sleep I need. How frequently can my father and Melissa walk in and out of the front door?

"Can a person get any sleep around here?" My voice sounds as cranky as I feel. Some people get grumpy when they are hungry; others—like me— cannot function with less than seven, or preferably eight, hours of sleep. Normally, I pride myself on my mellow disposition, but lack of sleep brings out a less gracious side of my personality.

Frustrated, I toss the blanket off my face, poke my head out, and see—standing by the door—a tall man with a scroll of paper in his hand and a faded blue baseball cap partially covering ink black hair, staring at me with a bemused expression on his face.

"Well, damn." One side of his mouth tilts up more than the other, adding a bad boy vibe to his already rugged appearance. A series of tattoos covers one arm.

"Look who finally woke up." He tips his hat with his free hand and takes his time openly appraising me.

I snatch the blanket over my exposed pink pajama top and glare at him. Speechless, bewildered, and more than a little frightened, I scan the room, searching for anything that I can use as a makeshift weapon to protect myself from this man, who, quite possibly, has broken into my father's home.

My eyes settle on the poker near the fireplace, but it's too far away. I open my mouth, preparing to scream, but I only emit a pathetic squeak. Clenching my hands, I clear my throat. "Don't try anything."

"Not unless you want me to." Obviously amused, he hitches his tool belt up higher on his hips before chuckling and briskly sauntering out the door.

"Jesus H. Christopher." Leaping up, I run to the door and lock it. "Who the heck was *that*?"

Chapter 8

*Miguel*

Striding past the registration desk in the front lobby, I'm preoccupied as I squelch memories of the big blow-up I'd had with my father when I was last here. Running a hand across my brow, I struggle to remember what it was about, and I'll be darned if I know. All I remember is that I couldn't wait to get back to Sunnyville and away from him.

"Miguel."

Lost in my thoughts, I hadn't noticed her standing off to the side, an electronic tablet in her hand.

"Taylor." Being back in the inn, knowing that I may encounter my father anytime, has me distracted and on edge. "Sorry, I didn't notice you there."

"No problem."

She's got a great smile. Probably could do one of those toothpaste commercials.

"Just don't make a habit of it."

"Huh?" I'm lost. Time to pay attention—focus on something besides my father and how irritating he can be. "Make a habit of it?"

"Ignoring me." She wiggles a finger in my direction. "Don't make a habit of not seeing me because I definitely see you, Miquel Montoya." She lays a hand across my arm, before stepping from behind the counter to stand beside me. "That would hurt my feelings."

"Wouldn't want to do that." Shrugging, I don't pay much attention to her words.

She's obviously one of those people who need to stand close to the person she's speaking to—closer than I would prefer. As Leah pointed out, the majority of my clients are women. I've had to adapt to the fact that many of them are prone to standing so close that I can smell their cologne. My tactic is to discreetly take a step or two away without comment. I figure it may be a men-women thing, with women more comfortable with being nose-to-nose while talking. No need to make a big deal out of it, especially not when these are some of my most dedicated clients who have made a commitment to their health and exercise routine.

"Where you going?" Taking a step forward, she holds out her hand. "Maybe I can help you."

She seems like the sensitive type, so I don't move away this time. "I'm going to talk to my father."

"Do you know where he is?" Tilting her head, she gazes at me expectantly, long lashes accenting her brown eyes.

"Not exactly." An image of him inspecting the orange groves or checking on his vineyards has me wondering where I should begin my search. Between his work on the Hartland Ranch and our property, he could be anywhere.

"I could help you." Raising her eyebrows, she gathers a fistful of her long black hair and tosses it over her shoulder.

"You're working, aren't you?" The truth is I'm eager to get over this initial meeting with my father. After all, I need to be patient with him, even if I know it's impossible to ever please him. According to my mother, he's had an injury and he's too proud to say he needs help. I'm not sure I can be of any assistance, but, while I'm here, I'll do my best.

"Don't worry about that," she says nonchalantly. "I'll get Toby to help."

"Who?" My mother can be a tough taskmaster. I'm sure she would not be pleased to find Taylor gone and someone else taking over her job.

"He busses the tables, but Rick is there to help in the dining room, so it will be okay." She speaks with an abundance of confidence, which could be foolhardy unless my mother has recently softened up. My mother is flexible about some things, but her business is *not* one of them. Most employees go out of their way not to incur her wrath. "We won't be long. I overheard your father saying where he'd be working today. It's easier for me to show you than tell you where to find him."

"Okay, thanks." She's got a point. If she knows *exactly* where he is, I won't have to waste time searching for him in the groves and vineyards. Better to get this meeting over with as quickly as possible. Unfortunately, my father refuses to carry a mobile phone with him while he's working, otherwise, I could call him. But *no*. That would be too easy, and nothing with my father is easy.

Taylor swirls around and heads into the dining area. While waiting for her return, I make my way to the far wall to the right of the red brick fireplace. I never took the time to give more than a cursory glance at the two photos, one of each pair of grandparents. The couples couldn't be more different, even while sharing some similarities.

The mischievous glint in my maternal grandmother's eye is evident even in the sepia-toned photograph. Twenty years younger than her husband, she's wearing a long gown with a form-fitting lace bodice. She was eighteen to his thirty-eight and he's glancing at her with unmistakable adoration, while she stares at the camera. No wonder my mother had had to learn to cook early, her mother liked to dance and sing folk songs and couldn't be bothered with domestic chores.

I turn from the photograph to study my father's parents, whose faces are stern even on their special day. My grandmother's bridal dress has long sleeves, a high collar, and hangs loosely from her slender figure, while my grandfather looks like he just sucked on a lemon.

"I'm back." Taylor sidles up to me. "Ready?"

"Do we need the car?" We step outside into the hot sun that has come out from beneath the clouds that had blanketed the sky earlier. This fluctuating weather pattern is known as June gloom, even though it can appear as early as May and is deceptive. A moist fog can last for four to six hours, eventually disappearing, only to be followed by an unexpectedly hot, blistering sun. "I don't know if he's at the orange groves or in the back near the cottage."

The Honeymoon Cottage, partially covered by a row of tall jacaranda trees, its delicate flowers create a purple path to the spacious one bedroom suite for couples who want privacy from other guests.

"We can walk." She links her arm through mine while looking up innocently at me.

"Great." Not wanting to hurt her feelings, I don't jerk away, but, really, this is a bit much. I can't help but wonder if my mother hinted to Taylor that I'm available. I wouldn't put it past her. I could be wrong, so I won't say anything yet. After all, it may be that Taylor's simply being helpful to the boss's son.

"He's in the groves, but it's not far from here—just over that small incline there." With a tilt of her chin, she indicates the path that leads from our lands to the Harts' property. "You seem like a man who could easily handle any type of exertion, including a short walk."

"You're right about that." She clings to my arm as we make our way past the parking lot, which is beginning to fill with cars. "Are a lot of people checking in today?"

"Yes. It's a sorority group convention that's being held in town." She taps a long tapered fingernail on my chest. "But let's get back to *you*. Tell me about yourself."

"Not a lot to tell." Slowing my pace, I make sure my strides aren't too long and that she's able to keep up. "You're right, I can definitely handle a little exercise. I'm a fitness instructor."

"Ah hah!" She stops long enough to let her eyes roam over me. "That explains so much. You look awesome." Pausing, she sucks in her bottom lip before continuing. "I remember you being… well, you were *really* cute. Still are but, you were—"

"Go ahead and say it." I let out a puff of air. "I was a fat kid. You won't hurt my feelings if you say it." How I hated those trips to the department stores for new school clothes. Shopping in the section with the *Chubby* signs was humiliating.

"I would never say that." Her face turns pink as she

releases my arm long enough to place a hand over her mouth before she resumes walking up the steep hill.

Lush green leaves adorn the trees, but it's too early to see any fruit. In a month or two, the buds will bloom, signaling the start of the growing season.

"Sometimes, I'm guilty of speaking before thinking. Sorry about that."

"It doesn't matter. You can call it whatever you want. It won't hurt my feelings. I remember what I looked like. My mother said I was pleasantly plump, and my Uncle Thomas said I was big-boned. Now, that sort of seemed like a compliment—until I later learned no one really has significantly larger bones than anyone else." No need to mention how my father was disgusted—and possibly embarrassed—by my appearance.

"Well, look at you now." Smiling, she glances in my direction. "No one would ever know. I always thought you were adorable."

"Really?" I look at her incredulously, wishing my memory of her wasn't so faint. Back then, I'd been a shy kid who'd mostly avoided eye contact with other kids as much as possible.

"Absolutely. Look what you've made of your life. Your mother tells me you were in the military, too."

"Joining the Marines was the best decision I ever made."

We are at the top of the hill, and faint voices, one of which is my father's, can be heard in the distance. Part of me wants to avoid any contact with him, which is why I asked to live with my Aunt Esther. Somehow, my father has a knack for making me feel like a failure, which made it a no-brainer to escape this place as quickly as possible. I know it'd been difficult for my mother to share me with her sister-in-law, but she'd placed my happiness before anything else. By the time I was twelve, the tension between my father and I had grown unbearable.

"My dad was military, too, so I'm familiar with some aspects of military life. We briefly lived in Oakland, at the Army Base there, before moving down here when I was six." Her eyes are warm as she flashes me with an appreciative grin. "Thank you for your service."

"Thank you." It feels good to have people respond positively to my being in the military, unlike previous war-era veterans. I've heard their stories, especially those of the older Vietnam War vets. They really had it bad. I can't imagine how it must have felt to come back from fighting a war, witnessing death and, upon their return, have their country treat them badly.

We walk on in silence, me dreading seeing my father, not feeling like dealing with the inevitable confrontation that will ensue. A few more steps and there he is, his back to me, standing beside Elaine, one of my two god-sisters. A twig snaps as Taylor takes a step forward and both my father and Elaine turn around at the same time, surprise showing on their faces.

"Miguel." Elaine rushes toward me, arms outstretched, as she envelops me in a warm embrace. "I'm so happy to see you." She shakes her head. "It's been too long."

"I agree." Neither of us adds that it's been since her father's funeral. "And you managed to get married since then." I know Elaine had a particularly hard time coping with the sudden loss of her father and then having to take over running the groves with no help from her Uncle Robert—who remained bitter because he hadn't inherited the groves. She'd done a great job, though, but this is no surprise, given her passion for the land. No doubt my father wishes I was as interested in carrying on our family legacy as Elaine is in carrying on her father's vision.

Elaine glances toward Taylor. "Hi, Taylor. Thanks for bringing us such a great surprise."

"I knew you'd be at the groves today, so it was easier for me to bring Miguel here than trying to describe the spot on the side of the hill where the two properties meet."

"If my son came home more often, he would know where to find me." My father's voice is gruff, as usual. "Miguel." He nods in my direction.

"Dad." Okay, so not exactly the warmest greeting, but, really, that's no surprise. The man will never change. I am *not* the son he envisioned, and don't I know it. "I'm here now, aren't I?"

My father's brow crinkles. "Elaine's right, this *is* a surprise." With flaring nostrils, he loudly snorts like a bull that's about to stampede. "To what do we owe the pleasure of your company?"

Taking a deep breath, I silently count to five and feel the tension along my shoulders and back. He doesn't know that I'm here because my mother said he's ill and needs my help.

"Taylor." Elaine's voice slices through the awkwardness of the moment. "I've got to give you some oranges before you go back to the inn. I know your brother loves them."

Taylor's eyes dart from my father to me as if she's

undecided whether she should make a dash to escape this real-life family drama or should stay and see what will happen next. Yep, my father and I are a regular telenovela, filled with the predictable drama and tension.

When Taylor doesn't say anything but stays rooted to the spot, Elaine approaches her. "Let's pick some oranges." She nudges the other woman while my father and I glare at each other. "It's early. I have one tree that's already bearing fruit."

"Right." Taylor, with a startled glance, finally acknowledges Elaine. Maybe she sees my father and I aren't in any rush to resume our conversation, if it can be called that. With a thumbs-up gesture, she enthusiastically adds, "Aaron loves oranges and yours are the best."

After the two women leave, an awkward silence stays wedged between my father and me. He hasn't changed much, a little grayer at the temples, but from the looks of it, he's still trim, probably from years of working the land, both the Harts' and ours. In recent years, his work has involved more recruiting, hiring, and managing than the physical labor of his youth.

"Mom said you haven't been well." I break the impasse—the first to try to steer the conversation in a more positive direction. No use expecting him to take the high road.

"I don't know what she's told you," he snarls, and deep frown lines crease his forehead. "Do I look *ill* to you?" He balls his hands into fists before settling them on his waist.

"No, you don't." Maybe he's recovered since she called me last week. Good. I'll contact Leah and we can get out of here before nightfall—but what if she's having a great time and doesn't want to leave yet? "Mom said that something was broken." Come to think of it, she hadn't mentioned *what* was broken.

Sputtering, he shakes his head. "It was my toes," he barks out.

I look down at the heavy, black work boots he's always worn, the type that lace up high on the ankle. "You broke *all* of your toes?" The tension is still there, streaking across my shoulders like pinpricks of heated needles.

"No. Just two." He curses under his breath, but still loud enough for me to hear. "Blasted steps. I can't tell you how it happened, so don't ask." He shrugs, looking perturbed—as if someone had asked him to complete a complex crossword puzzle in two minutes or less.

"Sorry about that." I'm not sure how I can be of help here. How did my mother think I could be of any assistance to my cantankerous father? "Are you in pain?"

"It doesn't hurt." Pulling a handkerchief out of his pocket, he swipes it across his brow.

The sun has broken through the gray clouds and replaced the earlier chill with a penetrating heat. Sweat trickles down the back of my shirt. "Let me know if there is any way I can help."

"You?" He slaps a hand against his thigh as he peers at me incredulously. "How could *you* help?"

"I don't know." Exasperated, I hold my hands out, fighting my own mounting frustration. "That's why I asked *you*. That's why I came here."

"Really? Well, you picked a fine time to help. We have a big group of ladies checking in today and you're taking one of their rooms, which means you are causing us to actually *lose* money, so you sure aren't helping there."

"Fine." I do know that the inn does a robust business, and the vineyard has a strong reputation for producing some good California merlots and pinot noirs that are selling at the local wine shop in town. "I wouldn't want you to lose money by having your son staying at the inn. I'll move out of my room as soon as I go back and relocate to the cottage." Raising my brows, I no longer attempt to suppress my own frustration. "If that's all right with you."

"Great," His voice is sharp as shards of broken glass and his eyes are cold as a glacier. "Sounds like a good idea. You do that."

Turning on my heels, I stomp off, aggravated and confused by yet another irrational conversation with my father. I can't wait to contact Leah to see if she's ready to get out of Santa Lorena as soon as possible because I sure as hell am.

I have enough adrenaline coursing through my veins to sprint down the hill. Of all the ungrateful people in this world, my father is at the top of the list. I go out of my way to check on him, and he can't appreciate the gesture. Sweat trickles down my chest by the time the cluster of buildings comes into view. The parking lot is now full, with women clustered in groups and greeting each other. Some pause long enough to take in the sight of me. I stomp past, finally reaching the door, which I jerk open, before striding across to the counter.

Stopping by the front desk, I pick up the key to the cottage before heading down the hall to my room. I open the door to my room, the one I always use when I'm in town. My father doesn't want me using the main building? Fine. I won't. This won't take long; it's not like I had much to unpack since I'd only planned on staying for a couple of days anyway.

In a matter of minutes, I've gathered my toiletries, tossed them in my duffle bag, and after running down the stairs at the end of the hall, I'm out of the building. Beyond a wooden fence, is a tree-lined brick path leading to the secluded honeymoon cottage that luckily for me, is vacant. I'm sure my father would have gleefully notified me if it were currently occupied by paying customers.

Inside, I head straight to the bathroom, eager to rid myself of my damp shirt. After pulling it off, I take my time splashing cool water on my face. How my father manages to get me worked up and pissed off in a matter of seconds is beyond me. I'll need to pace myself since I've been here less than forty-eight hours and am already planning my escape. Maybe I should take a shower, and reconsider calling Leah, especially since she's probably enjoying her visit with *her* father right now. No need for me to be selfish because my father and I can't have a civil conversation. It's not like I have to be around him for the next day or two, not when the cottage is available. By leaving, I have avoided any chance encounters in the elevators or halls.

Walking back into the bedroom, I pick up one of the three bottles of water in the room. Unscrewing the top, I down half the bottle in one gulp and decide that talking to Leah will be the perfect anecdote to my negative encounter with my father.

Cell phone in hand, I kick off my shoes first, pull

off my jeans, then click on her name before lying back on the mattress.

"Miguel." Leah, unlike my father, always sounds genuinely happy to hear from me. "I was going to call you later."

"Looks like I beat you to it." At least she was thinking of me and not her ex. It's a beginning. "What's up?"

"Great question. I wish I knew the answer." There's hesitancy and a quiver in her voice. Something is obviously wrong.

"If you want to talk about it, we can meet up." Obviously, she has something on her mind, so I'm not about to bother her with my problems.

"That would be great."

She sounds relieved. Did she think I wouldn't be available for her anytime, day, or night? If only she knew the truth and hopefully, soon she will.

"Should I come over there?"

"God, no." I blurt out, and immediately regret it, thinking that she may mistakenly believe that I don't want her here, when the truth is, I don't even want to be here myself. "I mean you don't have a car, so I'll pick you up. We can eat somewhere in town. Does that sound okay?"

"I can be ready in twenty minutes." Her voice sounds less shaky now, almost eager.

"Leah—" Before I can respond, I hear pounding on my door and wonder if it's my father coming to apologize. Right. Like that would ever happen, but who knows? My mother may have spoken to him about his lack of appreciation for me leaving my job to return home to check on him. "Hold on a second." Phone in hand, I get up from the bed and open the door.

"Oh my, don't you look delicious." Taylor, a wide grin on her face stands there openly ogling me and I remember that I'm only wearing my briefs. "I like how you looked in clothes, but practically naked… Well, you are *quite* the specimen."

"Excuse me a minute." I rush over to the bedroom and shut the door before picking up my pants and pulling them on—and remember that Leah is on the phone. Dang. Why hadn't I remembered to mute it? What would she make of what she just heard?

"I love the bed in here." Opening the bedroom door, Taylor walks in and runs her fingers across the king-sized bed "No wonder they call it the lovers' retreat."

"I'm having a private conversation." Glancing toward the phone, I don't bother to correct her by clarifying that it's *not* called the lovers' retreat; it's the *honeymoon* suite, reserved for newlyweds or, in this case, a son who has been told that staying in the main building is causing the family to lose money. "Can you wait in the other room?" I'm relieved to see that Leah hasn't hung up.

"Take your time. I'll make myself at home."

Shutting the door behind her, I grab my cell from off the nightstand. "Leah, I thought you had hung up." Taylor's timing could not have been worse, but at least I'm finally getting a chance to speak with Leah. "Sorry about the interruption."

"No, I'm sorry to interrupt you."

I can't say what it is, but there is definitely something different about the tone of her voice.

"I didn't know you had a girlfriend in Santa

Lorena."

"What?" She can't possibly think that Taylor is my girlfriend. I barely know the woman. "You've got the wrong idea."

"I'm pretty sure that wasn't a guy talking. I should go. Let you spend time with your girlfriend."

"That was Taylor." As soon as I say the words, I know that they don't mean anything to her. She doesn't know Taylor's just a girl I went to elementary school with, not a love interest.

"You don't owe me an explanation. I shouldn't have assumed you'd be available."

"Leah, it's not the way it seems." Why do I feel like I'm not getting through to her? My frustration is mounting as I struggle to explain. "Take my word for it."

"I know I'm not the best at interpreting things, but, this one, I *can* figure out."

Before I can say another word, she disconnects the call. Well, I blew that one.

Rubbing a finger along my jaw, I have to admit Taylor's greeting could have easily been misinterpreted. This misunderstanding isn't going to help me plead my case to Leah and make her see me as more than just a friend—not when she mistakenly believes there's another woman in my life.

"It's getting lonely in here," Taylor calls out.

What does she mean by that? It's not as if it's my job to keep her company.

"I'll be out in a minute." What is she doing here anyway? Has my mother sent her to fetch me? No, my mother wouldn't do that. If she wants to speak with me, she wouldn't send a messenger. So why has Taylor tracked me down? So far, this day has been nothing but frustration, first with my disapproving father and, second, with my too-brief conversation with Leah.

"It's not nice to keep a lady waiting."

Taylor laughs and I think at least there's one person who's in a good mood.

## Chapter 9

*Leah*

That was an eye opener. I didn't know Miguel had someone in Santa Lorena. What had the woman said? Something about him not having any clothes on. I'm happy for him, even if I'm disappointed that he can't come get me.

As soon as the cocky stranger retreats outside, I hop off the couch and head to the bathroom to get dressed. The more I think about it, the more I'm certain that I overreacted. The guy has got to be doing some construction work on the house, hence the tool belt and the key to let himself inside.

A pink T-shirt and my powder-blue jeans are perfect for hanging out around here. Since Miguel is busy with his girlfriend, I have *got* to talk to someone now. While heading into the kitchen, I call Jenny.

"So, what's the skinny?" Jenny asks as soon as she picks up the phone. "Did you talk to your dad to find out what he's doing with the student?"

"Jenny," I say, exasperated. "You really have to control your imagination. That is absolutely *not* what's going on here." I open a few cabinets, looking for the cereal, which I find in the pantry between containers of flour and sugar.

"Oh." She sounds disappointed. "I guess I was

wrong then. So, your father said there was no hanky-panky, huh?"

"I didn't ask him." Opening the refrigerator, I find oat milk and decide it will do fine for my bowl of cereal. "They were gone when I woke up."

"What?" Sighing loudly, she continues, "Are you saying you *didn't* talk to him about the woman in his house?"

I can imagine her shaking her head. "She is not a woman." I pour the granola in a bowl. "She's a girl."

"Do you know how crazy that sounds?" Her signature loud laugh echoes through the phone. "You said she's in her mid-twenties."

"At the most. Maybe younger."

"Well, in any case, being in her twenties qualifies her for adulthood. Stop fooling yourself. We aren't *that* much older that you don't remember what it was like to have a crush on one of our handsome professors."

"I remember no such thing." I should have known Jenny would refuse to see logic, what with her magic incantations and spells. "There's no hocus-pocus going on here."

"No. I'd say not." She chuckles. "If you don't want to remember Professor Larsen, our very bohemian art history teacher, well, good for you. Even *I* was attracted to him, and that's saying something."

"Okay." Of course, I remember him, but I'm not about to share that with her so she can gloat in satisfaction. My father is nothing like Professor Larsen, who had loads of sex appeal. He'd probably been in his late thirties or early forties, tall and rangy-looking, with a slightly disheveled look, messy hair, and crumpled clothes that looked like they'd been purchased at a secondhand store. He'd consistently appeared excited to discover he was teaching art to an excited group of students who he may or may not have noticed were mostly female. "I didn't ask my father about the living situation because, by the time I came back in the house, they were in bed."

"Together?"

"Jenny!" After choking on my cereal, I wipe my mouth with a napkin. "No." Although, really... how would I know? But the thought is too ridiculous to seriously consider.

"Go check now," she orders. "See if it looks like she's using the second bedroom and he's using the other one." Jenny can be very bossy.

Normally, I admire her directness, but not so much right now. "I'm not going to snoop around my father's house." I chew on a mixture of crushed almonds, coconut shreds, and pumpkin seeds. Obviously, this cereal is eaten for the health benefits, not the flavor.

"Don't be silly," she says impatiently. "That's exactly *why* you can snoop. All kids wait until their parents leave the house before they embark on a treasure hunt to discover what bounty they can unearth—candy bars, love letters, perfume samples, etc. You apparently missed out on some of those important developmental milestones. Go now and call me back when you're done."

"I'm not sure," I say hesitantly, while the idea begins to make sense. After all, they aren't here, and it will just take a minute.

Taking my bowl to the sink, I quickly wash it, then set it on the drying rack. "Okay, you're blowing this whole thing out of proportion. You'll see I'm right."

"Want to bet?" she asks eagerly.

"Not really." Now that I've decided to check out the rooms, I'm eager to get off the phone, so I can prove my point.

"If I win—or perhaps I should say *when* you see that they are sharing a room—you owe me a crystal of my choice."

"Fine. And you owe me one when you find out that she's renting a room and nothing more."

After disconnecting, I set my phone on the table and walk to the back of the house. My father's room is the first door on the right.

I twist the nob and cautiously peak inside. Same teakwood headboard on his double bed that is clearly unsuitable for two people. The beige curtains cover two windows, and the oblong brown-and-beige rug is on the floor at the foot of the bed.

Stepping inside, I make my way to the dresser where there's one bottle of expensive designer cologne. My hand shakes as I pick up the bottle, looking for an indication if it's for a male or female—but there's no designation either way. Maybe I should check in the closet. If the girl's sleeping in this room, she'll have to have some clothes in the closet.

Just as I'm about to slide open the door panels, a deep voice behind me says, "What do you think you're doing?"

It's the construction guy, a drill in one calloused hand, and a stern expression on his lean face.

"Hey." Startled, I jerk away from the closet door and hit my hip against the sharp corner of the dresser. "Ow." I rub the spot where the wood jutted out. "I'm looking for something." Women's clothes to be exact, but he does not need to know that. "I could ask you the same question. What are *you* doing here?" I feel guilty but also apprehensive since I'm alone with a stranger. Truth is, he probably *does* know what's going on here, even if I don't.

"I'm working on the other room." He tilts his head across the hall. "I didn't mean to startle you this morning." He looks at me sheepishly, a grin beginning to spread on his face. "I'm Aaron and you're a friend of the professor?"

My face grows warm, and I look down as I remember the short pajamas I was wearing earlier. No need to think about that, not when I have things that are more important on my mind. Maybe I should befriend him since he's apparently harmless and knows more about my father's situation than I do.

"You're not..." His brown eyes are filled with questions. "... an acquaintance or should I say a special *pal* of the professor, are you?"

"No, I'm not." My response is quick since I'm unsure of the direction he's heading. Obviously, Jenny's gotten into my head with her overactive imagination. Not knowing when Melissa or my father will return home, I am now eager to leave the room.

Edging my way past him, I can't help but notice how he smells—like a combination of sweat and musk, a strangely appealing mix on him. "I'm Leah Ann."

"Nice to meet you, Leah Ann." Grinning, he follows me out of the room into the hall. "Is that one word or two?"

"Two." I'm on a mission and not in the mood for small talk, even if Aaron appears to be a decent guy. "Don't let me stop you from doing your job." Glancing past him, I focus on the second bedroom door that he's blocking. I feel like reaching around and grabbing the handle. And why shouldn't I? It's my father's house after all—the place that I spent time in during school breaks. It doesn't matter if I had fun or not.

"What, with the other room being taken, I guess you had to sleep on the sofa." Scrunching his nose, he makes a face. "Doesn't look that comfortable."

"It was okay," I lie, remembering how uncomfortable I'd been.

"Here." He slips a hand into his back pocket, pulls out a business card, then hands it to me. "At your service. My number's there if you need me."

I take a minute to read the card. *Aaron Wong. Construction.* His name is in bold, blue print, with a picture of a red crane in the background. A phone number, website, and a contractor's license number are listed. "I won't be needing this, but thanks anyway. I've got no plans to remodel anything. I'm just visiting my dad for a couple of days." Feeling awkward about entering the other room now with him looking on, I saunter past the closed door.

"Really?" Following me down the hall, he adds, "I didn't know the professor had a daughter." He nods, looking at me appreciatively. "You must be excited."

"I am," I say confidently, having no idea what he's talking about, but I don't want Aaron to know how little I know about what's going on in my father's life. "Very," I say emphatically. I'm eager for him to go so I can finish my snooping. What am I supposed to be excited about? It would be too weird for me to ask him what he means. After all, we *are* talking about my father. "Don't let me hold you up." I wave a hand. "I

125

know construction runs on deadlines."

"We're just getting started." Opening the front door, he continues, "I've been working for the professor for a while." He shrugs before finally stepping onto the porch. "I do odd jobs here and there, although this is a bigger project. Anyway, it's nice meeting you."

"Nice meeting you, too." I wave my hand again, before shoving the door closed.

After he leaves, I rush to the other room. As I'm about to enter the bedroom, I hear someone at the front door. Impatient, I rush back down the hall to see who's here now.

"I thought of something." Aaron's hands are jammed in his pockets as he stands on the porch, a sheepish expression on his face.

"Yes?" How am I supposed to inspect the other room if Aaron keeps distracting me? I slowly uncurl my fingers from where they clutch the door handle. It's too early for either Melissa or my father to be returning any time soon—or... is it? What if he has only one class to teach today and Melissa's running an errand that takes a short time to complete? "Did you forget something?"

"You're here to spend some time with your father, right?"

"Correct." Now I'm puzzled. He now wants to talk about how I'm going to spend my time? I glance at my watch.

"Probably Melissa, too, am I right?"

"Hmm." Saying *no* could be construed as rude, so I murmur something unintelligible. *Why* is this man assuming that I'd want to spend time with one of my father's students? Strange.

"I know you said you're only going to be around

for a couple of days, but there is a new Italian restaurant in town." With a grin, he holds out a hand. "Do you like Italian?"

"I do." He has a great smile and his tattoos are sexy, but I'm not interested in going out with anyone at this time—even someone as ruggedly attractive as Aaron.

"Great. Want to get a bite to eat later? How about six? I can pick you up or we could meet in town."

"Thank you for the offer, but I'm good." This guy works fast. Maybe if I lived here, I'd take a chance since Raymond has someone and so does Miguel. But I need to stop hanging onto the past and move forward. "I'll be gone in a couple of days, so…"

"Say no more. It's cool. You have my number."

As he walks out the door, I hear him call out, "Call me if you change your mind. You have to eat while you are here."

Chuckling, I shut the door behind me. I'm certain there's no shortage of women he can wine and dine, but, right now, I have one mission, which is discovering what's happening in my father's house.

Rushing back down the hall, I grasp the doorknob, confident I'll be able to report to Jenny that all of Melissa's things are in the spare room.

But, before I can turn the knob, I hear my name being called.

Feeling like a thief with her hand on stolen jewels, I jerk my hand away, but not before Melissa has time to appear at my side.

"Hi, Melissa." I drop my hand so fast I slap my thigh.

"Good morning." Twirling a strand of hair, she

sighs. "I know that couch isn't comfortable, but with the other room under construction, we don't have much choice."

"Speaking of that, what *is* happening with that room?" Time to utilize a direct approach since my father didn't say anything last night and I keep getting derailed.

"I'd love to fill you in on *all* the details." Her blue eyes sparkle with excitement. "After I make this quick call to my doctor, we can catch up while I prepare dinner." She rubs her hands together. "I'm glad we can get to know each other."

"Me, too." I echo the sentiment, although I hadn't known she existed until yesterday. Apparently, my father had shared that he has a daughter. Since I'm not that much older than her, she's probably been curious about me. Well, I'm curious about her, too.

When she walks into the spare room, I expel a relieved breath. It's just as I thought; she's a boarder and they are remodeling the room.

Once I'm back in the kitchen, I pick up my phone from where I'd left it on the counter and see Jenny has sent me a text with two simple words.

—*What's up?*—

Of course—what, with Aaron's interruptions and then Melissa popping up—I forgot to get back to her regarding her crazy theory that my father and Melissa were an item, which is just insane. He's *way* too old for her.

—*Inconclusive at this time*—

I'm slipping my phone in my pocket when Melissa returns and heads straight to the pantry where she takes out a jar of marinara sauce, a white onion, and a box of spaghetti.

"I might as well start dinner, now that I got that call out of the way." Opening a drawer, she removes a knife and cuts the onion in half before peeling off the outer layer.

"Let me help." I wash my hands at the sink. "What can I do?"

"You don't have to do anything." She dices the onion into small squares.

"I know." The pasta evokes a memory of how much I enjoyed cooking with my mother. Eggplant Parmesan and lasagna were two of her favorite dishes. "I'd like to help."

"If you insist. There's parsley in the refrigerator. Can you chop it and then we can sauté it with the onions before adding the sauce?"

When her eyes meet mine, she quickly looks away. Is she upset about something the doctor said on the phone?

We work in silence for a few minutes before I ask, "Everything okay? With the doctor, I mean?"

She blinks nervously, and I hope she doesn't think I'm being nosy. She doesn't have to answer if she doesn't want to. "Everything's going smoothly. Sometimes, I feel queasy, which is pretty normal—considering."

"Considering?" I inanely echo her words as my thoughts scatter. Chemo can make a person feel queasy. Maybe she's ill. A stomach flu possibly.

Removing a large saucepan from the bottom cabinet, I add olive oil and set it on the stove to heat, before looking at her expectantly, hoping that she'll share more.

Dalia Dupris

She stops chopping and meets my eyes, with a determined expression on her face. Setting the knife down, she squares her shoulders, before answering. "Not that many people know. Of course, Aaron *is* fixing the room, so he knows." She fidgets with her fingers and inhales deeply. "But you know how small Santa Lorena is. People are already beginning to put two and two together."

"I'm totally lost." I stop adding the snipped parsley to the pan and focus on what she's saying. "Two and two together about what?"

Stepping closer, she places a hand on my shoulder and the scent of onions brings tears to my eyes. "We are beyond excited about this. We didn't know I'd be expecting so soon." Her smile is so radiant that it transforms her face, giving it an ethereal glow.

"Expecting *what*?" A package in the mail? Graduation from college? Earning a degree? *What* is she expecting? "Can you give me a few more details?"

"My mother would say that your being here is serendipitous. She's an avid reader, so she's got an awesome vocabulary." The onions sizzle as she sprinkles them in the heated pan.

"That's great, but you were telling me about your expectations." Following Melissa's train of thought is starting to feel like a maze and my gut is telling me that I need to keep her on track.

"Ed was going to call you, but you coming here now is perfect timing. I'm glad that he shared the good news with you last night."

"That's just it, he didn't tell me *anything*." Shifting away from the stove, I peer at Melissa, trying to comprehend where this conversation is headed. "What do you *think* he told me?" The calmness of my voice belies the knots in my stomach.

"Oh snicker doodle." A look of panic and dismay crosses her face. "I *thought* he told you. We discussed this. Ed was supposed to tell you."

"Melissa, my father said he was too tired to talk last night, so, basically, he didn't say much." *As usual*, I want to add, but decide against it. "What was he *supposed* to tell me?" I'm practically shouting now. Sucking in a gulp of air, I continue more quietly, "I'm sorry. Can you tell me what it is that you thought my father had told me?"

"Sure." There's sheer panic in those blue eyes as she eases into a chair at the dinette table. Eyeing me apologetically she adds, "I'm pregnant and your dad's the father."

"No way!" I blurt out. "He's too old. I mean... I thought, well, he's obviously not." I smell the vegetables burning on the stove but don't care. "Really? With all the eligible handsome college guys out there, you couldn't find a man closer to your own age?" It's too late to censor my thoughts or words. How could a man who never seemed to care for me or even know how to *speak* to me bring another child in the world?

"They are so immature." Her voice is defiant as she rises from her seat. "Compared to your father, they're just boys. I've always been attracted to older men."

"Oh, great." Clasping my hands, I notice the smoke rising from the stove as the alarm shrieks. "That explains it."

"What do your parents think?" I ask while turning off the burner. Somewhere, in the back of my mind, I know this is an irrelevant question. This grown woman is with child—my *father's* child. I can't be in denial anymore.

"They don't know yet." She opens the jar of marinara sauce and pours it over the charred onions and parsley. "But your father and I are happy and that's all that counts. You're about to be a big sister."

I can't process her words. The man who barely spoke two sentences to me when I visited on weekends is now embracing parenthood. "His parenting skills leave something to be desired." She needs to know that even if it's too late. Then again, it's not my place to dampen her joy about becoming a mom. "He wasn't—"

"Don't say it." She holds her hands out, as if to block my next sentence. "He's told me how he was with you, but he'll be different with *our* baby. I just know it." She turns the heat up under the sauce again, before stirring it with a metal spoon. "He really wants *this* baby."

"Excuse me?" My face grows warm as her implication comes clear. "Are you saying that my father didn't want *me*?"

Taking a couple steps backward, she picks up a dishtowel and swipes frantically at the smoky air. At least the alarm has finally stopped going off. Not looking at me, she says, "Nothing. I shouldn't have said anything." She throws her hands in the air, but not before I notice her guilty expression. "This is between you and your father. I have nothing to do with it." Throwing the towel into the sink, she stomps out of the room, leaving the ruined sauce boiling over on the stove and me simmering in my emotions.

Chapter 10

*Miguel*

"I hope I didn't interrupt anything." Taylor is sprawled on one of the white chairs near the fireplace, her legs stretched out and crossed at the ankles as her gaze flits across the room.

"I'll call her back later." Sitting across from her, I'm eager to know what she wants so I can finish speaking with Leah. She sounded as troubled as I feel about my frustrating conversation with my impossible-to-please father. "How did you know I was here?"

"I was outside getting my briefcase from my car when I saw you headed in this direction. I figured, where else could you be going?" Her eyes linger on the crystal vase of fresh roses on the table, their heavy scent filling the room. White eyelet curtains cover the windows, with glints of sunlight breaking through. A hand-carved loveseat faces the fireplace. "I've never been in the Love Shack."

"It's the honeymoon cottage." I don't point out that Love Shack has a totally different connotation.

"That's quaint." Chuckling, she saunters over to the fireplace and smells the vase of pink roses and jasmine on the mantel. Running her hands along the back of one of the chairs, she adds, "Hardly anyone gets married anymore. It's an antiquated remnant of the

133

past."

"I hardly think that's true." Why am I defending the institution of marriage to her? I know it's not antiquated. Regardless of my relationship with my father, his relationship with my mother is as strong as ever.

Eager to get to the point of her visit, I join her in front of the fireplace.

"Yeah it is." She chuckles, "But I love it that you are an old-fashioned type of guy who still believes in that kind of stuff. I find it endearing. You don't have to tie yourself up in legal contracts and potential property disputes when you can have everything you want free and clear." Those last words are spoken in a breathless whisper.

"Taylor, is there something I can do for you?" With her jet-black hair, dark eyes, and sultry voice, Taylor is attractive, but our views on relationships and commitment obviously clash—not to mention that I'm in love with someone else. I wonder how Leah feels about marriage. What if she doesn't want marriage and children one day?

"I came here to make you a proposition." She runs a finger along my jaw before returning to the chair. Crossing her legs, she leans toward me.

"Really?" I force myself to shut down thoughts of Leah and focus on what Taylor's saying. As a fitness instructor, I'm used to women coming on to me on occasion. It comes with the territory, but I'm not expecting it from one of my mother's employees. I make it a policy to never date a client—not that Taylor is a client, but still. It's not going to happen. "What did you have in mind?"

"My purpose in working here is two-fold. I've been helping out, so I can get a feel for the place. Your mother hired me to do an assessment and then figure out how to increase the inn's profit margins."

"From what I saw, business is booming." Confused, I run a hand across my brow. "That's why I'm in the cottage—because all of the rooms are booked."

"You haven't been here for a while, so you wouldn't know how much the last fires damaged the local economy. I'm good at marketing. I don't have a degree, but I've started my own business and have been hired by many of the shop owners, including your mother."

"I see." A rush of guilt hits me like a punch to the gut. Why didn't I know the inn was struggling?

Because I was too busy, developing my own customer base in Sunnyville, that's why.

"It can't be *that* bad," I say. "Not with all of the main rooms occupied."

"The rooms are occupied because I reached out to the Alpha Phi Philia sorority. They normally have their semi-annual meetings in large cities, so I reached out to their organization and worked out a phenomenal package for them here and at the Hawthorn Hotel in town. I gave them a great price—with your mother's approval, of course—and some extras, and, well, they couldn't refuse." She flashes her hand in a sign of victory.

"I'm impressed—although, I can't see how Santa Lorena can compete with the attractions that San Francisco or New York have for out-of-town guests." So, there's more to Taylor than meets the eye. It's possible I misjudged her. She's obviously good at her job, and, for that, I'm grateful. I know how much the inn means to my parents, especially my mother. Since she was a teenager, my mother had a dream of owning a place where people dine on delicious food at reasonable rates. The joyous sound of happy voices and appreciative feedback helps her feel less isolated from other family members who live in other cities.

"You haven't been here in a while." Tilting her head, Taylor pierces me with an intense look. "You should check out downtown. We now have a yoga studio."

"I saw it when I drove in." Shrugging, I continue, "Yoga has been popular for a while." And not something I would be adding to my fitness training; I know my limitations.

"We also have several new trendy restaurants, a small playhouse, a movie theatre, and a gallery," she boasts. "With the fire recovery money, people have been excited to go to the next level. We even have a massage parlor." She raises a brow, as if that last piece of information would be of particular interest to me.

She's wrong. The only massage I want is one that would involve Leah.

"That's quite a bit." Sighing, I try to process this new information. "I'll have to take a tour."

I have barely finished my sentence when she chimes in enthusiastically.

"I'll take you."

"If you don't mind, I prefer to explore on my own. You're right; a lot has changed. From the sound of it, the town is thriving, and your strategy to bring business to my mother's inn has been successful." So why is she still here, when her marketing plans have paid off? "You said you had a proposition for me?"

"I'm in a bind." She joins me at the fireplace. "Part of the sorority package includes free yoga lessons each morning. I just got off the phone with Kathy—the yoga instructor. She pulled a muscle or something while demonstrating a downward facing dog for her advanced students and is at her chiropractor's office. He's recommending she rest her muscles for the next week."

"Bummer." I'm familiar with how injuries must be treated—usually with rest, heat, ice or both. "Does she have another instructor to fill in for her?"

"No." She taps her long red fingernails on the mantel. "The other instructor is on vacation in the Dominican Republic and won't be back until Saturday, which is the day the sorority ladies are checking out," she continues, "I hate to ask you. But… the women were very excited about the yoga class."

"No way. I see where you're going with this." Stepping away, I shake my head. "I don't do yoga. I can't help you."

"Okay, fine." She looks at me pleadingly. "You can do whatever kind of physical activity you want. It can be hiking or even line dancing." She shrugs before folding her hands together. "Line dancing would be a big hit. The main thing is that we don't want the guests to feel like they didn't get their money's worth and write negative reviews, which can easily destroy a business."

"Let me make this clear—I'm *not* leading a line dance class." I see now why my mother hired her to increase business; Taylor is *very* persuasive. And persistent. She drives a hard bargain. How can I say no when I'd be doing something to help out my mother's business? But how will Leah feel about being here a few more days?

"Whatever you want." Her eyes turn somber. "You're the fitness expert. What activity would you prefer to offer?"

"A morning hike is something that even sedentary people can participate in. Nothing too rigorous. It's the best time of day to get out—before the sun has emerged from behind the clouds. I'll decide on the time after I look at their scheduled activities and meetings."

"All of their meetings begin at 10:00," Taylor eagerly chimes in, smiling broadly.

"You can notify them of the change in activities, from yoga to walking. We'll leave promptly at 8:00. That gives them time to grab a bite to eat, then shower before their first meeting. We'll meet in the lobby." How could I not say yes when it affected my mother's business? I already feel crummy about being completely unaware that reservations are down, and broken contractual agreements can destroy the inn's reputation. Since my father can't figure out how I can be of service, helping my mother will show him I *do* have a skill set, even if it's one he doesn't approve of. He's made his opinion clear that exercising or running around in shorts, as he puts it, is *no* way for a grown man to earn a living.

After I open the door, Taylor flings her arms around my neck, but not before she presses her lips against my mouth.

"Hey." Startled, I remove her arms and take a step back. "Affectionate, aren't you?"

"Not with everyone." A mischievous sparkle lights

her eyes. "But, with you, I found myself wanting to show my appreciation."

"I'm doing this for my mother." Shaking my head, I indicate that it's time for her to leave.

"I'd like to think you are doing this for me, too." She looks coy, but her actions tell another story.

"Nope, just for my mother." Opening the door wider, I grit my teeth and hope she'll get the message and leave without needing further prompting. I think I've made my feelings clear, but one never knows.

"Oh?" Looking uncertain, she pokes out her bottom lip.

"You don't need to thank me for helping my mother's business in any way I can."

"But I would enjoy thanking *you*." Chuckling, she's obviously *not* offended by my rebuff. "If—or should I say *when*—you change your mind, you know where to find me."

Needing to clear my head after two equally unpredictable encounters with both my father and Taylor, I grab my keys and drive toward Leah's father's house. I need to speak to someone rational. Leah's disposition is a big part of what appeals to me—that and how she cares for her students and what a loyal friend she's been to Jenny, Sandy, and Rebecca. *Especially* Rebecca. Not many women would be part of a bridal party where their ex-boyfriend is marrying their previous best friend.

Three blocks from the house, I spot Leah, a distracted expression on her face, as she makes her way down the street.

Pulling over, I open the window and call out to her. "Leah."

Startled, she abruptly stops and notices me. "Miguel." Her smile doesn't reach her eyes as she glances furtively at the quiet street. "What are you doing here?"

"I could ask you the same thing." Unlocking the passenger door, I reach across, and open it. "Hop in."

"You sure?" Her eyes are red and puffy as if she's been crying. "I don't want to bother you."

"You could never bother me." She doesn't have a clue that I'm in love with her. "I was coming to see you."

"Really?" It pains me to know that Raymond's rejection has left her feeling insecure. On the other hand, his loss creates an opportunity for me to demonstrate genuine love and loyalty that has never wavered.

"Yes, really." I gesture for her to stop stalling. "I was going to call you back, but I didn't want to interrupt your time with your father."

"Believe me, you would not have been interrupting anything." Sniffling, and with a defiant tilt of her chin, she finally opens the door and slides into the seat. "I don't care if I never see my father again in my life."

"What happened?" I've never seen Leah this angry.

I drive toward the newly renovated downtown area. One of those fancy overpriced coffee shops might come in handy right now. From what I can tell from my clients, coffee with caramel, whipped cream, and lots of sugar is their go-to drink. "Let's go someplace we can talk."

"I don't want to talk about it." She presses the palms of her hands over her shut eyes. "I wouldn't even know where to begin."

"How about the beginning? We've been here for less than forty-eight hours; how much could have happened?" In my case, it's been *too* long, but I can't imagine that Leah and her father have problems on my scale. But what do I know? One fifteen-minute conversation with my father and I'm ready to return to Sunnyville—and I would if my mother didn't need my help.

"No offence, but I can't talk about it now. It's too confusing." Removing her hands from her eyes, she sighs. "Do you think an older man—say, a professor possibly—should date a student?"

"Don't schools have rules about that sort of thing?" I recall that her father is a professor, and, if this question is any indication, he's dating one of his students. No wonder Leah is unhappy.

"Yes, exactly my point!" Twisting around in her seat, she faces me while pounding one fist against the dashboard. "There are *rules*. Rules are meant to be followed. Is it too much to ask for some simple decency?"

"Sounds reasonable." I drive a couple more miles until I see the familiar coffee shop ahead. "Let's go inside and you can tell me what has you stressed out." I'm not a coffee drinker, but, apparently, everyone else in town is. It takes me ten minutes to find a place to park in the crammed parking lot.

"I can't go in there, Miguel." She rolls her eyes. "People might overhear our conversation. Plus, as I told you, I can't talk about it."

"All right." I'm willing to do anything to be supportive to the woman I love, who is obviously in distress, even if it means not saying a word. We sit in

141

the car, in silence, for several seconds before she releases a shaky breath.

"Oh, Miguel." Leaning over, her head drops to my chest. "I'm so confused, and I've been awful." She snuggles closer to me before wiping the back of her hand across her face.

"I'm here for you." Wrapping my arm around her shoulders, I inhale the soft scent of flowers. The feel of her body leaning against me feels as good as I've imagined. "Sometimes it helps to talk about it, but that's up to you."

"I know that and I'm grateful. You and Jenny are the best friends a girl can have." Some of the tension leaves her body. "What would I do without you?"

"You're my best friend, too." Although I wish it were more. "Don't worry about me going anywhere. It's not going to happen." I run a hand down her arm. If I could have fallen in love with someone else, it would have already occurred. The women I've previously dated have only solidified my feelings for the woman sitting beside me right now.

She sighs contently. "I need to find a room. I can't go back to my father's house. I really need space." She shoves back the curls that have fallen on her forehead.

"Okay." I try not to moan with pleasure when she places a hand on my chest, and I try to figure out what's happening in her home. What has she told me about her relationship with her dad? Not much. "But isn't all your stuff over there?"

"Yes, but I had to get out of there and left my cell phone and everything else. At the time, I didn't know I would be uncomfortable returning. Now that I've had time to think it over, it's not a good idea for me to be there—for *so* many reasons, that I don't want to discuss."

"I see." That's a lie. I have no idea what she's talking about. As much as I want to support Leah, I'm not sure I'll have any useful answers. My own track record with family dynamics is dismal. How can I possibly understand her dilemmas when I'm unable to decode what my father expects of me?

"I don't want to ruin your time with your parents, but if I could stay somewhere else, even for one night, it would be a big help." Her eyes open wide and I can't ignore the desperation in her voice. "I wouldn't ask, but I know your family has an inn. I would pay, of course."

"You aren't paying for anything." I continue caressing her upper arm, making sure to keep it comforting and nothing more. "There's one problem. Our inn doesn't have any vacancies and the hotel in town is completely booked with a convention."

"Really?" Her eyebrows shoot up, a look of incredulity on her face. "Everything is booked in Santa Lorena? How can that be possible?"

"A large organization is having their semi-annual meeting in town."

She's sitting up now, no longer leaning against me and I miss her warmth. "That's great!" She presses her fingertips against her forehead. "Why am I *not* surprised? I'd sleep on a park bench before I return to my father's house. It's probably more comfortable than the couch I slept on last night anyway."

By now, I know better than to ask for more details, like why she was sleeping on a couch and not a bed. Maybe her father had converted her room into an office. Come to think of it, it's amazing our paths never crossed when she was visiting her father before. I was probably working in the groves with my father, while she was hanging out with hers. At least we met once I moved to Sunnyville. "I have a suite at the inn. Come home with me."

Her eyes narrow as she shakes her head. "I couldn't inconvenience you." She runs a finger through her hair. "I don't want to be a nuisance. I'll figure something out, even if I don't know what it is yet." Her voice trembles even though she sounds determined.

"You could never be a nuisance. I'm staying in a cottage. It's big enough for two people." I quickly decide not to mention that it's the honeymoon cottage; I don't want her to think I'm trying to make a move on her when she's vulnerable. "I promise you that the place is spacious." Faint, crescent shaped shadows under her eyes confirm her sleepless night. "Say yes."

"Okay. I'll do it." Her head falls back against the seat. "I'll stay for one night. I need time away from the situation at my father's house. A good night's rest won't hurt either."

"No problem." Leah in the honeymoon cottage; that's what I call temptation. It's going to be one long night and a true test of my willpower. She doesn't suspect that she stole my heart almost twenty years ago and there's never been anyone else. Is this the time to come clean and let her know that my interest in her isn't platonic?

Chapter 11

*Leah*

"I could eat something now." After assessing the
puffy-faced image that stares back at me from the
mirror on the flip side of the car visor, I take a deep
calming breath knowing that I look like what I am—a
woman who's muddling her way through one too many
crushing blows. I knew Raymond's wedding would be
challenging, but I'd had time to mentally prepare for
that day. However, I'm totally blindsided by the fact
that my emotionally unavailable, middle-aged father is
having a child with a woman who, not that long ago,
was one of his students.

"I can always throw something together at the
cottage. My mother taught me a few recipes that are
pretty good, if I say so myself. We don't have to go to a
restaurant if you're not up to it." Miguel's thick brows
come together as he glances in my direction. His dark
eyes reflect the concern in his voice. "You sure you
want to eat out?"

"Yes, I'm sure." A surge of guilt surfaces as I
reflect on how I've leaned on this man's broad
shoulders so many times for understanding and support
during my predicaments and he's never once
complained. The truth is that Miguel's presence puts
me at ease and pulls me back from despair over my

male relationship issues. First, it was Raymond, and now it's my father. I can't expect him to cook for me, too. "The hot dog stand I loved as a child is still there." Looking up, I peer through the rear window. "We drove by it earlier."

"Dippity Dog?" He laughs before fastening his seat belt and starting the car. "I remember that place. They had the best chili cheese dogs."

"Right." Smiling, I recall the extra-long hot dogs and buns, dripping with chili sauce and chopped onions. "They were the best. I didn't know what a calorie was when I was a kid."

"I didn't either, which is probably why everything tasted so good." His hand briefly rests on my knee before he backs the SUV out of the coffee shop parking lot. "Let's enjoy our food and *not* think about nutrition."

"Can *you* do that?" I don't mean to sound incredulous, but, as a fitness coach, he's probably always thinking of food, calories, and exercise. "I mean, it's part of your job to always consider healthy choices, isn't it?"

"Sure, but sometimes I have to give myself a break and not worry about if a food is a good or bad carb." He shrugs before steering the car in the opposite direction of the recently remodeled downtown area with all of its shiny new storefronts.

As Miguel continues down the road, the landscape shifts to fewer trees and dim streetlights. A sense of nostalgia looms as we pass the older familiar businesses that were able to survive the damage of the most recent Santa Anas. Here, the structures are weathered, the signs faded and frayed but still intact. There's definitely something comfortable about the familiar, even if it's tattered and torn.

"I consume my share of snacks and junk food, just like everyone else."

"Makes sense." Why is this a surprise to me? Have I placed Miguel on a pedestal, not realizing he's a normal human being like the rest of us? "You're always active—jogging, weight lifting, cycling. From what I've seen, you do it all on a consistent basis. If that's not disciplined, I don't know what is."

"I am, most of the time, especially when it comes to my work." He concentrates on maneuvering past a slow-moving truck before continuing, "I've noticed you're the same way. It's one of the things I admire about you."

"Me?" Frowning, I think I *must* have heard him wrong. We are *nothing* alike. I mean, sure I have *some* discipline, but nowhere near Miguel's level. I've seen him running in the morning, golden-brown muscular legs effortlessly piling up the miles while I look out from my dinette window, enjoying my giant blueberry muffin that probably has over the daily recommended numbers of calories and carbohydrates in one bite.

"Don't sound so shocked." He parks in front of Dippity Dog Diner, with the same red and blue awning and the oversized, tan, neon wiener dog wagging its mechanical tail from the roof. "I've seen how you prepare your materials for your students. All the care you take with making posters and decorating your bulletin boards with their names and birthdays…"

"I was going to ask how you know that, but then I remembered the day you came to my class last winter." It'd been a rare Southern California day—drizzling and gray, without a hint of sunlight peeking through the clouds. On my drive in to work, the engine had made a sputtering sound, so twenty minutes before the end of the school day I had sent Miguel a text, asking if he could come by when school let out.

Always punctual, he had shown up early enough to hang out in my classroom for the last few minutes of class, before he checked out my car.

"I enjoyed observing you in action with those children." His chuckle echoes in the car. "I don't know whose face contained more pleasure, the students or yours."

"I would say mine, no doubt about it." I do love working with the students; he's got that right. They do bring me joy. "By the end of the day, they are antsy and can barely wait to escape my classroom."

"That's not what I saw," he says dismissively before hopping out of the car and opening my door. "Those kids were hanging on to your every word."

We make our way inside the classic diner with the familiar red booths and checkered tablecloths. Nothing has changed, including the jukebox in the corner and the black-and-white linoleum floor. The dog theme continues inside with an array of black-and-white framed photographs of dachshunds on the counters and walls.

"Welcome." Fine lines etch the face of the silver-haired waitress.

She appears vaguely familiar, and I wouldn't be surprised if she's served me and everyone else in Santa Lorena at one time or another.

"I'm Dotty and I'll be your server today." She waves a hand toward the booths. "Sit wherever you like."

Heading toward the back, we make our way past a group of giggling teenage girls and a blonde woman encouraging a toddler to eat a miniature hot dog. Scooting into the last booth in the back of the diner, I clasp my hands, trying to keep them still as I release a shaky breath. "I owe you an explanation."

"That's up to you."

His eyes are apprehensive, which is entirely understandable, considering the mixed messages I've been dishing out all day.

"Don't feel like you have to share what's going on if you don't want to."

"I know that and appreciate your letting me decide to share or not, but I need to clue you in on my situation." My fingers nervously tap against the table. "I've been more than a little crazed today and I'm not sure where to begin. In all the years we've known each other, we've never revealed much about our families." Swallowing the lump in my throat, I glance away from his gaze; instead, I focus on the streetlight outside the window and the brightness of the moon's glow and how it looks like there are circles around it. Why is talking about family so difficult?

"No, we haven't." He pauses when Dotty sets down two menus and tall glasses of iced water. We decide what we want and wait for the waitress to return for the order before he continues, "It's easy to feel removed when you have a parent—or, in my case, two—living in another city. It's not far, but it can feel like a world away."

"You're right." I stop tapping long enough to stretch my fingers out like a fan. The familiar aching pain of no longer having my mother engulfs me, trapping my words in my throat. "Everyone knew my mother. She didn't like Sutton, the town we moved to when I was in high school. I wasn't crazy about it either. It's hard to relocate as a teenager when all the cool cliques have already been firmly established. When I graduated from college, we were both eager to resume our lives in Sunnyville. She loved the proximity to the beach. After her retirement, it was her favorite place. She'd stake out a spot facing the ocean where she could sit for hours, contentedly listening to the waves and sea gulls and the occasional loud-honking seals, and would read a medical romance novel that she loved." I've boxed her stacks of paperbacks, along with several hardcover books. All that's left is to donate them to the library, but part of me wants to hold on to something that I know she held in her hands and which brought her such joy.

Shaking my head to clear the memories, I refocus. "Sorry about that. I'm digressing."

I stop long enough for the waitress to bring us two blue baskets with a Dippity Dog special in each and a red basket of fries for sharing.

"I'll be back with the milkshakes." Dotty is surprisingly spry as she pivots on her heels and heads toward the shiny chrome milkshake machine behind the long counter.

"This looks great." Unfolding my napkin, I carefully spread it across my lap, glad there's a napkin dispenser on the table. Consuming chilidogs is a messy affair, and since I'll be wearing the same clothes tomorrow, I need to proceed with caution.

Miguel takes a big bite of his food and smiles as

bright as a ten-year-old on Christmas morning. "Man, this is good."

Dotty returns with Miguel's chocolate shake and a strawberry one for me. We eat in silence for several minutes, concentrating on the flavors of diced red onions, spicy ground beef, cheddar cheese, and a grilled hot dog on a toasted bun. Taking a sip of my shake, I savor the thick, icy chill as it slides down my throat.

"So, you were telling me about how happy your mother was to move back to Sunnyville."

"Right. It's easy to talk about her because we were always so close. My father is another story, one that's a bit of a mystery. The thing is, I've never had a good sense of him. Who he is, I mean. My parents divorced when I was young and when I visited him, he was distant." When I grab a fry, my hand collides with Miguel's, and, for a minute, I want to clutch it—feel the warmth of it and hold onto it like it's an anchor in my turbulent world of uncontrollable losses and pain, but, instead, I pull away. I blink and the moment is gone as I stuff the fry into my mouth. "Anyway, he never spoke much or asked me about my life. I don't know him. He's there, but… *not* there." Tension fills my chest as I continue, "I know that sounds crazy, but that *is* exactly what my relationship, if you can even call it that, with my father is like."

"That must have been hard." Miguel nods as if he understands me completely.

I release a breath, relieved that he doesn't tell me that I'm not making any sense. "It was." The truth is that our relationship is fragmented, like shards of broken glass, and I've never understood why. Was it something I said or did as a child? Something I can't remember, but is unforgiveable to him, even now, all of these years later? Is that why our conversations are stilted? "I have never voiced how my father and I aren't able to connect."

When I set down my drink, Miguel shifts toward me, reaches out, and then covers my hand with his. There's no judgment or pity in his eyes when they meet mine.

"When you dropped me off at my dad's, there was a woman in the house—a student of his. Let me correct that—I'm certain she's a past student, because otherwise..." Shaking my head, I banish the thought of any other, more disturbing, scenarios. I know universities have rules about student–teacher relationships. I'm a hundred percent certain that Melissa's and my father's relationship would be breaking the rules if she were still in one of his classes. "In any case, she's living there." My voice is a hushed whisper—as if university administrators are sitting behind us. "In my father's house. *Alone* with him."

Miguel's head jerks up and his ebony eyes double in size. He looks as stunned as I felt after learning about my father's dalliance. "*That* had to be a surprise."

"That's putting it mildly." I push my half-eaten hot dog aside. "I was in shock and probably in denial. I called Jenny for a reality check, which reminds me, I was supposed to call her back." Another thing to feel guilty about. First, I made *no* attempt to disguise the truth that I'm less than thrilled when my father's girlfriend announces she's pregnant and, second, I've forgotten to get back to Jenny. Great.

"You can call her from my phone." Picking up his napkin, he swipes at a drop of chili on his cheek before reaching into his back pocket and pulling out his cell.

"Thanks." I don't pick up the phone, though, knowing that I'll have to confess to Jenny that her assessment of the situation was correct. "Jenny knew right away what was going on. I didn't want to believe it. There are rules about that sort of thing—professors not fraternizing with students. And then there's the fact that Melissa is young." Lowering my head, I press my fingers against my temples, attempting to ease the tension.

"You *have* had a lot on your mind." He runs a hand across the nape of his neck. "I can see how you could have been blindsided."

"That's not the worst of it." I throw my hands up. "She's pregnant."

"What?" He opens his mouth as if to say more, but no words come out.

"Exactly!" To be on the safe side, I lower my voice even more as I lean closer to Miguel. "I couldn't believe it, but I didn't have a choice."

"On the positive side, you get a little brother or sister out of this."

I have to love him for trying to be optimistic or not saying that my dad is a lecherous old man—oh, God. If Miguel had said *that*, I would've disappeared under this table. "I'm an only child and always thought it would have been nice to have a sibling or two. You know, someone to commiserate with about how confusing and aggravating parents can be."

"I get it. I mean, it *would* be nice except…"

I focus on the vinyl tablecloth until the red and white lines blur. "Except that, number one, the woman who is my potential stepmother is freaking younger than me and, two, I don't think my father even *likes* children and, believe me, I'm saying that from personal experience."

"Leah." Miguel's voice deepens and I can feel his understanding and empathy wash over me. He finishes the last of his milkshake before leaning back in the booth. "Some people have difficulty showing it, but maybe he does like children."

"Well then, he must have changed, because he sure as heck *never* liked me." Finally, I've given voice to what I've believed in my heart for years—a deep disconnection from my father. "No matter what I did, it *never* pleased him." Two emotions compete for center stage: relief at no longer holding my feelings back and the discomfort of stating such a painful truth. "I never said a word to my mother about any of this. I know it would have saddened her and I never wanted to cause her any stress."

"I hear you." There's sympathy in his eyes as he slides toward the end of the booth.

During my darkest moments, Miguel has been by my side, always ready to lend support without judgment or blame. He has never made me feel any shame for my thoughts or feelings.

"Ready to go?"

"Yes." Brushing curls off my forehead, I reflect on how many emotions I've kept bottled inside, and now the top has broken off and previously unexpressed feelings are tumbling out like a waterfall over a rocky cliff.

Miguel picks up the check, and, after the meal is paid for, we head outside. Most of the shops have closed. Not much stays open late in Santa Lorena. The shutters are drawn, and most people have already made it home. The sun has almost set as streaks of orange and purple light the horizon. A mild breeze blows as Miguel opens the passenger door for me.

"My mother wanted things to be good between us, so I never told her how miserable I felt at my dad's. Sounds crazy, right? I don't feel bad about keeping the truth from her. She'd ask how the weekend had gone, and I always said it'd gone well."

"I get it." We drive in silence for several minutes before Miguel turns on the heat, causing a blast of warm air to blow into the car. "More than you know." He reaches out, resting his hand palm, side-up, on the console between us.

Placing my hand in his, I marvel at how his touch leaves me feeling safe, secure, and settled in my soul.

I'm halfway asleep by the time we leave the center of town. The scent of oranges hangs heavy in the air as we pass row after row of citrus trees, their bright green leaves barely moving in the night breeze. The parking lot in front of the sprawling inn is completely full. Miguel circles around the building until he finds a space marked RESERVED.

In the dark, we make our way to a building that's smaller than the larger building in the front. We are almost at the front door when Miguel abruptly stops, an expression of concern in his dark eyes. "Sorry about the mess. If I'd known you were coming, I would have straightened up." Facing the door, he pulls a key card out of his pocket and, with a shove of his foot, he steps aside so I can enter first.

Stunned, I stand inside the entrance and look around at the assortment of flowers on the coffee table and over the fireplace mantel. Pictures of red and pink hearts and a heart-shaped sculpture on the fireplace capture my attention. A plush white rug covers the maple wood floors and the scent of fresh roses wafts in the air.

"Are your parents here?" I can't stop staring at how immaculate and beautiful everything looks. The off-white sofa is adorned with pink, heart-shaped pillows.

"No. They live in the main house." Miguel picks up a pair of shoes by a plush, oversized chair and sets them down near the wall. "I live here by myself."

"This is really nice." I stroll into a kitchenette. "I got a sofa bed with wires poking me in my back and your parents give you your own house." Rolling my eyes, I notice that his brow is furrowed and his lips are tight. Have I offended him? "I like the whole heart-shaped theme." Continuing my self-guided tour, I open the door to the bathroom and gasp when I spot twin sinks and a sunken whirlpool tub. My breath catches in my throat when I enter the wood paneled bedroom. A king-sized canopy bed is in the center of the room. The matching dresser and desk are off to the side and an enormous window reveals a panoramic view of majestic mountains set against a moonlit skyline.

Rushing out of the room, I face Miguel, who's now sitting on the small sofa and switching television channels with the remote control.

"Miguel, this place is gorgeous." Sitting beside him, I make a mental note of the small sofa size, and angle my legs to the side, trying not to brush my thighs against his. "You have your own house; how did you bring yourself to leave?"

His Aunt Esther's Sunnyville home is nice, but nothing like this elegantly welcoming cottage.

When he doesn't respond, I continue, "The view is gorgeous. The mountains, the sky… Honestly, I'd never want to leave." I can't prevent comparing my sleeping arrangements at my father's house with Miguel's in this place. "Now, this…" I fling my arms wide, "… this would make me feel genuinely welcomed."

Finally, I stop blabbering long enough to notice that Miguel has a far-away look in his eyes and his lips are sucked in. My gushing has obviously made him uncomfortable.

He pauses the game show he's watching and faces me. "Leah, this isn't where I grew up." His voice is flat as he stretches his long legs.

"I don't understand. I thought you brought me to your home." Now I'm confused.

"I was staying at a room in the main house, but my dad and I got into it. He made it clear that they needed the room I was staying in because they have a big group here this week. I gave up my room and took this place." Turning away, he refocuses on the television.

"*This* is where you sleep when you and your father disagree on something?" Looking at him suspiciously, I add, "If this place is the punishment, I'd want to stay here all the time."

"Well, it's not all ways available. My mother keeps it ready year-round just in case there's a booking." Eyeing me apologetically, he murmurs, "It's the honeymoon suite."

"What?" I'd scoot away from him on the sofa, but there's nowhere to go if I don't want to land on the floor. "Oh, I see." Heat creeps up my neck as I flush with embarrassment. "That makes sense. That's why the sofa is so small—it's a love seat. The hearts should have been another clue." Feeling obtuse, I shrink farther into my corner of the couch. "How could I have missed all the signs?"

"I'm guessing that, unless you're keeping something from me, you've never been in a honeymoon suite before." There's a mischievous glint in his eyes. "Is there something you need to tell me?" He chuckles.

"Funny." I jolt up, suddenly self-conscious. I shouldn't be here. This is a special romantic place for two people who are in love, not two buddies. "I shouldn't have imposed on you." Wishing I could disappear, I recall the distinctive voice of the woman who'd been in the room with him when I called. "You probably had other plans for how you wanted to spend your time in this room. And here I come, messing everything up." First Raymond, then my father, and now Miguel. When will I ever learn how *not* to force myself on men who don't want me? "I can go." I bite my lower lip. "I have no idea where that will be, but I'm sure I can find someplace." Honestly, all I can think of is a park bench, but I'm not about to say that.

"Leah," Miguel responds sternly as he stands, too. "You aren't going anywhere. I offered to share my place with you."

"I don't recall you asking me to stay with you. I *assumed* that I could stay with you because I'm uncomfortable at my father's house. I see now that I put you on the spot." I grasp my hands to prevent me from wringing them like a wet towel. With a sinking sensation, I face the fact that I am the queen of being someplace where I am not wanted.

"Don't be ridiculous." Taking my hands in his, he gently squeezes them. "You are *not* going anywhere. I appreciate your company. Always. You know that." He gives me what I assume is meant to be a reassuring smile. "Please stay."

"Speaking of company, what would your girlfriend say about me being here?" I force myself to focus on my words and not how closely we're standing to each other—which isn't unusual, but now that I know we're in the honeymoon suite, well, it somehow feels different.

"What girlfriend?" Miguel drops my hands as his brows come together, a look of confusion on his face. "I don't have a girlfriend."

"When I called, I heard a woman's voice in the background." Now that I think of it, she'd been saying something about him not having clothes on, but I'm not about to mention that I overheard their conversation.

Miguel continues to look perplexed for a few seconds before he releases a loud laugh. "That was Taylor," he says nonchalantly. "She works here. She's helping to drum up business. She's *not* my girlfriend." As if the matter is now settled, he returns to the sofa and picks up the remote control, eyes focused on the show he was watching.

"I see," I say, which is totally false. Apparently, he's moved on from the subject and I probably should, too. Who Miguel spends time with when he's back in Santa Lorena is no business of mine. Plus, I honestly don't know where I would go at this time of evening. If Miguel says it's okay for me to stay here tonight, then that's what I'll do. "I'm really tired. Is it all right if I

Dalia Dupris

take advantage of the tub?" Yawning, I give up trying to figure out relationship puzzles.

"Sure," he says, never taking his eyes from the television screen. "Help yourself."

"Uh," I hesitate before leaving the room, but there is one more thing that I need to bring up. "About the bed."

"Oh damn." That gets his attention. Startled and with a look of sheer panic, he peers at me as if I suggested we have a threesome. "Right. The bed. It's yours." He rubs his chin before continuing, "I'll sleep out here." He holds two thumbs up as if that has resolved the sleeping arrangements.

"No, you won't." My voice is firm. I'm not about to allow Miguel to squeeze his practically six-foot frame onto a love seat. He'll have all kinds of aches and pains tomorrow morning and will probably end up on the floor. "We'll share the bed."

"I'm not sure that's a good idea."

Clicking off the remote control, he faces me. I've never noticed the muscle twitching in his jaw before and a slight sheen of perspiration dots his forehead, even though the temperature in the room is perfect.

"You need your space and a good night's sleep after last night."

"I'm not arguing with you about it." Forcing my eyes to stay open, I stifle another yawn. "Look, I'm too exhausted to analyze our options here. I have enough energy to take a bath and then I'm crashing. That bed is humongous." I use my firm teacher voice, which works every time with my students.

Walking over to stand in front of him, I bend down to run my fingers through his midnight black hair. "We

160

are two adults. I'm sure we can manage to sleep together peacefully. I don't take up much room. I tend to sleep curled on one side and don't move much during the night, so I won't accidently roll over on you, if that's what you're thinking."

"Not what I was thinking." Miguel's voice is muffled with a hint of agitation. "But you don't have any pajamas."

Does he truly believe that would be a problem? Considering that he's the one insisting I stay, he's making this more complicated than it needs to be. "Any one of your T-shirts will do fine." I'm already moving toward that wonderful bathroom where I'd seen the generous size containers of bath salts and bubble bath along the rim of the tub. "Leave it on the door, and I'll get it when I'm finished."

I'm grateful to see the drawers are filled with a generous assortment of amenities, such as a travel toothbrush, mouthwash, floss, toothpaste, shower gel, shampoo, and lotion. There are also two fluffy white robes hanging on the back of the door and matching white slippers. They've really thought of everything.

The tub and its pulsing jet sprays don't disappoint, and, by the time I step out, I'm more relaxed than I have been in several days. I lather on the complimentary citrus-scented lotion and brush my teeth before cautiously opening the door and grabbing the T-shirt that's hanging on the handle. Even before I hold it up to my nose and inhale, I recognize Miguel's scent, a subtle mixture of mossy green woods and blue ocean waves.

Still warm from the bath, I shuffle to the bedroom and choose the side of the bed that faces the open window with the spectacular view of the Santa Lorena mountains. Shaking my head, the last thought I have before I fall asleep is that this bed is so huge, Miguel will forget I'm even in it.

Chapter 12

*Miguel*

The television is on, but it doesn't make any sense for me to pretend that I'm concentrating on anything besides the fact that *my* Leah, the woman I have pined for, is *naked in my bathroom*. When soft moans emanate from the other side of the door, I groan and spring up from the sofa. Now would be a good time to do fifty push-ups. Dropping to the floor, I assume the correct exercise position, legs back, arms straight and supporting my upper torso. *Down and up. Take a deep breath and repeat. Anything* to rid myself of the image of the luscious woman of my dreams, skin glistening with warm water and bubbles, stepping out of the tub, looking like a goddess sent from Heaven to tempt my resolve to do the right thing.

Twenty minutes later, I'm drenched with sweat and experiencing muscle fatigue when the bathroom door squeaks open.

"Oh crap." I've been so busy visualizing her curves that I forgot to hang a T-shirt on the outer doorknob. Jumping up from the floor, I sprint to the bedroom, grab the first shirt I see and rush to hang it on the doorknob seconds before Leah's fingers reach out and grasp it.

This is going to be one long night. Being here with Leah is a dumb idea. If I'd had a lick of sense, I'd have checked to see if there was at least one room available despite my father's assertion that he needed the room I had originally checked into. Had his statement been his way of letting me know how little he thought of me or was it accurate? If I had given it a second thought, I would have touched base with my mother, but none of that matters now. As uncomfortable as the situation is, I'm pleased to offer Leah a way to decompress after the challenges she's been experiencing, first, with Raymond and, now, with her father.

In the kitchen, I grab a paper towel and swipe the perspiration from my forehead before chugging down a bottle of water. I can't complicate her life further by telling her how I feel. At least, not now, but her being here is a huge trial. One bed for two people—one of who happens to be in love with the other person— would be a test for even the most disciplined man.

I have to keep my hands to myself and not share what's in my heart. Opening the front door, I peer into the dark night and let the brisk air cool me down. No streetlights out here, so all I see are the stars and sometimes the moon. I remind myself that I've been in love with her for a ridiculous number of years. What's one night together in a romantic suite?

Shaking my head to clear it, I acknowledge that it wouldn't matter if we were in a two-star motel; my desire for Leah would be the same.

Time to suck it up and develop a fool-proof strategy to get through this night. I'll take a cold shower, then I'll put on sweats—no sleeping in the nude tonight. I'll be sure to stay on my side of the bed and not move. I especially won't look at her in my bed and I *definitely* won't touch her—not her hair, not her shoulders, not her thighs or any other body part. I have to remember that she still thinks of me as nothing more than a good friend… which, I guess, is better than not being thought of at all.

After all, it's just one night. Once she gets some shut-eye, she'll be refreshed and ready to return to her father's home for the remainder of the week and I won't be up half the night thinking about how nice it would be to have her in my bed for keeps.

After my cold shower, I cautiously make my way into the room, mindful of not walking into anything or making noise. I don't want to wake her and have to resist *that* temptation. She's left the curtains open so there's enough light for me to make her out, sprawled in the middle of the bed, arms flung wide as she lies on her back, a mass of curls covering her eyes. So much for her sleeping on one side of the bed.

How the heck am I supposed to get in without touching her?

Placing one knee on the bed, I bend down, and whisper in her ear, "Leah, move over."

She mumbles unintelligibly before turning onto her side. Lord, this woman smells good. I recognize the familiar fragrance of the toiletries we keep in each room, but when mixed with Leah's natural fresh scent, it presents a one-of-a-kind, seductive temptation. If I can move her a little farther to the right, I'll have enough room to lie down.

Cautiously, I place one hand under her arm and another under her knees and gently lift her more toward the other side of the bed. The sheet falls off and reveals my T-shirt twisted around her middle and molded to the contours of her body. As I remove my hands from her,

I'm not sure if *I* moaned or she did.

Even with the cold shower, it's a long night, filled with lustful dreams of the woman I love being in my arms. It takes every ounce of willpower I possess to stay on my side of the bed.

Finally, after what feels like hours later, I'm able to close my eyes and fall asleep.

I hardly move when I sleep, so when I feel something warm on my chest, I know I'm not the one who shifted position. The sun has begun its ascent over the horizon and Leah is resting her head against my chest and snuggled up to my side. I may not be able to control how my body is responding, but I can use my mind to stay very still and enjoy the magic of the moment.

I carefully remove her arm before edging my way out of the bed. Is it possible to have the best and the most difficult night of my life at the same time? I can't recall how many times I've dreamt of Leah sharing my bed, but under totally different circumstances. Not being able to tell her how I feel and knowing it would be wrong to make a move makes for a rough night.

I'll be working out hard today and am glad I'll be leading the sorority ladies on an early morning stretch and walk—anything to distract my mind and body from wanting a woman I can't have. In the military, I learned that timing is everything and that discipline and patience will get you further than a rash decision, so I will wait.

Duffle bag in hand, I head for the bathroom and change into my running shorts and a short-sleeved cotton shirt. After preparing a cup of coffee and grabbing a protein bar, I head out the door toward the front of the inn where Taylor and the sorority ladies will meet me. There's a clear area directly off to the side of the porch near the herb garden that can easily accommodate up to twenty people. Taylor sent me a text last night informing me that fifteen women had confirmed for the one-hour walk.

"Hey, Miguel."

When I arrive at the designated location ten minutes early, Taylor is already there. In her snug fitting, super brief, black shorts and low-cut tank top, she looks more prepared to play beach volleyball instead of participating in a nature walk in the woods.

She peruses me slowly. "You're looking good, as usual."

"Morning." I decide not to mention that it can be a little chilly this time of day when the fog hasn't completely evaporated. "You got here early."

"I like to be prepared and not leave anything to chance, that way I get what I want."

"Sounds good." I'm not sure what she's talking about, but I don't ask for clarification. When she begins to stretch, I raise my brows, wondering if she'll join the class. "Plan on participating?"

"I'm feeling a little tense." She tilts her head slowly to one shoulder and then the other. "I figure a workout may be just what I need to unwind."

"Maybe so."

Several women make their way to the area. Most are wearing sweats or leggings and lightweight jackets with appropriate shoes, so there won't be a need for me to review how important proper footwear is in supporting the body, especially when exercising and preventing injuries.

"Is this okay?" Taylor asks, indicating her scanty outfit.

"As long as you can move freely and are comfortable, you should be good." Shrugging, I count the number of women that are chatting while waiting for the class to begin.

"I've been told I'm very hot-blooded." Spreading her legs, she bends forward, revealing a good amount of cleavage while stretching and touching her toes. "I'm super flexible."

"I'm sure that comes in handy." I suppress the impulse to remind her that I'll be leading a morning walk, not a gymnastics class.

"Absolutely." Standing straight, she pierces me with a laser stare. "I could show you all the things I can do."

"Maybe another time." I silently count the number of women who have shown up before glancing at my watch. "Time to get started."

"Of course." Tilting her head, she glances at the assortment of women who have gathered. "Can't forget about the class. That *is* why we're here, after all."

I don't know why she sounds frustrated since she's the one who suggested the class. In any case, I'm in no mood to figure out the workings of Taylor's mind. I'm here to follow through on the contractual agreement that an exercise class would be available to the members of this organization while they are guests at the inn.

After fifteen minutes of stretching, I begin the slow and steady scenic walk along my father's vineyards and the outer perimeter of the orange groves until we reach Pacific Ridge Road, which is an easy half-mile trek that leads to Point Matthew, a clearing surrounded by an abundance of California's state flowers, bright orange poppies in full bloom. Now that the sun has emerged from behind the clouds, we pause long enough to peer over the mountains, past scenic downtown Santa Lorena and enjoy a panoramic view of the Pacific Ocean. The walkers pull out their cell phones, and capture the images before we make our way back to the inn.

By the time we return, I'm eager to finish the warm-down and check on Leah, but first things first. "Did everyone enjoy their walk?"

A chorus of affirmative responses confirms that the women enjoyed themselves.

"It was a great walk." Taylor says, while flashing a thumbs up sign. She stayed close by me the entire time and although she chatted throughout our trek, my thoughts have been elsewhere. "I've really worked up a sweat." She pats her chest.

"Glad you enjoyed it. Sweating is good. Gets rid of toxins and cools down our bodies." Looking at the class, I raise my voice and demonstrate the warm-down exercise I want them to emulate. "Keeping your right leg bent, stretch your left leg behind you and hold it there for a minute. This will stretch your shin and thigh muscles."

"What about me?" Taylor waves her hand, signaling me to inspect her position. "Can you check my alignment?"

"Of course." I note that Taylor's legs are in the correct position. "Your legs look perfect."

"You really think so?" Taylor smiles before twisting to the side and frowning. "Whose that woman over there?"

I follow Taylor's gaze and spot Leah standing near the registration table. "That's my friend Leah and I need to speak with her."

"Wait." She clutches my arm. "I'm thinking of hiring a personal trainer. Interested?"

"Not really." I remove her hand. "Remember, I don't live here."

"Fine, but I'm not the type of girl that gives up easily." With a flip of her hair, Taylor faces the ladies who are still stretching while I head toward Leah.

"You look like you got some sleep." One glance at Leah tells me that she's feeling better than she did yesterday when I spotted her wandering down the street looking crestfallen. Her eyes are now bright and her skin has its usual soft glow.

"I did. That bed is comfortable. I thought you had finished with your group."

"Your timing is good. We're wrapping up."

"I didn't want to interrupt anything." Peering over my shoulder, she says, "The lady you were speaking with is headed toward us."

With a glance, I spot Taylor moving in our direction. Whatever she needs can wait until tomorrow. "Can you give me a second?"

"No problem." Leah takes a step back when Taylor walks up and stands between us.

"Don't forget about me... us." She giggles before adding, "I mean, the class. They are waiting for you to demonstrate the last stretch."

"I'll be right there," I say, suppressing the irritation in my voice and indicating that Taylor should rejoin the group.

"Go finish your class," Leah says. "I'll wait for you."

I give Leah a quick wink before returning to stand in front of the participants where I complete the final hamstring stretch before ending the class.

When I'm finished, Taylor joins me as I'm walking back toward Leah. What does this woman want *now*? I'm starving and in no mood to entertain Taylor's whims. I am eager to enjoy one of my mother's famous breakfasts with Leah.

"Can we debrief about the hike?" Taylor asks. "I think now would be a good time, since we just returned."

"Really?" What's to debrief about? Everyone obviously enjoyed the walk, but maybe she wants to talk about an evaluation, in which case we wouldn't distribute that until the end of the week.

"Not now." I spot Leah, who's exploring my mother's herb garden. "Maybe later."

"All right." Taylor sends a disapproving glare Leah's way. "I can see you're preoccupied." She pokes out her bottom lip and folds her arms before turning toward me, a tight smile on her face. "We'll talk later. After all, I'll be seeing you for the next few mornings." With a smug smile, she saunters away.

The dining area is bustling, but Leah and I manage to locate an available table for two in a back corner.

"I recommend the buffet." Squeezing her hand, I wonder how she's doing this morning. She's dealing with a lot of family issues. "Especially if you're hungry."

"You've twisted my arm." Rising from her seat, she adds, "The buffet it is."

"Good choice." I stand close to her as we survey the array of turkey sausages, bacon, ham, boiled, poached, and scrambled eggs, and Mexican pastries, which, as a child, I'd always thought were shaped liked various seashells. I point at my favorite one. "I must tell you; my mother is known for these. Not bragging. Just a fact."

"Say no more." She adds one fluffy, corn-based pastry to her plate. "That's it for me. My plate is full." She eyes my plate before looking up at me. "I know you aren't going to try to pile one more thing on there."

"Well." I look at her sheepishly. "Since you put it that way, it would be ridiculous, so I won't." I chuckle under my breath as she shakes her head. "I'll come back for the rest."

"Let's eat what we have before we think about getting seconds."

"Whatever you say." Back at the table, I set down my plate before pulling out her chair. "You're the teacher."

"Apparently, you are, too." She picks up a slice of bacon and nibbles on it before continuing, "So, was that your girlfriend?"

"What?" I sputter, practically dropping my forkful of eggs. "Or perhaps I should say *who* are you talking about?"

"The woman whose eyes were shooting daggers at me the entire time I was speaking to you." She takes a sip of her tea before continuing, "The one who was practically wearing underclothes as exercise attire." She rolls her eyes and smirks. "I have bathing suits that cover more skin than that get-up she had on."

"Jealous?" Even as I ask the question, I know it's

just wishful thinking on my part. Leah doesn't feel that way about me. "You're talking about Taylor. She's not my girlfriend."

"Okay." Leah shrugs. "I'm just saying that I don't think she got the memo."

"It's not like that at all." Eating the last bite of my sausage, I add, "She's helping my mother with marketing. She's the person who asked me to fill in for the yoga instructor who was supposed to be leading a class."

"She definitely has the hots for you." Leah takes a bite of her pastry and closes her eyes before sighing. "These are heavenly."

She's left a couple of crumbs on her bottom lip. Taking my napkin, I wipe them off. "There. That's better."

"Thanks."

She gives me a grateful smile, not knowing that what I really wanted to do was take my time and lick away the crumbs from her perfectly plump lips.

"Please tell your mother how much I'm enjoying her food, particularly the sweet breads."

"You'll have a chance to tell her yourself." My mother is very snoopy by nature. The last thing I need is her poking around my relationship with Leah, which technically, isn't a relationship as much as it is a friendship. But I'll be changing that status when the time is right. I hoped to introduce Leah to her at a different time and under different circumstances. I'm planning on us finishing our meal before my mother makes her morning rounds. So much for that, here she comes now in one of her signature pastel pantsuits.

"Great." Leah finishes the pastry seconds before

my mother reaches our table.

"Good morning." My mother nods at me before she raises one brow and looks at Leah with open curiosity. "I'm Miguel's mother, Lucia. I don't believe we've met."

"Mom, this is Leah James." There are only two seats at the table, and I'd really like to enjoy the meal alone with Leah, but I won't be rude. My mother trained me better than that. "Do you want to join us? I can pull up another chair." I know the right thing to do. "You can have my seat." Pushing the chair back from the table, I stand.

"Thanks anyway, but I can't. We've got a large crowd coming in for lunch and I need to oversee the kitchen staff." With a wave of her hand, she signals me to take my seat. "Nice to meet you, Leah. Miguel mentioned you to me before."

"Nothing bad, I hope." Leah's eyes narrow as she glances in my direction. "He's one of my very best friends." She reaches over and rubs my hand.

"He's said only good things." My mother tousles my hair, which makes me feel like I'm ten years old. "You live in Sunnyville, right?"

"I do, but I'm visiting my father."

I don't expect my mother to notice it, but I hear a tremor in Leah's voice.

"By the way, the food here is delicious. I especially love the pastries."

"Thank you, dear." My mother shifts her gaze in my direction. "I'm glad Miguel brought you by for breakfast." She pauses before continuing, "Are you, by any chance, related to Professor James?"

"Yes. He's my father."

"Many years ago, I enrolled in several university classes, including one of your father's history classes. Of course, that was before I had opened the inn and had more time. He was a good professor. Very approachable. Had an open-door policy."

"I'm sure he did," Leah says with a barely perceptible touch of bitterness to her voice, but she's soon smiling again. "He may be too friendly as far as I'm concerned."

"Oh?" A flicker of surprise crosses my mother's face, before she nods her head, as if in understanding. "Children are frequently critical of their parents' actions. Speaking of which," she focuses her attention on me, "I need to talk to you about *your* father."

"Maybe later." I'm sure my father slanted the story so I appear to be the unreasonable one, even though I came here because I thought he needed me. "I've got a couple of things I've got to do with Leah first."

"No problem. By the way, I'm very pleased you're offering the guests a morning hike in exchange for the yoga class they were promised." She gives my shoulder an affectionate squeeze. "Taylor can't say enough good things about you."

"Humph." Leah mumbles with a smirk. "I bet she can't."

"Pardon?" My mother asks, while peering at Leah.

Leah coughs while pointing a finger at her throat before saying, "'I think a piece of bacon got stuck in my throat."

"Oh dear. We can't have that." My mother picks up a glass of water from the table and hands it to Leah. "Drink this." Once Leah's impromptu, coughing fit ceases, my mother continues, "Nice meeting you,

Leah."

This is not how I expected to introduce my mother to the woman I plan to marry, but, in time, she'll learn Leah isn't only my best friend. My mother is obviously clueless about the fact Leah spent the night with me in the honeymoon suite.

"Your mom is nice." Leah takes another sip of her water and I'm curious to see if she'd still feel that way if she knew my mother has been plotting for me to see Taylor as future marriage material.

"I love her like crazy, but I think she's eager for me to settle down and provide her with some grandchildren." I hadn't planned to share that, but now that I have, I wonder how Leah feels about marriage and children. Just because someone is good at working with children doesn't mean they want their own.

"I guess that's normal." She shrugs before swiping her mouth with her napkin. "If you actually like your children, you probably can't wait to love your grandchildren." Abruptly standing, she pulls her shoulders back. "It's time for me to face my father."

Chapter 13

*Leah*

"I owe Melissa an apology." Squirming in my seat, I reflect on how poorly I behaved yesterday. "It's not like it's her fault she fell in love with her professor, is it?"

"Nope." Miguel keeps his eyes on the narrow road winding down from the inn past the vineyards.

"I'm sure it happens all the time." Holding out my hands, I inspect them. "Young, impressionable student, handsome older professor; it's kind of a cliché." Biting my bottom lip, I glance out the window at the white orange blossoms and the lush green trees lining the side of the road. "But I'm certain acting on it is against university guidelines."

"Probably." Miguel nods.

Does he think my father is a bad person? Although, I guess the bigger question is do *I* think he is a bad person?

"But here's the thing… " I talk to the side of his face, somehow never having noticed before that he has a distinctively handsome profile; even nose, long lashes, and lips that are perfect for his face. "… If I'm being completely honest, it's not his morals I'm thinking about." There, I've said it out loud.

"No?" He looks confused, which is understandable

since I'm skirting around the real reason I was obnoxious with Melissa. "What was the main thing that bothered you?"

"I'm aware that this will sound childish." Pausing, I attempt to swallow the golf ball-sized lump lodged in my throat. "But what really both annoys and perplexes me is that he's chosen to have another child when he so clearly doesn't like the one he already has." The admission leaves me emotionally drained and feeling stupidly vulnerable. My eyes fill with tears, and I concentrate on not blinking so they don't escape. Slumping in my seat, I sniffle before taking a deep breath. "Sorry." Embarrassed, I stare at my lap. "Right about now, you're probably regretting inviting me to join you on this trip."

"Are you kidding me?" He glances at me before reaching for my hand and squeezing it. "You're my best friend."

"I thought Sammy is."

"Sure, he's my best *guy* friend, but you're my best *girl* friend." His lips curl in a smile.

"Huh?" I stiffen, fighting the urge to tug my hand out of his. Later, I'll figure out why I'm having this irrational reaction to an innocent statement. "I thought you said you don't have a girlfriend," I say accusatorily. I must be losing my mind. The situation with my father is making me needy, even to Miguel, in whom I have *no* romantic interest at all.

"I don't." He taps his hands against the steering wheel. "I meant you are my best *female* friend."

"Ah. I'm sorry." Pulling my hand back, I add, "I'm feeling unusually testy. Just ignore me. I'm not making any sense. Between losing my mom, who I was super

178

close to, and losing Raymond, who I probably never really had, it now feels like I'm losing my father, too."

For the longest time, silence hangs heavy in the air. Miguel's jaw is clenched; I can see the muscles twitching and there's a crease between his shiny black brows. I've probably done it now. Miguel is no doubt sick of my whining and ready to dump me along the side of the road. I can't blame him. I'm tired of my *woe is me* attitude, too, but I don't know how to change it, at least, not now, when I'm about to talk to the man who doesn't seem to love me at all. My father, the professor who everyone thinks is so great and friendly, so accessible… Hah!

Pulling up in front of my father's home, Miguel turns off the engine, before facing me.

Feeling ashamed of my erratic behavior, I avoid eye contact.

"Look at me." He lifts my chin with the tip of his finger, while piercing me with the intensity of his gaze. "You will *never* lose me." His raspy voice skirts along my nerves for some odd reason. "I will always be here for you. Always."

This is a different side to Miguel. It's probably his serious military side that gets his subordinates to do whatever he tells them to do.

"Understand?"

Nodding, I don't dare look away. "Yes."

"Never forget I will always be here for you."

Between the muscle jerking along his jaw and the firm set of his mouth, I know Miguel is a man of his word.

"I won't." Reaching up, I give him a quick hug. "I'm so glad you're here." Pulling back, I shake my head. "I don't think I could do this without you."

"You don't have to worry about that." The intensity of his eyes and the gravelly voice are gone. "What's the plan? Are you ready to sit down, and a have a face-to-face conversation about your feelings?"

"Well." Sucking in my lip, I twist my hands together. "Not quite." I grow warm under his unwavering scrutiny. "I was thinking about it on the way here. I can't have a private discussion with him while Melissa is at the house. It wouldn't feel right. I already know I acted horribly, and I owe her an apology. She hasn't done anything wrong and she's so excited about the... baby." I take a deep breath, before continuing, "But the conversation I need to have with my father should be a private one and it's about my relationship with *him* not Melissa or... my future brother or sister." An unexpected twinge of joy fills my chest at the thought of me becoming a big sister.

"So what are we doing here?" Miguel rubs his chin, not attempting to hide his confusion.

"I can't go back and stay there, and not just because the couch felt like a torture device. I'd like to stay at the inn a little while longer—that is, if it's okay with you." I bring a hand to my brow. "I forgot to ask how you slept."

"Fine." His voice is clipped and there's a scowl on his face.

"You can say no if you want." I pat his hand. "I can see if a room has become available at the Hawthorne."

"It hasn't." Tapping the steering wheel, he continues, "The sorority conference won't be over for a couple more days. I slept," he pauses long enough to clear his throat, "well and you are welcome to stay as long as you need to. Remember what I said earlier. I'll always be here for you, for whatever."

"Thank you." Although his words are reassuring, I can tell something is still bothering him, and finding out what it is will go on my To-Do list. So far, he's the one man whose love I've never had to question. I definitely don't want to test the limits of his loyalty, no matter what he says.

"I still don't understand why you wanted me to bring you to your father's place, since you don't believe you'll be able to speak with him now."

"To get my clothes." I point at my outfit—the same one I had on yesterday. "I need my suitcase with my clothes, toothbrush, and makeup."

His eyebrows rise. "But you don't wear makeup and you certainly don't need it."

"You dear sweet man." I chuckle before continuing, "If only you knew. I appreciate the compliment, but this," I indicate my bare face, "is not how I want to face the world the whole time I'm here." I grab his hand and give him my most pleading look. "Could you go and get my suitcase for me?"

"What?" He yanks his hand away. Shaking his head and looking doubtfully at me, he adds, "You want me to walk up to the door and tell your father I need your clothes?"

"Yes." I smile and shamelessly flutter my eyelashes, which is something I've never done in my life. "Don't worry. I think he must be conflict-avoidant or something because he never talks to me about anything serious, so he certainly isn't going to say anything to you."

"I don't know about this." He taps his fingertips against the steering wheel. "Woman, what I wouldn't do for you..." He unlocks his door.

"You are the best." I bring my hands together as if in prayer. "I owe you one."

"Don't I know it," he says ruefully before stepping out of the car and striding toward the front door.

Several minutes after he rings the doorbell, Melissa opens the door. I can't hear what they're saying.

"Leah Ann." Aaron suddenly appears from out of nowhere next to the car window. "How's it going? I missed seeing you on the couch this morning." His smile is crooked as he hooks a finger into his tool belt.

"Hey." Leaning to the side, I strain to see what's happening on the porch, but Aaron is blocking my view. "I'm not staying here."

"Cool." He leans against the car. "Want to get a bite to eat later?"

"No, she doesn't." Miguel is back and he stands next to Aaron, looking like he's ready to get into a fight. "She's busy tonight, aren't you, Leah?"

For a minute, I'm speechless and confused. Am I busy tonight? I can't think straight as I watch my father stomping toward the car. "Tonight isn't good."

"I can see you're busy," Aaron says easily, looking from Miguel to my father. "I'll catch you later." He points a finger in my direction as he strides off.

"No, you won't!" Miguel calls out after him.

Why does Miguel sound angry? What did my father say to him?

Before I can ask him for details, my father has reached the car. For the briefest of moments, I contemplate sinking down into the seat, kind of like I did after the wedding when I'd hid in the back seat of my car, too drunk, embarrassed, and pitiful to be seen. That was ridiculous. Time for me to get my act together.

"We need to talk." My father's voice is stern, and clearly agitated. Is it because I insulted his girlfriend?

I'm not about to back down on my decision to speak to him somewhere other than here.

"You are always welcome to stay here. It's your home, too."

"I agree, we should talk, but not there." I indicate the house, which never felt like a home. "I need my suitcase."

"If I can't convince you to stay…" His voice trails off and I wonder if he's not secretly relieved, since he didn't really try to convince me to go inside. "I'll be right back."

When he leaves, I turn to Miguel, who's now sitting silently beside me in the driver's seat. "Thanks for trying. I'm sorry to involve you in all this family drama."

Before he can respond, my father returns, a pained expression on his face and my suitcase in his hand.

For the first time, I notice the vertical lines bracketing the sides of his mouth.

"I'll take it." Miguel opens the trunk before stepping out of the car and taking the suitcase from my father.

While he's gone, my father, solemn-eyed, clears his throat. "Melissa will be at her parents' home tonight. Can you come by for dinner at six? We can talk then."

I wish I knew what he was thinking, but I have

never been able to figure him out. Will he really talk to me, for once?

"I'll be here." This is what I wanted, isn't it? An honest, genuine conversation with my elusive father, the man other people find approachable. So why am I holding my breath and clutching my hands together so hard the color drains from my knuckles?

"Good." His voice is devoid of any emotion. "Someone's been trying to reach you." Reaching into his shirt pocket, he removes my cell phone and hands it to me.

"That will be Jenny. She's probably worried sick." A surge of guilt surfaces when I see how many times she's sent text messages.

"Jenny?" Shoving his hands into his pockets, he looks at me questioningly.

I'm reminded how little my father knows about my life. He's never asked for details, and I've never volunteered any. Why bother? He's never been interested.

"She's my best friend." My eyes find Miguel and warmth spreads through my chest. "Of course, Miguel is my other best friend."

"I see."

For a minute, he stands rigidly, peering at me, and I can't help wondering if he's as confused about me as I am about him.

"Tonight then." His mouth twists in a downward slant, and, with rounded shoulders, he makes his way back toward the house, his steps slow and steady.

As Miguel pulls away from the curb, neither one of us utters a word. My mind is cluttered with unanswered questions. My father didn't look very thrilled at the thought of having a conversation with me. Nothing unusual about that. Why hadn't I gone to Melissa when I saw her standing in the door and apologized for my previous behavior? How had I missed the chance to tell her congratulations on her pregnancy? Why is my timing always off with everyone?

Closing my eyes, I lean back against the headrest while massaging my temples. *Is life supposed to be this hard?*

"He had some nerve," Miguel says as he rounds the curve in the road.

"Who?" I've been lost in my own thoughts and haven't been paying attention to Miguel, but I look at him, see how tightly his hands grip the steering wheel, and hear the distinct edge in his voice. "My father?" Had my father said something to offend him?

"No." His eyes shift to me for a quick second before he refocuses on the road. "Aaron." He spits out the name. "Taylor's brother."

"Oh. I didn't know they were related. I gather you don't like him." Is there some history I don't know about between the two men?

"I don't *dislike* him." He scoffs. "I just think he has some nerve walking up to my car and asking you out on a date when you are with another man." His speed increases until it's clearly past the limit. Finally, he jerks to a halt at a red light.

"I don't think he meant anything by it." Seeing that he's obviously upset, I speak softly before placing my hand on his arm, which feels as stiff as a piece of iron.

"The hell he didn't." The light turns green and, this time, he drives within the speed limit. Taking a deep breath, he clears his throat. "You're with me, and he

has the nerves to approach you and ask you on a date."
He shakes his head. "He's lucky I'm highly disciplined
and didn't want to create a scene in front of your
father's house."

"You'd never do that." My voice is reassuring,
although, honestly, this is a side of Miguel I've never
seen before. Why is he so angry with Aaron, who
appears to be a decent guy? It doesn't make sense. Then
again, I didn't understand why Raymond was dating me
when he was obviously in love with his ex-girlfriend.
Men! I'll never understand them. "I met Aaron the
other day. He's doing some work at my dad's, and he
walked in while I was sleeping on the sofa. He kindly
volunteered to show me around town."

"I'm not surprised." Eyes on the road, he shakes
his head. "All I know is he better not try something like
that again."

"I could have answered him myself." I trust
Miguel. He's the big brother I've never had, but
sometimes—like now—he goes too far with being
overprotective. "I know you mean well, but you can't
make decisions for me."

He doesn't immediately respond, just keeps driving
without saying anything else until we pull up at the inn.
He parks in the designated space for the honeymoon
cottage. Grasping my hand, he says, "You're right. I
overstepped my bounds."

He slowly rubs his thumbs across my fingers and a
shiver passes through me.

"I know you can take care of yourself."

When he smiles, his face lights up and he looks
like the Miguel I know and love.

"I'm... not sure what came over me."

His voice is husky and, for a minute, it seems as if he wants to say more. "It's fine." Distracted by how nice it feels to have his hands now gently massaging my fingertips, I struggle to recall what I was about to say. "Uh… we… all have our crazy moments." Needing to think clearly, I pull my hands away and immediately miss the warm sensations his touch aroused. Miguel doesn't feel that way about me. I don't know why I'm reacting to his touch like this—probably because I'm feeling vulnerable and apprehensive about my upcoming meeting with my father. "You've certainly seen enough of mine."

Needing to clear my head and sort out my jumbled thoughts about everything in my life, I leave Miguel standing at the door to the cottage, impulsively deciding that, since I want privacy to call Jenny back, now would be a good time to explore this rustic northern part of Santa Lorena that contains both the Montoya Property and the Hartland Orchards. This area is only twenty-five minutes from town, but my father never brought me here as a child, and I had never thought to visit when, as an adult, I'd come to see him.

The grounds surrounding the inn are filled with lush green foliage that provides a natural canopy of shade as I stroll along the winding path in the back of the picturesque cottage, and I completely understand why a couple would choose this location for a romantic, post-wedding retreat from the rest of the world. The mixture of delicate pink cherry blossoms, crinkly purple jacaranda petals, and the sturdy white eucalyptus flowers create a sense of being in an isolated pastoral garden of Eden, free from all worries. I roll up my sleeves and head toward a clearing up ahead that contains a wooden bench. Taking a seat, I inhale deeply and enjoy the heady fragrance of the surrounding jasmine flowers.

The phone rings once before Jenny picks up. "Finally. It's about time you called. I was just about to get in my car and drive to Santa Lorena."

"I'm sorry." Sighing deeply, I continue, "First of all, I'm fine."

"Good to know. I was worried. The last time I spoke to you, you were about to have a talk with your father's, er, um roommate."

"Geez, Jen, that feels like it was a hundred years ago." Stretching out my legs, I brush a wiry lock of hair off my forehead.

"You're telling me." She snorts. "I'm the one waiting for the call back."

"I left my phone at my father's house." I shake my head, even though she can't see me. "Nothing new there. Unfortunately." I tap my foot against the ground. "You were right. The redhead is his girlfriend. That doesn't sound right, but it sounds better than saying his lover."

"I knew it. Didn't you say she was super young?"

"Super young for my dad. I mean, she's old enough to be his daughter and why did she have to be the one to tell me?"

"Don't get mad at me for saying this, but it happens all the time."

"I know." I kick a fallen branch. "But I always thought my father was shy and conservative."

"Apparently not *that* shy or conservative." Jenny sums my misjudgment up perfectly.

"Exactly. I don't even know who he is." Pausing, I

focus on a hummingbird flitting nearby. "You haven't heard the most shocking part."

"There's more?" she asks incredulously. "Do tell."

I visualize Jenny now, sitting slightly forward, intently listening to every word. She's a great listener, to both what I say and what I'm *not* saying. She knows how to read between the lines, which is sometimes beyond irritating.

"Are they secretly married?"

"Oh no, I hadn't thought of that." I shrug, wondering why I hadn't considered that possibility. "Not that I know of, but, then again, getting anything out of my father is nearly impossible."

"What is it then?" Jenny's voice is barely above a whisper.

"They're having a baby." My attempted chuckle sounds more like I'm gasping for air.

"Wow! Well, that's unexpected." She makes a tsking sound with her tongue. "How do you feel about becoming a big sister?"

"Good question." I stop tapping my foot against the dirt and purse my lips together before answering. "I haven't had a lot of time to think about it, but I like the thought. You know I love children, and even though I'm going to be old enough to be my sibling's parent, I think I'll enjoy it."

"That's a good way to look at it," she says with obvious relief.

"But I initially handled it poorly when Melissa told me. I was so thrown off-guard by the whole thing. My father has been so distant with me that I couldn't imagine him actually wanting another child when he so clearly doesn't enjoy parenting."

"Leah Ann, that may not be true. Maybe he enjoyed being a dad, but he was never good at it." She pauses before continuing, "Have you ever thought of that?"

Sucking on my bottom lip, I think about Jenny's suggestion. "Could be. I don't know anything anymore. I just can't figure anything out. All I know for sure is that I owe Melissa an apology."

"What about your dad? Did the two of you ever have that talk?"

"No. I left and am staying with Miguel right now. My room is being turned into a nursery and I couldn't sleep on that couch one more night, plus I needed some space. My father and I will be having dinner soon and we'll talk then when Melissa is visiting her parents."

"Wait just one minute. Did you say you are staying with Miguel?"

She raises her voice and I have to move the phone away from my ear. "It's no big deal. There's plenty of room in the honeymoon cottage." I regret saying the words as soon as they're out of my mouth. Jenny's imagination is going to run wild.

"The *honeymoon* cottage, you say?" Her laughter booms loud and clear through the phone. "It's about darn time."

"It's not what you think," I say sternly while I remember the way the mere touch of his fingers affected me. Maybe it's been too long since I had a real date and hunger pangs are starting to set in. Aaron seems like a good guy, and it might not be a bad idea to accept his offer for dinner on the town.

"Hah!" she says smugly. "Maybe, my dear friend, it's not what *you* think." And with those last words, she bursts into laughter.

****

"You don't have to keep doing that." Miguel takes his time examining the green shirtdress I've decided to wear to dinner. Once again, we are parked in front of my father's house, and I can't keep my hands still.

"Doing what?" With an open palm, I run my hands down the front of my dress as if I'll be able to smooth away the wrinkles that set in the fabric from being folded in the suitcase.

"That." Glancing down, he indicates the constant motion of my hands. "Your dress looks fine."

His earlier irritable mood continues to baffle me, but there are no traces of it now as a smile lights up his face. "You're only going to see your father; it's not like it's a job interview."

"I know," I mumble while folding my hands in my lap. "Of course, you're right, but you probably wouldn't understand how difficult my relationship is with my father."

His eyes grow somber as he covers my hands with his. There it is, that same warm feeling that makes me want to stay here forever instead of getting out of the car and hearing my father tell me what's going on in his life with his ex-student-slash-soon-to-be-baby-momma.

Taking a deep breath, I remind myself to not go there. After all, this child will be my brother or sister and I'm looking forward to being in his or her life.

"Try me."

Miguel looks at me as if there is no one else in the world and as if what I have to say matters to him. Taylor is a lucky woman.

"What has you so uptight about speaking with your

father?"

"Even though we got here early, we don't have time to go through the whole thing." Pursing my lips, I glance out the car window, noticing the brightness of the sky even though it's almost six. "The reason we're here early is because I know my father is a stickler about time."

"That's not so bad."

"I know, but it's more than that. If I'm one minute late, he's mad at me even if he doesn't say anything." Sighing, I glance down at my dress. "I just feel like whatever I say or do, it's never good enough." I throw up my hands. "It's a losing battle and he never talks to me. He's living with a woman and she's about to have a baby and if I hadn't come on this trip with you, I wouldn't have known any of this."

"Dads can be tough." When Miguel looks at me, I see complete understanding. "I know a little about trying to please a father, but that's another story for another time." He looks at his watch. "That's all about to change tonight. Your father wants to speak with you and it's time for you to go inside."

"I thought this is what I wanted, but, now, I'm not so sure." I steady my breathing and hope Miguel doesn't feel the dampness of my palms. "You go on. I'll get a ride back to the inn with my dad. Don't wait for me."

"I'm not going anywhere." Reaching into the back seat, he picks up his tablet and sets it on his lap. "I've got plenty to keep me occupied. I'm developing some new workout routines. Take your time." Leaning forward, he brushes his firm lips across my cheek.

Hopefully, Miguel can't see the blush that spreads

across my face and warms me from the inside out. If the brotherly kiss on my cheek leaves me wanting more, what would it be like if we ever went further? "This shouldn't take too long, considering how my father typically doesn't have much to say."

I remind myself that this is what I wanted as I make my way up the path to the front door, which my father opens before I touch the doorknob.

"I thought you were going to stay out there forever." He steps aside and ushers me in with a wave of his hand.

"Miguel and I were talking." Following him into the kitchen, I ask, "Is there anything I can do to help?"

"I like Miguel." He opens the oven door and I smell two of my favorite dishes, which happens to be the only meal my father knows how to prepare: baked chicken and extra cheesy macaroni and cheese.

"I do, too." That's when it hits me, that I *do* like Miguel and for more than his role as a friend. Feeling flustered, I wonder when *that* happened.

"I know his father must be proud that he served his country." After slipping on oven gloves, my father removes the food before replacing it with a pan of garlic toast.

"I suppose." It dawns on me that I've been so busy using Miguel as a sounding board, I haven't taken the time to get to know about his relationship with his parents. What had he said about his father? And the bigger question is… what about his girlfriend? I peer at my father to focus on what he's saying, not my nonexistent love life.

"Would you like a glass?" He holds up a bottle of white wine. "I believe this is from a local vineyard." He pauses long enough to study the colorful label. "It's the Montoya Vineyard. Isn't that Miguel's last name?"

"Yes, it is." I try not to stutter.

Had Miguel mentioned a vineyard? What else don't I know about the man I've probably gone and fallen in love with? My chest constricts and my heart pounds as the truth of that statement sinks in. It's Miguel who's always been there for me, who has never shown me anything but kindness and compassion. At some point, my feelings have grown from friendship to something more, even though his feelings for me are platonic.

I've come to lean on him, trust him, and, now... there's love. I thought I'd loved Raymond, but it doesn't compare to what I now feel for Miguel. This feels deeper, like the difference between wading in shallow water and swimming in the ocean.

But... there's Taylor. During the class, she couldn't take her eyes off him. When I had previously called his room, she'd been there. I'd heard her voice, which confirms that they have a relationship. Have I gotten myself into another love triangle? Am I destined to always being the one looking in from the outside, wondering if I'll ever be the one chosen to be loved in return?

It's better to shove those thoughts to the back of my mind because the last thing I need is another complication in my already chaotic life.

I turn my attention back to my father, deciding it's best to concentrate on one man in my life at a time.

He removes two goblets from the cabinet and fills them three quarters of the way full. He seems unusually relaxed, until I notice his hand slightly shaking as he hands me my wine.

"You can get the salad from the refrigerator and place it on the table."

Startled, I try not to stumble. On my other visits, we'd seldom sat at the table. We'd either eat standing in the kitchen or at the small counter where we never had to face each other. No doubt, sitting at the table was Melissa's idea.

"This looks great." By the time the food is set out, the bread has browned. Mouth watering, I sit across from my father. "Thanks for preparing my favorite meal."

"As you know, chicken and mac and cheese are the only two foods I can cook without burning." He chuckles, which is a rare occurrence.

"Well, there's that." Rolling my eyes, I concentrate on eating, all the while wondering who's going to be the first one to move beyond small talk and broach the reason I'm here.

After a few moments of silently enjoying my food, I set my fork down. "I wish *you* had told me about the baby."

"Oh." Sputtering so that the wine he's drinking dribbles down his chin, he picks up his napkin and wipes his face before his eyes meet mine. "That would have been better."

I wait for him to say more, but when he continues eating, I know it's on me to keep talking. "I got the feeling you didn't like kids a whole lot… or was it just me?" There, it's out. I've said what I've always felt. It would be great to have him reassure me that I'm wrong, but he doesn't.

"I'm not sure what to say."

Not the response I was hoping for, but no doubt honest and unrehearsed.

"I loved you the best way I knew how. I see now that it wasn't enough." His mouth tightens as perspiration dots his forehead.

"I never felt like *I* was enough." My voice cracks on the last word, and I shake away the memories of feeling alone when I was with him.

"Perhaps I should start at the beginning." Clearing his throat, he takes another drink of wine while pushing his chair away from the table.

"Please do." My voice is resolved as I face the fact that he *knows* what I'm talking about. How what I had felt was *not* a figment of my imagination as my mother had implied, on the rare occasion when I had hinted at not wanting to visit my father.

"Your mother and I were young when we married, and later, we were both busy in graduate school—your mom in med school and me working on my doctorate. We were both focused on our future careers." His eyes roam upward as he studies the ceiling as if the story of his life is written there. "We wanted to get married, but children weren't part of the picture." His eyes are nervous when they meet mine, before looking up again. "At least, not at that time, but when your mother finished her residency, she changed her mind. I think it was working with premature infants in the neonatal intensive care unit that kicked on her maternal instincts." He drains his glass of wine, before continuing. "I wasn't happy with her changing her mind, but I warmed to the idea—sort of."

"*Sort* of?" I blurt out. Hearing the verbal confirmation of a lifetime of feeling unwanted stabs me in the gut, and a mix of hurt and anger has me clutching the edge of the table. "You never did warm to the idea—or to *me* for that matter—and you can't deny it." I don't recognize the shrillness of my voice as I glare at him.

My outburst leaves him stunned, and, for a minute, he hangs his head before deciding to bring the wine to the table. After he's poured himself another glass, he holds up a hand. "You wanted to hear this, so let me finish. I don't know that I'll ever want to talk about this again. But you wanted to know, so listen."

"Okay." Taking a deep breath, I struggle to control the sadness that threatens to engulf me. The pain in my chest feels like my heart is shattering in a thousand small pieces.

"We tried for two years, and I thought," he shrugs his shoulders, "that was that. End of discussion. But not your mom. Once she got an idea in her head, there was no stopping her, which meant we went to a fertility clinic." He pauses for several seconds while swirling the wine in his glass. "They said my sperm count was low, and I most likely would be unable to father a child. I was shocked, of course, but not bothered."

"I don't understand." No longer hungry, I cover my plate with my napkin. "But then you had me, so you *could* have a child, even if you weren't happy about it." I knew it all along. I wish I didn't, but I did. I was a disappointment to him.

"Not exactly." Tilting the chair back, he laces his fingers around his head, his face flushing a darker shade of brown. "Your mother made an appointment at a sperm donation center." He lets the chair down with a thud and there's a sharp bitterness to his voice. "That's not what they're called, but basically that's exactly what they are."

"What?" I gasp, totally surprised by this revelation. It's so crazy that I thought I knew my family, but now, I don't know what's real. Do I even want to know where this is going? "Without you knowing?"

"No, no." He waves his hands in the air. "I knew, and I thought I would be okay with it." He pounds a fist softly against the table. "I loved your mother and I'd do anything to make her happy, but this tore me apart in a way I hadn't anticipated. I said yes, and immediately regretted it, but I never told her how I really felt. She was so goddamn happy, I didn't want to take that away from her, even if I felt like I was in hell. I couldn't get over the fact that she was carrying another man's child. It's ridiculous. I'm intelligent enough to know that, but—"

"Stop." I thrust my hands in front of me, as if to block a blow, before jolting to my feet. "I've heard enough. I get it." I choke out the words as nausea has my stomach cramping.

Rushing to the bathroom, I collapse on the floor in front of the toilet, everything I've eaten gurgles up and rushes out of me.

When I'm done vomiting, I force myself to stand, even though I still feel sick to my stomach, and my head begins to ache. After rinsing my mouth, I study the face in the mirror, and wonder how, all these years later, I am learning that my father is not my biological father.

Tears stream down my cheeks as I absorb the idea that my whole life has been one big fat lie. How could they do this to me? How could my *mother* set me up like this?

Shaking my head, I run out of the bathroom and grab my purse from off the kitchen counter. Ignoring my father as he calls out my name, I rush to the front door, then out to the car, ready to put this whole nightmare behind me.

Chapter 14

*Miguel*

The front door of Leah's father's house slams shut, and, glancing up, I see Leah making a frantic dash to the car. Leaning over to open the door for her, I notice she's upset and has been crying.

"You okay?" It's a dumb question because she's unsuccessfully trying to blink back tears that are staining her cheeks.

"Really?" She raises one eyebrow and the eyes that meet mine are filled with sorrow. "Please, let's get out of here before my father comes to the car."

"Of course." Reaching into the back seat, I pull a tissue out of the box and hand it to her before pulling away from the curb. What happened back there? It's none of my business because it isn't my family and, Lord knows, I have father issues of my own. On the other hand, Leah is the woman I've loved since the moment I set eyes on her, so everything she experiences matters to me, so it *is* my business.

After five minutes of listening to her sobbing, I place my hand on her thigh, trying to comfort her with my touch and let her know how much I care. Whatever he told her, she's clearly shattered.

"Want to talk about it?" Why hadn't I asked her that sooner? Maybe she was waiting for me to say something to let her know I'm not one of those men who avoid difficult conversations.

"No." Sniffling loudly with hunched shoulders and holding her head in her hands, she adds, "Not yet. I'm… trying to… process what my father told me." She places one slender hand on mine and keeps it there for the rest of the way back to the inn.

By the time I pull into the parking space, a cool breeze has set in and the air is ripe with the scent of the fresh fruit that remains on the vines surrounding the area.

Walking around to her side of the car, I open the door for her, and she immediately falls into my arms. Her soft curves feel good pressed against my chest, as her jagged breathing slowly subsides. When her arms encircle my waist, I release a slow moan of pleasure, but I'm not about to take advantage of her when she's so vulnerable.

Focusing her hazel eyes on me, she reaches up behind my neck, and places those lips I have *literally* dreamt of kissing forever on mine. I forget about my silent pledge to not take advantage of her current state and I put everything I've been holding back into the kiss.

Brushing my lips against hers, I take my time first kissing the corner of her mouth before I slowly prod her lips open with my tongue. As the kiss goes deeper, my body responds, and I know I need to pull back before we do something we may later regret.

*Not now*, I tell myself. Not when she's this fragile and doesn't know what she's doing. The last thing I want is for her to ever regret anything she's done with me. Plus, what kind of friend would I be if I took this opportunity to push the limits of our relationship?

I muster all the willpower I possess to break contact. "Let's go inside." I need time to cool off.

"Okay." Her voice is barely above a whisper.

She drops her arms and I wonder if she's regretting the kiss—the kiss I can't believe she initiated, but, when I look at her, she doesn't look sorry at all. In fact, it almost looks as if some of her original sparkle has returned to her eyes.

As we make our way to the cottage, she takes my arm and holds it close to her side, causing her shapely thigh to brush against my leg. I'm in so much trouble right now. I don't know what she's doing. Of course I want her, but not when what she needs most is for me to be a trusted friend.

"You go ahead." Removing the key card from my pocket, I open the door. "I'm going to take a walk right now. I'll be in later."

"*Now?*" Her eyes widen in surprise, before she crinkles her brows. "But it's so late."

"I love late-night walks." I'm lying, but I can't go into the cottage with her right now, not when my desire has surged, and I don't want to test my willpower any more than I already have. A long walk in the night breeze will help me keep my hands to myself—that and sleeping on the couch.

"Do you want me to go with you?"

In the moonlight, I can see her tears have finally dried, even though they've left streaks down her cheeks.

"God, no." I blurt out without thinking. When I see she looks hurt, I continue, "You need your rest. Don't wait up for me." Would she? That would be sweet, but tonight, that would be bad. *Very bad.* I don't need to see her in her pajamas or nightgown or whatever she wears to bed, sitting up and waiting for me. "I meant to say, I prefer to walk by myself… solitary walks."

"What about your morning group hikes?"

Twisting her bottom lip and twirling a strand of hair, she looks at me as if she's trying to figure out if I'm telling the truth.

"That's not by yourself."

"Work is different." Shrugging, I turn on my heel and head to the trail in the woods behind the house.

Trekking my way up the steepest hill, I continue past the rows of grapevines, surprised to see how much they've grown since the last time I was home. For a minute, I wonder if this is still home. Or is Sunnyville my home? With resignation, I know this land I grew up on is in my blood, even if my father thinks it doesn't matter to me. It does, but I also needed to forge my own path and figure out who I was without the dominant personality of my father breathing down my neck, telling me what I had to do, who I had to be. From an early age, it was an expectation I, too, would work for the Harts, but that'd never been my dream, even if it was his.

Perusing the area, I take in the effort my father has put into maximizing the lands wine producing potential. Rows of recently added vines are visible as far as the eye can see. The deeply colored fruit is flourishing here in this remote area of land near the jagged wooden fence that divides our property from the Harts'.

Pausing to catch my breath, I peer at their renovated home. Two and a half years ago, a burst of fast-moving flames had caused massive destruction that destroyed the local trailer park and numerous other homes, including Hartland. But there's no evidence of damage now, and the family had been able to start remodeling as soon as it was safe to do so. The renovated Spanish-style stucco home with a wrap-around porch and large patio area surrounded by magenta bougainvillea trees is still distinctive.

If it weren't so late, I'd stop by to say hello and catch up with my god-sister, Elaine. I haven't seen her since I'd returned and, this morning, my mother had informed me my other god-sister, Morgan, and her family were back in town. They'd both lucked out with finding their true love, Elaine with David, and Morgan with Dakar, both great guys. Their families were continuing to expand. Elaine and David had their baby, Twyla. Morgan even got a bonus with Dakar's daughter, Bailey, from his first marriage, and Trisha, their adopted daughter.

Facing the opposite direction, I'm now ready to head back to the cottage and Leah. Will she ever see me as a man, not just as a buddy whose shoulder she can lean on in tough times? No matter what, I won't take advantage of her vulnerability.

Cautiously opening the door, I stop in the kitchen long enough to pour myself a glass of water, before tiptoeing past the bedroom, where relief washes over me as I hear the soft hum of her sleeping.

Once I'm in the bathroom, I quickly peel off my soaked shirt and take off my pants. The hot water feels good trickling down my skin, and even though Leah is asleep, I turn on a blast of cold water before I get out of the shower, just to make sure I don't go getting any ideas.

After removing two blankets from the hall closet, I make my way past the bedroom and into the living room. Grimacing at the small couch, I know it's going to be impossible for me to get comfortable in that compact space, so I won't even bother trying. Instead, I create a makeshift bed on the floor, and as I'm dozing off, I'm startled by the sound of Leah's footsteps, probably heading for the bathroom.

Through half closed eyes, I sense Leah, standing by my makeshift bed.

"What are you doing here?" she murmurs drowsily.

I close my eyes, but not before noticing what she's wearing—the flimsy top and bottom are semi-sheer, revealing the outline of her full breasts and the bottoms barely reach the top of her deliciously thick thighs.

Maybe if I don't say anything, she'll think I'm asleep. I can't believe I'm doing this, but I turn my back to her before releasing an imitation of a loud snore. The question is, will she fall for it? Did she see me checking out every beautiful inch of her before I snapped my eyes shut? God, I hope not. Why didn't she stay in bed? Is she intentionally trying to test me? If that's the case, she's doing a great job. I am definitely being challenged by her presence.

Her clean fresh scent engulfs me, as I feel her fingers raking through my hair. "Miguel, I know you're awake." She giggles and runs a hand across my jaw. "You can't sleep here. You have a class tomorrow. Now, stop being silly. I'm not going back to sleep until you join me in bed."

Even after she returns to the bedroom, I don't move or acknowledge I've heard anything she's said. I don't let on that the lingering sensations of her fingers smoothing back my hair or caressing my cheek had my body burning with desire for her to touch even more and for me to return the favor.

"What do I do?" I whisper in the dark, torn between honor and desire.

*I release a loud groan. Face it, man, she knows you're awake. And you're a soldier who's stared down enemies and fought for your country. You slept with her one night without touching her; you can do the same tonight.*

But… the truth is there's something different about her tonight, and I'm not sure what it is or that I *can* handle it. I want Leah when she's not rebounding from conflict with her father or anyone else.

"I heard you." Her giggle fills the silence of the night. "Get in here, or I'm going to join you out there."

"Hell." She's not making this easy for me.

In one swift movement, I'm up and headed to the bedroom, leaving my blankets scattered on the floor. Sometimes, there aren't any good options, and a man does what a man has to do. "You win."

In the room, she's pulled the covers back on my side of the bed and is curled up on the other side, with her eyes closed and the corners of her mouth lifted in a triumphant smile.

Yawning, she says, "I can't let you sleep on the floor while I'm in this giant bed alone."

How did my long-held fantasy of Leah beckoning me to join her in bed turn into this brutal test of my willpower? I stay on the edge of the bed, as far away from her as possible for good measure.

Eventually, I fall asleep, only to have my sleep disrupted by life-like dreams of Leah's soft hands sensually caressing my chest and her lips gently kissing the side of my neck while I stir restlessly, intent on restraining myself from putting one hand on her.

Finally, hours later, the sweet tortuous dream fades, and I'm able to drift to sleep.

I manage to get out of bed and make myself a cup of coffee before heading outside to meet the ladies early the next morning. Several new faces have joined the group, and some of the others have already begun stretching on their own.

"Good morning, ladies," I call out. "Good job with the stretches. You're all looking good." I hold a thumb up before adding, "We'll get started in a few minutes."

"Miguel." Taylor, in skintight pink shorts and a matching midriff tank top, rushes toward me. Placing a hand on my arm and smiling she gushes, "Can you believe it? I emailed an evaluation form after the first class, and the ladies gave you glowing reviews, *and* invited their friends to join us." She runs a hand down my back. "I knew you would be a hit."

"Thanks for the vote of confidence. I'm glad the women enjoyed the walk."

"Enjoyed it?" She chuckles. "They *loved* it. Let's face it, they loved *you*. *You're* the magic sauce." Lowering her voice, she adds, "Just look at you; what's not to love? Following a handsome man with an impressive physique isn't exactly torture."

"Taylor." I'm growing tired of dealing with her insinuations. If the class weren't valuable, the women wouldn't come, regardless of what I look like. She's gone too far now. "My workouts are not a male burlesque show, and I hardly think the other women are here to watch my ass." Is this what women regularly experience when they're being judged by how they look instead of for their skills?

"Sure." Shrugging and smiling with a smirk on her face, she continues, "In any case, I took the liberty of sharing the evaluations with your mother, and she was very excited."

"I'm glad to hear that." I walk away, gladly shifting my focus to the class participants. "Follow my movements and don't do anything that feels uncomfortable. Remember, this is the time to *slowly* warm up those muscles." Calmer now, I take a deep breath and remind myself I'm only going to be here for a couple more days, and then Leah and I will be on our way back to peaceful Sunnyville.

Fifteen minutes later, we reach a clearing where blackberries grow in abundance.

"Help yourselves to the fruit." I distribute the small plastic bags my mother provided for the ladies, who eagerly begin filling them.

Twenty minutes later, after they've enthusiastically gathered their blackberries and we are trekking back down the trail toward the inn, Taylor catches up with me.

"I didn't mean to offend you earlier." Her head's down and she appears contrite.

"It's fine." Glancing over my shoulder, I slow my pace, giving the stragglers plenty of time to catch up. "Fitness is serious business."

"I know it is and I didn't mean to imply otherwise." She has a mischievous glint in her eyes as her gaze meets mine. "But you've got to know you're a handsome man."

"Thanks." I know my voice still carries more than

a hint of annoyance. Hopefully, she'll drop the subject. What do looks have to do with anything?

A part of me still feels like I'm the chubby kid who's a disappointment to his father. In school, I was the fat kid who was always the last person chosen for any team. The Marines whipping me into shape was the best thing that ever happened to me. It'd made exercise a way of life. I enjoyed sharing fitness routines with others who may have gone through similar experiences. Regardless of an individual's body type, weight, dress or shirt size, I want them to feel good about themselves. After all, I know, firsthand, the pain of feeling inadequate.

We are silent the rest of the way to the inn and when we begin our warm-down routine, I notice out of the corner of my eye my father stiffly standing off to the side, his eyes focused on the class.

Once we are finished and the ladies have left, my father walks over to me. First Taylor, now him. My back stiffens. We haven't spoken since our earlier disagreement a few days ago.

"Can we talk?" he asks gruffly while scratching his chin and looking down.

"Sure." Does he want to critique my exercise techniques? I'm hoping this father-son conversation is brief because, at this point, my thoughts are on Leah and why she was so upset after speaking with *her* father.

"Are you up to walking some more?" His black brows furrow as he scans the road beyond the parking lot.

"Sure." My shoulders tense as I wonder what I've done wrong now. I'm in no mood for another frustrating encounter with my obstinate father, but I don't have much choice. We've managed to avoid each other for the last couple of days, but I knew that before I leave town, I'd have to endure another conversation with him. "You can lead the way."

Neither of us speaks as my father takes steady strides along the cleared path that leads to the grapevines behind the cottage. His breathing grows heavy when we reach the slight incline, and it reminds me he's growing older. When my godfather, Thomas Hart, had died suddenly from a heart attack, I'd been reminded of my own parents' mortality, something I didn't want to think about then or now.

"The vines look great." We've stopped now in front of the new growth. "I didn't know you had expanded so much."

"I decided what the heck." He pauses long enough to rub his hand across his chest. "Why not make this a real vineyard?"

"Looks like you have a couple of different varieties of grapes." I notice how the wiry green tendrils wrap around the supports before meeting my father's eyes. "I thought you were all about the orange groves." It was an interest I'd never shared and the cause of much of my father's frustration with me. On my visits home, he'd bring up how much he enjoyed working at Hartland, and I could never pretend I shared his enthusiasm.

"I was—back then." His mouth twists and he glances up at the sky before continuing, "I enjoyed overseeing the orange groves and working with Thomas. You know we went back a long way. It's not easy to lose a best friend. When he... died... so did some of my pleasure in working at Hartland." He inhales deeply as sadness sweeps across his face before he resumes walking at a slower pace. "Elaine does a damn good job of taking care of things," he says with pride.

"She loves it." Even as a kid, she'd marveled at how fruit would replace the delicate white blossoms on the trees, as if it was a miracle, which, I suppose, it actually is. Her younger sister, Morgan, and I were never as interested, but the orange groves had always been Elaine's happy place. The land belongs to both sisters, but it's Elaine and her husband, David, who live at Hartland and keep the citrus business profitable. "Uncle Thomas would be proud."

"I've already told her this will be my last summer at Hartland." His eyes are somber now and there's resolution in his deep voice.

"What?" I'm shocked. The man has lived and breathed the orange groves. I never expected him to stop working there.

"Close your mouth, son." The fine lines around his eyes deepen as he chuckles. "Time moves on and it's best if I do the same. I'm going to focus on the wine— Montoya Vineyards." His gaze is intense as his eyes probe mine. "You never commented on the name. What do you think?"

"It sounds good. Grandpa, if he were still alive, would be happy to see the family name stamped on a label." I take my time looking at the even rows of grapevines covering the land as far as the eye can see. I can't believe we've managed to have a conversation this long without getting into one of our usual arguments, and he's actually asking for my opinion for once instead of telling me how I should think or feel. This is a first.

"Good for you." Stuffing my hands into my pockets, I add, "I can't say I'm not surprised."

"Sometimes, you have to get old to get wise," he says with more than a trace of what sounds like regret.

"You're not old." As I look at him now, noticing the new lines around his eyes and mouth, I face the reality that my parents are at the ages when people begin to think of retirement or doing something different with their lives.

"Old enough to now know better than to try to force you into doing something you aren't interested in." Pausing, he runs a calloused hand across his furrowed brow and peers at me sheepishly. "Seeing you out there with your class, I finally got it. You *are* doing what you love and that's all that matters."

"I know it's not what you wanted for me." For the first time I say it without rancor, understanding this land has given him a good life and he's wanted the same for me. "You meant well." I let that thought sink in, for both him and me, before continuing. "Now, tell me more about the grapes. I've been told the wine industry is booming. I have to admit I don't know much about it, but I have a friend who's into visiting local wineries and recently joined a wine club." I think of Sammy, who's an intrepid reporter by day and budding wine connoisseur by night. As a newlywed, he enjoys visiting vineyards with his wife, Cindy.

"I didn't know that much myself, but, with your mom's business thriving and guests always asking about visiting local wineries, it seemed like the next logical step." He says it matter-of-factly, as if starting a new business adventure is no big deal.

"I never thought you'd leave Hartland." It's true. He's lived and breathed those orange groves. How does my mother feel about this new direction? Of course, my parents have the kind of love where they support each other's dreams. I can relate, because that's how I feel about Leah. She's probably wondering where I am, because she knows the class is only an hour long and I've been gone longer than that.

"Timing is everything. Sometimes, you have to know when to alter your course. If I had to do it over again, I wouldn't change one single thing." He scans the landscape. "Enough about me." He shifts his gaze. "You're obviously a great teacher. I saw how those women were enjoying your class."

"Thanks," I manage to mutter, now truly stunned by the turn of the conversation. I've waited all of my life to feel like I'm good enough to be his son, to have one single discussion that doesn't end in a shouting match or resentment, and now that he's finally acknowledging me, I'm at a momentary loss for words.

Straightening my shoulders, I say, "During my stint in the Marines, I learned that being fit can be a matter of life or death, such as when you need to get the hell out of a location fast."

A painful recollection from my military days flashes in my mind. There'd been bullets and an unexpected explosive device. We'd had to get out of the line of fire and retreat as quickly as possible. We'd lost Jimmy that day. He was a great guy, with a wife and four children at home waiting for his return. If he'd made it to the shelter one minute sooner, he'd have been able to return home with the rest of us, instead of in a body bag.

"Son, you look like you saw a ghost."

The concerned words pull me back to the present.

"Are you okay?"

"Yeah, I'm fine. I got distracted for a minute, that's all." Blinking back the haunting scene, I refocus on my father who's intently peering at me. Inhaling deeply, I mentally block out the disturbing images that occasionally disrupt my sleep. Luckily, these flashbacks don't happen often, but I understand certain memories never completely go away. "What were you saying?"

"That you should follow *your* heart." His voice is raspy as he pats me on the back. "I'm proud of you, son, for serving our country, and following your passion, not mine."

"I learned from your example." It's true. He'd followed his passion and had never looked back, and I'm trying to do the same. I never thought the day would come when my father would see me for who I am and be proud.

"And, if you're serious about that girl your mother tells me you're shacking up with in the honeymoon cottage, go for it." His laughter surprises me as much as his words. "You know your mother knows everything that goes on around this place."

"What?" I sputter, uncertain how to respond. Of *course*, my mother has figured out Leah is staying with me. Why hadn't I thought of that before? Plus, my parents share everything. Not to mention, there are no secrets in Santa Lorena. "It's not like that." Unfortunately.

"Who are you trying to fool?" With a knowing look on his face, he points a finger at my chest. "I know my son. If you brought a girl here and she's staying with you, it's got to be serious."

We continue to walk in silence and are standing in front of the inn before I respond. Defining my relationship with Leah isn't easy. If only I could say she was more than a friend, but that wouldn't be the truth.

"It's complicated." I look at the cottage and wonder what Leah is doing now. Will she want to speak to her father again and give it a second try? "She wasn't supposed to be staying with me. She planned to stay in town with her father."

"Sure, whatever you say." My dad dismisses my words with a wave of his hand. "I suggest you clear things up with your mother before she begins planning your wedding to Taylor. She happens to think the two of you make a great match, and you know how your mother is when she gets an idea in her head." Laughing, he strides past me.

"What the hell?" Perplexed by his last comment, I follow him, wondering where my mother got the crazy notion I have any romantic interest in Taylor, a woman I barely know. She's obviously a smart businesswoman, but my heart already belongs to someone else.

It's beyond time for me to reveal my true feelings to Leah. Whatever had her so upset last night, she needs to know she doesn't have to go through it alone. It's still early, but, if she's up, she's probably hungry. I'll just grab a couple of pastries, bacon, and fruit to take back to the room with me.

"Oh, there you are." My mother, looking every bit the proprietress in a beige pantsuit, greets me as I'm about to enter the dining room. "You're just the person I wanted to speak to."

"Good morning, Mom." Giving her a quick peck on the cheek, I marvel at how she's managed to still look beautiful despite the passing of the years. She looks more like forty than sixty years old. "I'm just about to dish up some food to take with me to the cottage."

"So you and Leah can eat together?" She raises one perfectly arched eyebrow.

"Yes." I didn't see that coming, but after my conversation with my father, I can't really be surprised. "That's the general idea."

"That sounds lovely," she says innocently. "However, I really need to speak to you right now."

"Now?" Twisting my lips, I release a low groan.

"Yes, now." She lifts her chin. "Look, I'll have someone prepare a to-go box for the two of you while you and I have a quick chat." She pierces me with a disapproving scowl. "And stop looking so put out. This will only take a few minutes of your time."

Taking a deep breath, I relax the muscles in my neck that had bunched up at her insistence we meet now. The one thing I don't need is to have a discussion with my mother about my love life or lack thereof.

Glancing at my sports watch as we walk into her office, I take a seat across from her desk.

"Let me put your order in first."

Tapping my fingers impatiently against her desk, I wait while she contacts the dining area, then stretch my legs. There's an assortment of family pictures behind her desk, and it's like watching a silent film of moments from my life, including the pictures Aunt Esther regularly sent her from Sunnyville.

Done with her call, my mother, bright smile on her

face, clasps her hands together. "Taylor tells me the classes are going exceptionally well. We even have some of the locals wanting to know if we're now offering personal training." Leaning back in her chair, she's beaming with contentment. "This could provide the revenue boost we need to get us out of the red."

"That's great." Is she forgetting I'm only visiting and don't live here? "Before, this trip, I didn't know that business was down." A surge of guilt surfaces as I realize how disconnected I've been from what's happening in my parents' lives, including the winery and my mother's financial challenges with her business.

"I didn't want to bother you." Her eyes dart away from mine. "After the fires, it's taken a while to get the town renovated and for people to start traveling again." Reaching across the desk, she gently tugs on my earlobe, a gesture of affection she hasn't done since I was ten. "But, with your help and Taylor's, I think we'll be just fine."

"About that... I'm *visiting* here," I say firmly. "I'm holding classes for this week only." I look at her intently, knowing she could *not* have forgotten the agreement.

"Of course, dear." She smiles sweetly. "Whatever you say." She swivels in her chair, looking completely confident. "You and Taylor do work well together."

"We have worked well together for this limited amount of time." I'm impatient to leave now before my mother attempts to push me into making a bigger commitment to the inn. Of course, I care about the business, but my life is not here. "Do you think the food is ready?"

"Not yet," she says abruptly before eyeing me

inquisitively. "I like the two of you together, but if you prefer Leah…" she shrugs, "I'd be happy with her as a daughter-in-law, too."

"Mom!" I can't believe how smoothly she slipped that in. "There have not been any wedding proposals, not to anyone." I abruptly stand. Now would be a good time to go.

"Hey, I'm easy." Opening her eyes wide, she looks at me innocently. "Either one will do." Abruptly rising from her chair, she reaches around me and opens the door. "I can see you're eager to get going. Don't forget your breakfasts."

Five minutes later, breakfasts in hand, I'm shaking my head and walking back toward the cottage, wondering if all parents are as confusing as mine.

When I finally let myself inside, I'm surprised it's completely quiet—no television or music. Normally, Leah would be blasting some neo-soul tunes.

"I'm back." Setting the food on the kitchen counter, I walk through the small living room area before checking the bathroom and finally the bedroom. No sign of Leah anywhere. Maybe she's on a walk. Why hadn't I thought to ask her if she wanted to join the group? My chest tightens as I open the closet and notice that her suitcase is gone. Now that I think of it, her toiletries were missing from the bathroom counter.

Where could she be and how far could she go without a car? Maybe she went back to her father's house. But the more I think about that possibility, the more it seems unlikely. After last night, she'd been in no mood to talk *to* him or *about* him. Who else does she know in Santa Lorena? After all, she did spend time here off and on during her childhood.

I'm ruling out Aaron since she just met him. Frustrated, and mad at myself for taking so long to come back to the room, I sink down onto the bed and decide the most logical thing to do is call her, but, as I reach into my pocket to remove my cell phone, I see a note in Leah's writing, taped to the dresser mirror.

Chapter 15

*Leah*

"You did what?" Jenny's voice goes up a couple of levels. I've got her on the speaker as I drive the compact sedan I just rented in town. "Why would you leave the *free* honeymoon cottage and pay for a room in town?"

"I need space." I steer the car down Main Street, knowing the Hawthorne Hotel is two miles ahead.

"From Miguel?"

I'd always thought Jenny had a sultry voice, but, as she squeals our friend's name, I see I've grossly underestimated her vocal range.

"*I'm* not even into men, and *I* wouldn't walk out on him like that."

"Exactly." Closing the driver's side window, I turn on the air conditioner. It's not yet noon, and already sweat is dripping down the front of my blouse. "In the past, I never saw Miguel that way, but now, everything is different." Just thinking about yesterday and how much I'd desired him has me flushing with embarrassment.

"I am so confused," Jenny mutters, clearly exasperated. "What happened last night?"

"Okay, if you want the details, here goes." Pausing, I clear my throat, then take a breath before continuing.

"I kissed him and then, later, when we were in bed together, I almost seduced him. I had to force myself not to. And, by the way, he did *not* want to sleep with me. He preferred to sleep on the floor in the living room, but I forced him to join me in the bed. For God's sake, Jenny, I was out of control."

"Hallelujah! It's about dang time you let go of some of your inhibitions and stopped being the proper kindergarten teacher." She laughs. "That's what I'm talking about." Jenny cheers me on, as if I've just crossed the finish line of the Boston Marathon, instead of almost seducing my best friend. "I'm proud of you."

"You don't get it." After my stomach loudly rumbles, I steer the car toward a drive-through restaurant that's up the road. "I didn't eat before I left the cottage and I'm about to order myself a breakfast sandwich, hashbrowns, and a cup of coffee."

"Maybe some food will help you think more clearly. It sounds like you recognized that Miguel is not only good-looking, but he's also nice. Honestly, Leah Ann, he's one of the good ones."

"Yes, he is." After paying for my food, I pull into the parking lot, prepared to provide some clarification to Jenny. It's better if I'm not driving when I break the shocking news that I'm about to share with her. "That's the problem. I now see I definitely have a more-than-friendly feeling toward Miguel." I unwrap the bright yellow paper and take a bite of my sausage-egg croissant before continuing. "Girl, I'm so tired of lying to myself about how I feel."

"Humph. Interesting. I'm glad you figured out what I always knew. You two are good together." Her voice is smug, as if I'm not telling her anything new.

"But what made you see the light, and why abandon the man when you could be snuggling with him in a honeymoon suite?"

"Cottage." I correct while sipping my coffee.

"Huh?" Jenny asks, clearly confused.

"It's a cottage." I already miss the soft linens and the view of the mountains from the bedroom window.

"Okay, whatever." She makes a dismissive sound. "The point is, why *leave* the man?"

"He has a girlfriend." Brushing crumbs off my lap, I sigh before continuing. "I've seen them together. They are a great couple. Perfectly matched." No need to disguise the disappointment in my voice. "They could both be cover models for *Fitness Magazine*, if there was such a thing."

"Please." She drags out the word. "Miguel is crazy about you. He loves your curves and lush figure. I can see it in his eyes every time he looks at you." She pauses before continuing. "I wish I had a woman who looked at me like that. I'd never leave her side."

"Are you forgetting I've been through this before?" I take the hash browns out of the bag. "I'd thought Raymond was into me, but he wasn't. I was a placeholder until Rebecca returned. I get it, but I don't ever want to be in that position again. I deserve to be number one to the man I eventually give my heart to." Sighing wistfully, I push against the pressure that fills my chest.

"Don't you get it?" She's back to shrieking, which is totally out of character for Jenny. "That's *you*. You've known him forever and *you* are the one he wants."

"Don't try to make me feel better." Smiling, I take

another sip of hot coffee. What does it say about me that I love this two-dollar cup of coffee more than the six-dollar cup they offer at the fancy coffee shop down the street? I shake my head. "The point is, after speaking to my father, I've decided to go with my instincts from now on."

"Whoa, that was a quick change of subject."

I imagine the bewildered look on Jenny's face.

"Hmm, so now we are talking about your father?"

"Give me a minute and you'll see how it's all connected. So, anyway, while Miguel was teaching his class, there was a knock on my door." I close my eyes, re-envisioning the scene that played out this morning before I'd even had time to get dressed. "I'd assumed it was housekeeping. Instead, I was shocked to find my father standing outside the door, looking like a hot mess."

"What?"

I hear her moving around and imagine she's walking through her studio apartment, probably tinkering with her camera equipment.

"Provide details, please."

"For one, he looked like he'd slept in his shirt and pants. His eyes were bloodshot. He said he felt terrible about the way things had ended the night before." Mixed emotions engulf me as I recall the shock of learning the circumstances of my conception. I can't say anything as I will myself *not* to start crying again. It's been a rough twenty-four hours. Actually, it's been a rough couple of months.

"How was your conversation with him?" Her voice is hesitant. "Did you get the answers you needed about his relationship with Melissa?"

"He acknowledged his relationship with her and that they are expecting a child." My voice is flat. "It's been difficult to imagine him wanting to start over with a baby."

"You always said your relationship with your father was strained."

I appreciate the compassion in her voice.

"Do you think he'll be different with this child? I mean, he's a lot older now and maybe he'll be a better parent the second time around."

"Probably." My attempt at a chuckle falters. "Apparently, Melissa and my father wanted a child and were trying, although he had been told he was unable to father a child. I don't think they expected it to actually happen." Suddenly, I'm exhausted and ready to go to my room at the Hawthorne. My mind is a jumble of thoughts, but I know what I have to do.

"Really?" She waits for me to elaborate, but when I don't say anything, she continues, "Did he have a vasectomy after you were born?"

"No." Looking out the window, I watch a neon yellow hummingbird whirl by. It briefly settles on a rose petal before flitting off. If only life were that simple—drink sweet nectar and go on to the next beautiful flower. We'd all be happier or, at least, everything wouldn't be so messy.

"He was told he was unable to have children. My mother used artificial insemination and it destroyed their marriage." I blurt out the words, eager to get it over with. All those years of not feeling loved and accepted were *not* products of an over active imagination. The awkwardness between us was real. "Last night, he confessed that, after he'd agreed to the artificial insemination, he'd immediately regretted it, but he never told my mother. He became obsessed with the realization that his wife was pregnant by another man, and it destroyed their marriage and probably my relationship with him, too."

"Oh... my... God." She stretches out the sentence before gasping. "That's awful."

Neither of us says anything for several minutes. "It's not often I leave you speechless." I half-heartedly attempt to lighten the mood as I shift in my seat. "I know this is a lot of information to process. I'm still struggling to put all the pieces together. Even your psychic powers couldn't have conjured up this scenario."

"You got me there, girlfriend. I didn't see this one coming." Jenny, a firm believer in all things mystical, frequently has visions which she is adamant will come to fruition. "I'm not sure what to say, except you were right about something being off about your relationship with your dad." She sighs before quickly adding, "Not that I ever doubted your feelings. What's so unfortunate is *not* the fact that your mother was artificially inseminated, it's that your father allowed the sperm donation to poison his relationship with his wife and daughter."

"Exactly." I vividly recall how uncomfortable he'd looked as he'd sat across from me in the cottage, shoulders slumped, head down, and his voice raspy with emotion as he'd asked me to forgive him. That was a *big* ask. Was I supposed to forgive him for not being able to love me? Sure, there'd been regret and sorrow in his eyes as he questioned me about the possibility of us starting our relationship over. But that was asking too much, too soon. Stunned and hurt, I couldn't give him the response he'd wanted. I need time to process this shocking and painful information.

"I see why you need to clear your head. You've been dealing with a lot."

Squashing the empty paper bag, I finish the last of my coffee. "It validates what I've always felt and known in my heart. Even if, as a young girl, I didn't have the words to express what I was feeling... something *was* off with our relationship."

"Exactly," Jenny says triumphantly, as if I'm finally grasping what she's been saying all along. "Trust your inner goddess to lead you on the path to enlightenment and love."

"Not sure that's what *I* just said." I burst into laughter as I back out of the parking lot.

"Sure it is," she says confidently. "The inner goddess is your intuition. It's what we know internally, and, now, you don't have to be in a fog anymore about your feelings. You have more clarity, don't you?"

"I do." I'm not certain my intuition is a goddess, but I like the way that sounds, so she won't get an argument from me. "You're right about the fog clearing. I understand now why I always felt like my father and I didn't connect. I'm done with the tears—for Raymond and my father. If they don't love me, it's not on me."

"What about Miguel?" she asks tentatively, as if she's unsure if she should mention his name right now.

"Last night, after I met with my father, I looked at Miguel sitting beside me, and it was as if I was seeing him for the first time." Warmth spreads through my chest as I loudly exhale and reflect on Miguel's outer and inner beauty. But what impresses me the most is his commitment to his family, his country, and anyone he cares about. "It's odd, even to me, to see him in this new light."

"No, it isn't." Her exasperation comes through the phone. "I always knew you two belonged together. Glad you finally got the picture. But the big question is what are you going to do about it?"

"Absolutely nothing." I spot the neon hotel sign straight ahead, about five blocks up on the left side of the street. "Not after last night, when I practically seduced him. After his rejection, I felt horrible. He so clearly did *not* want me."

"Now wait a minute—"

"No, listen. He's taken. I have to respect that. I'm not going after a man who's already spoken for. Not again. I can't endure having my heart broken for the third time because I love people who clearly don't love me." Jenny doesn't need to know Miguel not sharing my feelings is breaking my heart. "Besides, I have a more important situation to focus on right now."

"Really? For goddess' sake, like, what?"

"Like meeting my biological father." I recall how my father hadn't meant to share that information with me, but I'd been relentless. After all the pain and rejection he'd put me through, I deserved to know the name of my biological father. Who knows? Maybe *he* will love me—after all, I *am* his birth daughter.

"*Really*? I get that you'd be curious. I mean, how could you not be, but isn't that confidential information?"

"Someone in a town this size has to know something." I hesitate, wondering if I should continue to refer to the man who helped raise me as my father. The fact is that he is the only father I've ever known— at least for now. "I don't believe I'm asking too much."

"Whew!" She makes a whistling sound. "You *do* know this is the stuff that reality television thrives on."

"I know." Grimacing, I roll my eyes. "Honestly, I wish this was something I was watching and not living." Glancing at the phone, I see Miguel's name on the screen. "Jenny, Miguel is trying to reach me." My palms sweat and panic surfaces as I contemplate what to say to him after practically forcing myself on him last night. Should I apologize? Tell him that I'm sorry and was out of line? I knew he wasn't sleeping or that tired that he didn't sense my presence, but he'd rather ignore me than hurt my feelings by rejecting me outright. Taylor is one lucky woman.

The bigger question is, is it my destiny to always come in second to some other woman?

Sighing heavily, I add, "I don't know what to do."

"Talk to him." Her voice is emphatic. "Share what you told me about how you feel."

"I don't think so." His picture appears on the screen. "I'll call you back later. Thanks for listening."

"You never have to thank me. That's what friends do for one another. Now, talk to Miguel openly and honestly. Love you."

When Jenny disconnects, I feel unanchored, uncertain how to navigate this new terrain of emotions and speak to the man I now recognize as the one I truly love. Why do I always want more than any man has been willing to give?

Great. Relief and disappointment surface as I glance at my cell phone. I've kept him waiting too long.

Miguel's picture, the one he took when he was wearing his black running shorts and a red tank top and standing in front of the gym last summer disappears from my phone screen. Seriously, not sure what would have been appropriate for me to say. *By the way, sorry I almost seduced you last night. That sudden burning desire to have your hands all over my body and to feel your lips against mine was powerful. Lust is something else, isn't it? I'm glad one of us showed some restraint and it certainly wasn't me. Ha-ha. It was probably a misplaced stress reaction from the father fiasco. Give my apologies to Taylor and have a nice life. I'm sure you two will produce beautiful babies together.*

After pulling into the hotel's parking lot, I discover all the spaces are taken, so I drive across the street to the overflow lot. Removing my suitcase from the car, I head toward the hotel entrance and enter a spacious lobby bustling with women who are all sporting similar shades of deep purple and light blue attire. I'm reminded Miguel's mother's bed-and-breakfast was also filled with sorority conference attendees, which is why Miguel was staying in the honeymoon cottage. Judging by the volume of suitcases, it appears that some of them are now checking out, which is likely the reason I was able to secure a room today.

Life has so many unexpected twists and turns. If I had been able to stay here instead of with my father or Miguel, my life would have resumed its normal course, uninterrupted by the knowledge of a surprise sperm donor father, and a powerful shift in how I feel about my relationship with Miguel. Oh, sure, I would have eventually found out about my younger-than-me future stepmother and baby brother or sister, but I don't regret learning about my parents' past and that I have feelings for a man I've always been able to count on.

However, the desire I feel for Miguel is unchartered territory—new, unfamiliar, and uncomfortable. No wonder my heartbeat accelerates as I recall how my imagination had taken me on a journey where Miguel's lips were pressed against mine and his well-defined arms held me close. Wiggling my nose, I wonder if the romantic ambiance of the cottage kicked in my previously dormant hormones. Moving forward would be easier if that were true, but I know with a certainty that what I feel for Miguel is anything *but* simple.

My cell vibrates as I take my place in the customer reservation line behind a stout older woman with bright blue hair framing her unlined face. Glancing at the phone, I see Miguel is calling again. Time to be a grownup and answer the man's call. No use avoiding the inevitable.

"Hello." I whisper, not wanting to be one of those people who has loud phone conversations in public places.

"I'm glad you answered the phone this time. I got your note. Can we talk?"

"Er… um… not really." I eye the blue-haired lady who has pivoted so that she's facing me. Frowning, I'm surprised she's obviously listening to my call. "At least not now."

"Your note said you needed space. What does that mean?" He sounds baffled. "Are you still in town or have you headed back to Sunnyville?"

"I'm still in Santa Lorena." After Ms. Blue Hair raises a brow, I move so my back faces her and lower my voice. "I decided it would be better if I checked into the Hawthorne."

"They don't have any vacancies." He mumbles something I can't understand before clearing his throat. "Let me come and get you."

"No." I can't be responsible for what I'd be tempted to do if I have to sleep in a room with him for even one more night. "I called this morning and was told someone checked out today."

"I see." He emits a low growl. Is he angry with me for kissing him last night? Was it too much? "I don't know why you left."

"There wasn't enough room for both of us." That was true. Seeing his sweatshirt tossed on the back of the loveseat had tempted me to run my hands across it before smelling the lingering and enticing scent that was uniquely Miguel.

"What did you say? This reception is really bad."

I *must* keep my distance from him.

"Not enough room there." I slant my head, checking to see if I still have an audience of one. Yep, she still appears to be listening. Shrugging, I decide it could be my imagination. Maybe she's searching for a friend or studying one of the prints hanging on the back wall.

"That's ridiculous." His terse reply is quick and dismissive. "It's a spacious cottage. Don't check in. I'm on my way."

Jamming my phone into my purse, I know I won't be returning to the cottage, regardless of what Miguel has to say. Of course, I'll speak with him, even though the note *clearly* stated I needed space and had to handle family business.

Glancing ahead, I see that the line has not moved. The same guest who was at the head of the line is still there, widely gesturing with her hands and jerking her head so that her long locks swing from side to side. This hotel is clearly short-staffed. I want to be checked in before Miguel arrives, but at the rate this line is moving, I'll be standing in this same spot at dinnertime.

"Men. What can you do?"

There's no mistaking it. The lady in front of me is speaking to me.

"They are exasperating sometimes, wouldn't you agree?"

"I would." No need to be rude. After all, she's probably trying to make the time go by more quickly by sparking up a conversation. She's not wearing the same colors of the other women, so it's unlikely she's part of the conference. Maybe she lives by herself with her seven cats and is desperate for company.

"I'm Leona." Her smile makes her look several years younger as her amber eyes twinkle in delight. "I'm on my fourth husband." Running her fingers through her spikey hair, she continues, "I change husbands more than I switch hair colors."

Not sure how to respond, I raise my brows. "That's something."

"I'm a hopeless romantic." She holds up her left hand, flexes her fingers, and admires her sparkling diamond ring. "What can I say? I love love. There's nothing quite as exciting. I'm sure you agree it's worth the risk." The grin that follows is mischievous.

"I suppose. I don't really know that much about love to be honest." That's an understatement if there ever was one. "It sounds like you have a lot of experience." I smile, hoping that what I said doesn't offend her. "I mean, in a good way." Straightening my shoulders, I add, "Four husbands… Wow!" I wonder how it's even possible that one person could find four men to marry. I've made so many mistakes falling in love with the wrong person, not once but twice, that I can't even imagine marrying that many times.

"The thing is, I'm a believer in taking risks." She gives me a quick wink. "That's the key. I don't like to sit on the sidelines; I like to jump in and play the game." She pauses, concern etched on her face, "You look confused."

"I am. A little. First, you were discussing your husband—er, *husbands*—and, now, you're talking about not sitting on the sidelines and playing the game. I'm not sure I see the connection."

"It's all the same thing." Light laughter follows. "Men, sports… it doesn't matter. I've bungee-jumped, sky-dived, and climbed Mt Kilimanjaro."

"Really?" I'm impressed. Leona can't be more than five feet tall, and she must be at least seventy years old. "I'd never do any of those things."

"You may change your mind one day." She has a distant look in her eyes as if remembering some of her adventures with men and life. "It's all about making the most of each moment. Going for the prize. Living life to the fullest is the only way to experience true joy." Her arms open wide. "But don't take my word for it; try it for yourself." Patting my hand, she tosses her lavender silk scarf over her shoulder and faces the front of the line, ready to check in and, no doubt, eager to experience her next adventure.

Twenty minutes later, registered and with my room

key in hand, I know I'm nothing like the daring Leona. I would never leap off a mountain, bungee cord or not. I'd be content to find one man who loved me as much as I loved him, but some of us don't have that type of life. Setting aside any thoughts of a *happily-ever-after,* I'm ready to begin my search for my biological father.

My stomach recoils at the thought of walking up to a stranger and informing him that I'm his child. What will I say? Heck, what will *he* say? Will I look like him? Will he spontaneously open his arms, tears of joy glistening in his eyes as he enfolds me in a warm embrace, thrilled to finally be united with the child he's always wondered about?

"Leah." Miguel's voice jolts me out of my father-daughter reunion fantasy. His strides are long as he rushes across the lobby toward me. The concern visible on his face has me feeling guilty about my hasty departure, but it was for his sake as well as mine. He doesn't know it, but, by leaving, I'm respecting his relationship with Taylor.

"I figured I'd find you here," he says triumphantly.

"I wasn't hiding." I don't add that I would if I could, but who can disappear in a town that has one hotel and one inn?

Stepping away from the counter and toward the set of seats in the lobby, I add, "I felt it was better if I had some time to think things through."

"You didn't have enough space at the cottage?" Clearly baffled, he peruses my face, hurt evident in his dark eyes.

"Not really." The last thing I want is to offend the one man in the world who has been honest and never lied to me about anything. But why had my mother intentionally deceived me, never revealing key details about my conception?

Releasing a shaky breath, I know I can't blame her, because I'm certain she did what she felt was right. She undoubtedly believed I had nothing to gain by learning the truth. Unfortunately, I can't agree with that sentiment.

"The bed was a little crowded." Blushing, I blunder on. "I know I was all over you last night." He doesn't need to know it was intentional and I had hoped he'd take the hint and know what to do from there.

"It's a king-size bed."

He ignores my comment, proving he isn't interested. Lucky Taylor. He's loyal and true.

"Can you at least tell me what's going on?" Leaning forward, he adds, "Was it because I was gone so long this morning?"

"Of course not." I dismiss the comment with a flip of my hand. I don't want to talk here, in the middle of a bustling lobby. "Want to follow me up to my—?"

"Yes." He smiles sheepishly. "Isn't it obvious I would follow you anywhere?" He places a hand under my elbow. "Lead the way."

Four other people are in the elevator with us, and even after they get off on the second floor, we are silent as we make our way to the eleventh floor. Miguel's familiar woodsy scent sparks an impulse to nuzzle my nose into his neck—but I control myself until he steps behind me as I swipe my key card across the magnetic reader. I feel his body heat and he's not even touching me. I'm glad I'm staying here and he's across town.

"Nice room." Even as I say the words, I know this room can't begin to compare to the honeymoon cottage.

We walk past a bathroom and into a small area containing a standard queen bed and a small wooden desk and chair.

"If you say so." He rolls his eyes before sitting on the chair. "Even our basic rooms are larger than this."

"This room is fine for me." Sitting on the edge of the bed, I cross my legs while tapping one foot on the speckled gray carpet.

"Why did you leave?" Reaching out, he takes my hand in his. "I know your note said your father came by to see you and you had to sort out some things, but why couldn't you do it at the cottage? We could do it together. No pressure."

"Actually..." How much do I say? This isn't going to be easy, but it's time for the truth and nothing but the truth. My palms grow moist, and I clear my throat before meeting his eyes. "It's two-fold. When I saw my father the other night, he told me that... well... that he isn't *actually* my father."

"What does that mean?" Confused, Miguel squeezes my hand, encouraging me to continue. "Were you adopted?"

"No." My shoulders tense as sadness and anger fill my thoughts. Did my mother have any idea her husband wouldn't be able to cope with her having a daughter he didn't physically father? "Artificial insemination." The two words say it all. "They thought he was sterile, which is probably no longer a politically correct word."

"Sterile?" His eyes widen. "The term may not be politically correct—and it apparently isn't true, in your father's case." He's visibly shocked as he looks at me with concern. Running a hand across his brow, he hunches his shoulders. "He's now having a baby with

Melissa. I don't get it."

"The doctors were obviously wrong." Tension has me straightening my back. "He's about to have a child of his own, and I've got to find my biological father."

"Hold on a minute." Miguel holds both hands up. "Isn't that confidential information that's kept safely sealed somewhere in a vault?" A vertical line appears between his brows.

"I'm sure that's the way it works in some places. But remember what you told me earlier?" Folding my arms across my chest, I try not to chuckle at his bewildered expression. "In a small town, there really aren't any secrets, although the donor's name was supposed to be confidential, my father was eventually able to talk to someone, who had a cousin who worked at the fertility clinic."

"I get the picture. Someone always knows someone else who can connect them to someone who knows even more information, until the pieces of the puzzle fit together." Miguel runs a hand across his jawline. "That's a lot to process."

"You're telling me." I don't attempt to mask the excitement in my voice. "My father eventually gave me the name of the sperm donor."

Chapter 16

*Miguel*

*"How are you?"* I finally give in to the urge to run a hand through the massive tangles of Leah's hair. It's obvious by the rigid set of her mouth that she's stressed, even if she's trying to sound matter-of-fact. I can't imagine what it would feel like to find out the man I've called father all of my life is not my biological father. Although, in my case, my father would probably not be surprised. Heck, he may even be delighted. "What can I do to help?"

I have a feeling that Leah is underestimating what it may take to actually locate her father. Even if she finds out his name, it doesn't mean he still resides in the state—or even the country for that matter. Maybe he doesn't want to be contacted by any of the children he fathered via artificial insemination. I have no idea about the contractual agreement he signed when he made his "donation," or if it had a statute of limitations, but I imagine the man must have *some* say in the matter of being contacted, even if it's decades later. But I don't want to burst her bubble, not now when she's finally feeling confident about being able to control something in her life.

"There's nothing you can do."

We are sitting on her bed now, and, as she moves

to face me, our knees touch. I should lean away, but I don't.

"This is something I need to do for myself." Her lips form a half smile, but the sadness in her eyes is unmistakable. She is struggling to keep it all together. Her shoulders are so tense, they practically touch the tips of her ears.

"I'm good with my hands," I say, not thinking of how that could be interpreted until I hear her chuckle.

"I believe you," she mutters, as she absently rubs my thigh, looking up at me with those hazel eyes.

"You could use a massage." The heat that surges from my thigh to other parts isn't good, and this definitely is *not* the time to let her know how I feel about her. Still, I don't move her hand; instead, I reach out and lightly touch her stiff shoulder.

She hesitates for less than a minute. "That would be great. It's been forever since I had a massage. Jenny and I were planning to get one before I left Sunnyville, but, that didn't happen."

Before I have time to process what she's doing, she unbuttons her blouse, takes it off, then drapes it over the back of the chair.

"Great," I mumble. It takes willpower to not go into a state of shock at the sight of Leah's full breasts in a cherry-red lace bra. I'll never understand why women wear bras that cover less than half of their breasts. It doesn't make sense, but, I must say, I do enjoy the view.

"I'm going to lie down." She props one of the pillows under her head before rolling over on her stomach in the center of the bed. "Is this okay?"

"Sure." The word sounds like a frog croaking. I can

barely speak. Desire kicks in hard, and the room feels suffocatingly hot. *Get it together, man; this is* Leah, *not someone you're hooking up with.*

Apparently, my fully aroused body didn't receive the memo. "I'll see if there's some lotion in the bathroom." Taking a deep breath, I sprint toward the bathroom.

"Good idea." Her voice is muffled, so she raises her head from the pillow. "Thanks so much for thinking of a massage. I know I'm tense."

"Sure." The perfect shape of her butt in those jeans distracts me, and I fight the impulse to squeeze it as I walk out of the room and into the bathroom. Damn. I need to splash water on my face.

Standing over the sink, I thoroughly drench my face. It does the job and cools me off. "What have I gotten myself into?"

"Did you say something? I didn't catch that."

"Nope." What I'm doing is *stalling*—trying to regain control of a situation that has created its own momentum.

"Got the lotion?" she calls out. "It's getting a little chilly in here."

I force myself not to imagine what a little cold can do to her body. *Wrong thought. Focus, man.* Good thing she reminded me since I was about to leave the bathroom without picking up the travel-sized plastic container of lotion.

"Let's get started," she says in a sultry tone—or is it my imagination? Probably. Her eyes are closed, and she looks completely peaceful, as she innocently lies there, waiting for me to give her a massage.

How is it that she is *not* affected by me the way I

am by her? She clearly doesn't view me as more than a friend. Whatever almost happened last night was based on stress and nothing more, which is a fact I'd be wise not to forget. She's experiencing a lot of emotional turmoil and probably doesn't realize what she's doing. Like right now—she has no idea how enticing she looks.

Inhaling deeply, I sit on the side of the bed. "Let's get rid of that tension." The lotion smells like a combination of lemon and ginger and I know it's going to smell great on Leah's skin. Brushing curls over her shoulders, I gently massage her skin, doing my best to gently smooth out the knots, and I concentrate on not allowing my hands to wander.

"Mmmm." Purring like a kitten, she turns her head to the side, eyes still closed. "Wouldn't it be easier if you straddled me?"

"Pardon?" I gasp, wondering if I'm losing my mind. "What did you say?"

"I think it would be easier if you straddled me so you don't have to lean over so much. That can't be good for you."

"Probably not." Clearing my throat, I don't immediately join her on the bed. Of course, I *want* to, but this is *Leah*—the woman I love and she's going through some stuff now and doesn't realize how I feel about her. As much as I want her, it can't be like this.

"And the pants," she says into the pillow.

"Huh?" My heart is pounding as I scan the room, looking for a camera. Maybe I'm being filmed for a reality television show where people's willpower is tested in impossible circumstances.

"How can you straddle me with those heavy jeans

on?" Swiveling around, she faces me. "I know I'd feel more comfortable if I took my jeans off, too." Leaning forward, she tugs her pants off, one leg at a time, which further exposes one of her breasts, causing it to slip partially out of her bra.

"Uh… something is falling out." My God. She has the perkiest breasts I've ever seen.

"What?" Wide eyed, she peers at me, totally clueless as to how she's affecting me.

"That." I want to touch her, but, instead, I drop my eyes. "One of your—"

"Oh. Thanks." She blushes bright red before placing her lush breast back into the too-small bit of fabric that's supposed to keep her covered. With one last tug, she shimmies out of her pants. "Your turn." She smiles as if stripping in front of me is the most natural thing in the world.

I stop before I reach for the button of my pants. What are we doing here? I'm a full-grown man and this full-grown woman is pushing me to my limits of restraint. Maybe she's experiencing some trauma-induced disconnect. That's probably what's happening here. She's in shock and is now acting totally out of character—even irrational. I'll have to proceed with caution.

"Slow poke." Abruptly, she jolts up from the bed and stands in front of me.

I'm sitting on the edge of the bed, pulling my jeans down, uncertain as to how I should handle the situation. I'll talk some sense into her, so she won't have any regrets. Or am I overthinking it? Maybe she simply wants us to be more comfortable.

Unfortunately, all those logical thoughts disappear

as I notice the tiny strip of V-shaped lace panties that dip down dangerously low in the front. Holy mother of St. Joseph.

"I'm not so sure about this," I use a firm tone, hoping to jolt her back to her senses. She probably needs a therapist more than she needs a massage. Why hadn't I thought of that sooner? Does she have any idea *what* she's doing? Maybe it's some kind of stress-induced amnesiac psychosis. There's a distinct possibility that all the men she knows are now a source of confusion. "I'm fine with my pants on."

"But I'm sure you are *more* fine with them off." She giggles and, bending down, she grabs my pants and yanks them off. Standing upright, her eyes roam over my legs before she places her hands on her hips. "I was right. You *do* look better."

"Are you ready for your massage now?" Maybe she's oblivious to what she's putting me through and I'm taking it to a whole other level. After all, I do still have my T-shirt and boxers on; it's not like either of us is naked. My imagination has gone wild. The woman wants to be comfortable for her massage. People take off more clothes than this when they get professional massages. *Get your head out of the gutter, soldier.*

"Ready and eager." She walks over to the side of the bed.

Jesus, why does she still have on her shoes? Who knew that simple white sandals and sexy lingerie could look so good together? I love the way her soft parts jiggle when she walks.

"Let's get this party started."

Party? She's clearly disoriented. It's time to use my best drill sergeant voice. "This is not a party. It is a therapeutic massage."

"Whatever you say." She giggles and stretches out on the mattress. "I can hardly wait."

She squirms on the bed in a way that sets a surge of heat through my body.

"Be still." If she wiggles like that while I'm straddling her, I can't predict what I'll do. Again, I scan the room, trying to identify any cameras that might be catching this whole thing—

*What* am I thinking? Leah would never do that. She doesn't have a deceitful bone in her luscious body. It's got to be the amnesiac psychosis.

"Let me know if you are uncomfortable." Because I sure as hell am as I straddle her, which causes me to sit right in front of her plump butt with my legs on both sides of the backs of her upper thighs. Neither of us speaks as I rub more lotion into my hands, then down her back, gently massaging it into her soft, supple skin. "Is this pressure okay?"

"Perfect," she says softly. "Keep going."

My fingers glide across her warm skin, and desire has me struggling to breathe evenly. She's not herself. She doesn't know what she's doing. She'll be better soon. Be a good friend. Nothing more.

Several minutes later, she turns around, and I groan as her sudden movement has me falling off her onto my side so that we now face one another.

"Thank you." Touching my face with the tips of her fingers, she adds, "That was great. I'm much more relaxed."

"Good." Focusing on her eyes and not her body requires a lot of willpower. I'm in no condition to talk now. I need to get up from the bed, put on my pants, and leave this room as quickly as possible.

But, instead, I stay exactly where I am, inhaling Leah's fresh clean scent, and gazing into her trusting eyes.

"The thing is, I've been thinking about what you said earlier—about letting you know if I needed anything."

"I meant it." Were her eyelashes always this long and did the tips always curl up so high they brush against her brows? How did I not know she had a beauty mark beneath her bottom lip?

She props her head on her hand. "The truth is, at this very moment I need more than a massage."

"What?" I run a hand along my jaw. "I'm not sure I heard you correctly."

"I'm not the same woman I was yesterday," she says.

Now I see it; there's something different in how she's looking at me. Something that looks a lot like desire.

"I'm trusting my instincts from now on." She wraps her arms around my neck, and softly brushes her lips against mine.

Before I succumb and kiss her back, I come to my senses. That kiss last night in my car was no mistake and neither is this. Now that I know that she's not reaching out to me just to escape her turmoil, I can relish this kiss and give in to what I've wanted for so long. This is so much better than what I've imagined— and I've imagined a lot.

As the kiss goes deeper, I'm abandoning any thoughts of putting on the brakes. A part of my brain says, *Mayday, mayday. Sinking ship. I need help.* But that voice—the voice of reason—fades into the background as Leah's fingers caress my chest and shoulders.

"Give me what I want and need," she murmurs while nibbling on my earlobe.

"Yes, ma'am." Rational thought is abandoned as I struggle to rip off those ridiculous panties. How can I deny her anything? There's urgency to her request. It's more of a demand, which is even more of a turn-on. This is a side of Leah I've never seen before—and I like the new *take-no-prisoners* tone of her sultry voice.

"Your turn." She shoves down my briefs. "Make love to me Miguel—just this once."

She's now straddling me; her hands are hot and feverish as they stroke me until I can't take it anymore.

"Leah, I need to make sure—"

"Don't talk." She presses three fingers over my lips. "Not now."

Hell. What's a man to do, but comply? The feel of her body on mine, beneath mine, beside mine, surpasses anything I had ever imagined. Everything feels so right: the arch of her foot, the pink toenail polish, the flush of color across her chest, the jagged panting, the rake of her nails across my back, and the whisper of my name filled with longing and then satisfaction as she mumbles incoherently before shuddering and collapsing against my chest, a blissful smile across her face, before the even sound of her breathing fills the room.

I lose track of time as we familiarize ourselves with each other's bodies. I want to memorize every detail of this time. Making love to Leah surpasses all my expectations. Being with her in this most intimate way, our eyes locked, our bodies connected as one, feels both natural and exhilarating at the same time. The fact that she came to me adds a surreal quality to every whisper and caress.

When her shapely arms reach up to circle my neck before she kisses me deeply and moans my name repeatedly, I know I'm not dreaming. Sure, there have been other women, but none of them could compare to the scent, the touch, and the flavor of Leah. The perfection of our lovemaking confirms what I have always known in my heart—we belong together, and this is the beginning of a new phase in our relationship that finally goes beyond friendship.

The room is now cast in shadow as the sun begins its descent. Stillness settles in, and it's as if we are cocooned in our own private world, away from all of Leah's recent pain—Raymond's betrayal, her father's detachment, and the knowledge of her biological father.

Kissing the top of her head and brushing a single strand of hair from her cheek, I know that, for the time we've been together in this room, she's been able to have a reprieve. I can't feel guilty about that, even if it did satisfy my own selfish desires to make sweet love to this incredibly brave woman. As much as I want to, I can't regret what just happened, and, with that thought, I finally fall asleep.

Rolling over, I'm awakened by the warmth of the sun beaming through sheer tan curtains. I remember in vivid detail every sensation that ran through my body last night as I made love to the woman of my dreams. Glancing around the room, I wonder where Leah is and how she's feeling this morning.

The scent of food fills the room, but what I crave has nothing to do with eating. Even though we made

Dalia Dupris

love twice last night, my appetite has not been satiated. I still desire her with a hunger that is all consuming.

*What now*? I run a hand across the crumpled sheets, where she'd laid beside me all night, nestled against my side. Her sensuality was a surprise. Her lust matched mine and she gave more than I had imagined as we'd moved in perfect unison.

I need her back in this bed beside me where I can let my hands roam freely over her velvety-soft skin and kiss her full lips before taking her again.

"Leah." Sitting up, I spot two covered food trays and a carafe of coffee on the desk, but there's no sign of her. Was I too much last night? Should I have stopped at making love once?

No, she'd clearly desired me as much as I'd desired her. Her body had made that fact abundantly clear. We'd been of one accord as we'd simultaneously reached the peaks of pleasure. Just as I'm wondering if she's left me here alone, she steps out of the bathroom and into the room.

"Good morning." Smiling, she makes her way to the bed, looking as beautiful and tempting as ever, which is amazing, since we hardly slept last night. "I wanted to brush my teeth, before doing this—" Leaning over, she softly caresses my jaw before kissing me.

"I could get used to this." I pull her down so that she's sitting near me on the bed. "Would you care to join me?" Lifting the covers, I give her my sexiest look, hoping she'll say yes, and that she isn't harboring any crazy notions about turning back to the way we were before last night.

"It sounds tempting." She smiles hesitantly. "But if I get back in that bed, who knows when we'll get up."

"I like the sound of that." Pulling her to me, I think that, if this is a dream, I never want to wake up.

"Honestly, I do, too." She glances at the food before continuing, "but I think we should talk—that is, as soon as you wash up."

"You're no fun." I groan.

"You didn't say that last night." Giving me an impish grin, she leaves my side and walks away from the bed. "Don't take too long. All of that late night-early morning frolicking has me ravenous."

"I already told you what I'm hungry for, but I'll comply. *This* time." Grabbing an end of the sheet, I wrap it around my waist before rising from the bed.

"What's that for?" Laughing, she meets my gaze. "I've already seen what you've got, so there's no need to be modest now."

"Fine." I drop the sheet to the floor and feel a sense of satisfaction when she gasps.

Following her orders, I quickly finish up in the bathroom before heading back into the room, where I slip on my pants before sitting beside her at the desk. "Was that fast enough for you?"

"Yes." She fills both of our coffee cups. "You are a man who knows when to be fast and when to be slow." She meets my eyes, a wicked grin on her face.

"I'll take that as a compliment." Smiling back at her, I'm relieved to see she's relaxed and that we're still good. For a minute, I was concerned there would be self-consciousness after a night of so much unbridled passion.

"As you should."

She removes the lids from both plates, and I see what had my mouth watering earlier: grits, biscuits, scrambled eggs, and crisp bacon.

"We forgot dinner last night." Suddenly ravenous, I focus on my food.

"We had other appetites to satisfy." She bites into a piece of bacon, and I almost miss the quick look of uncertainty clouding her eyes.

"About that… how are you feeling this morning?" Setting my fork down, I take her hand in mine. "Are we good?"

"We are always good." Sighing deeply, she continues, "I was being selfish last night."

"You couldn't have done it alone." Brushing my thumb across her fingers, I say, "I give you permission to be selfish with me whenever you like."

"I'm not sorry about telling you that I wanted you." Dropping my hand, she adds sugar and cream to her coffee.

"I'm not sorry either." Has she finally figured out that I've been in love with her for years?

"Since we've arrived in Santa Lorena, I've come to realize how much I depend on you—and always have, ever since your return to Sunnyville. You and Jenny are the two best friends a girl could have." She focuses on stirring her coffee before resuming, "I've told you that before. Lately, I've been viewing you in a different light. Your loyalty to your country, to your family, to me… well, it's special."

"I don't know about all of that." I make a dismissive gesture, not sure where the conversation is heading. Sure, she's complimenting me, but her tone is unsettling and has me on guard.

"I told you yesterday that I'm trusting my instincts more." She flicks a crumb off the desk. "I know you aren't expecting to hear this, but I'm going to say it anyway. Miguel, somehow I've managed to fall in love with you." Twisting her lips, and looking contrite, she adds, "I never saw this coming, but... there it is, and I don't want to lie."

"Why do you look so sad?" My spirit soars. I'm not sure why she looks like she just bit into a sour lemon. Coming back here was the best decision I have ever made. The woman I have loved for almost twenty years *finally* sees me and loves me in return. "I couldn't be happier."

"That's hard to believe." Pushing her chair back from the table, she folds her arms and glares at me. "Last night was incredible, but I'm not about to go down that road again."

"What are you talking about?" I'm confused. Maybe the lack of sleep has affected her. "What road?"

"Come on, Miguel." Springing up from the table, she retorts, "You know what I mean. Falling in love with a man who *has* a girlfriend and doesn't love me in return." Pacing in front of the bed, she balls her fists. "I'm not going through that again."

"Excuse me?" I stand up and take her hands in mine. "I have no idea *who* you're talking about."

"Please, spare me. I'm not naïve. I've seen Taylor and you together, and it's obvious there's chemistry there."

"No there isn't." Feeling like I've been sucker-punched, I take in a gulp of air and continue, "I don't know what you are talking about." And, just like that, the best morning of my life has abruptly taken a bizarre turn.

But Leah's reasonable. Once I explain that I don't

251

have a relationship with Taylor, she'll understand. "I don't know what you could have seen."

"On my way to the dining room, I walked by Taylor and you. Your hands were all over her, and she was looking at you with adoration."

"My hands have *never* been all over Taylor." Standing, I run a hand across the nape of my neck and struggle to figure out what Leah thinks she saw, and then I remember. Two days ago, prior to the start of the morning walking group, Taylor had had a cramp in her calf and I had massaged her muscle. Even though I hadn't seen Leah, she'd obviously seen us and had gotten the wrong impression. "She had a cramp."

"Uh huh." She smirks and rolls her eyes. "It's okay. Please don't try to explain. If I'm honest with myself, I always knew something was missing between Raymond and I, even before Rebecca came back to Sunnyville, but I chose to ignore it." Snorting, she shakes her head. "My mother was right. He was never the one for me."

"Leah, you've got to listen to me." I caress her cheek. "It's been you all along. Only you."

"Really?"

Her voice softens and I'm hoping that's a sign that she's finally hearing me—trusting me.

One eyebrow lifts as she eyes me suspiciously. "If that's the case, why did you have a condom with you? It certainly wasn't for me. I mean we normally wouldn't... you know, uh... make love." She looks completely vulnerable, before she continues, "Don't get me wrong, I'm glad you did." When she smiles, her eyes sparkle.

"Training." In an instant, I get a flashback of a

younger version of my father, a stern expression on his face, and a no-nonsense tone to his voice as he stands in the orchards and drills it into my head that a man should always carry protection with him because one little slip-up could change the course of a person's life.

"I find it hard to believe that your military training included directions to carry a condom with you." She raises a brow while looking at me suspiciously.

"They did say something, but it was my father's words that stuck with me." Frustrated, I add, "I was fifteen when my father gave me my first wallet. It had a condom in it. Carrying protection is just a habit, whether I use it or not, I know it's there. It *wasn't* that I had any plans—and certainly *not* with Taylor. You've got to believe me."

"Miguel, I can't afford to lose your friendship. It means everything to me. I told you last night that I loved you... and, well... if you loved me back, you would have said it then, wouldn't you?"

"Leah, please let me explain." Is that what she'd mumbled last night right before she'd fallen asleep? Her mouth had been pressed against my neck, and I'll be darned if I'd known what she was saying. "First, I wasn't sure what you said because you were half asleep and so was I. I knew you'd mumbled something, but I didn't know what." Walking over to the window, I feel like a thoughtless jerk. "I was so caught up in the moment. You don't know how many times I had fantasized about us making love and then to realize it was finally coming true, honestly, it left me speechless. Part of me felt like I was dreaming." Seeing how skeptically she's peering at me through narrowed eyes, I rush on. "Plus, I had rehearsed the way I wanted to tell you how I felt, and last night didn't fit into that scenario."

"You don't need to say that. It's not necessary. I've grown up a lot during the last six months, and I'm being brutally honest with myself about everything, even when it hurts like hell. I'm apparently *not* the type of woman men fall in love with." She straightens her shoulders. "I get it. You don't need to pretend like you feel something when you don't."

"Leah, you've got to listen. I couldn't fake what happened last night if I tried." I cup her face between my hands, looking into those eyes that carry so much pain, even though she's trying to be brave. "Last night was something that I've always wanted to happen between us. Granted, I didn't expect you to take the initiative, but I'm grateful you did."

"I shouldn't have." She moves out of my reach, but not before I see the pain that she's trying to hide. "I pushed and you consented. Miguel, you are always so gallant and accommodating. I admit, I am baffled. The last time I was baffled, I was ignoring all the signs, but not now. Now, I'm alert." Her shoulders slump forward as she nervously laces her fingers together. "You and Taylor. Me and you." Tensing, she twists her lips before shaking her head. "I cannot be part of another love triangle. No. I can't and I won't do it. That's it."

Chapter 17

*Leah*

Now that Miguel has left, the room appears much larger. His presence filled the empty spaces in both the room and my heart. It's a relief to cry freely without an audience. I don't need to worry about anyone's reactions to the mess that is my life. A growing surge of emptiness makes its way up my belly to my chest, leaving me cold and shivering.

The task of finding the man I've decided to call biological father is daunting, but compared to the threat of losing Miguel's friendship, it's nothing. I had to get him out of this hotel room before I lost it completely. The last thing I want or need is his pity.

And that's when the stark truth strikes me: what Miguel and I shared amounted to no more than a pity screw.

With that mortifying realization, I collapse on the bed and slide under the covers. If only I could delete last night from my memory. Hah! Even that's a lie. I loved every minute of it—of *him*—and I will always cherish this experience of what real lovemaking felt like.

I shudder as a flush of heat engulfs me as I recall the texture of his skin, the firmness of his muscles, and the tenderness of his touch. Ahhh, it was that tenderness that was my undoing, that left me clinging to him as if he was my only source of oxygen. It had been impossible *not* to surrender to every stimulating sensation, relish every single stroke and tender touch. I have never felt so valued and cherished as I did when he had peered into my eyes. It was as if he was seeing deep into my soul, branding me with his passion and it had left me shaken. Is this what lovemaking is supposed to be like? All this time, with all the other men, I'd just been going through the motions and hadn't known it. This time with Miguel has opened my consciousness about what connecting with another person is like… the beauty of it all. But I can't pretend that this was something *he* had initiated. I'd pushed and he'd complied, and therein lies the problem. There's no limit as to what Miguel is willing to do to make me feel better, even if it means responding to my need to be held and comforted.

My cell phone ring tone startles me out of my reverie, and I debate answering it. I'm not up to speaking to either my first dad, who it would be more appropriate to identify as *Reluctant Dad* or Miguel. It's *all* too soon. I haven't sorted anything out yet, except I do want to meet Bio-Dad. Kind of.

When the caller hangs up, and then calls again a second and third time, I decide I might as well answer.

Looking at the phone, I'm relieved to see it's Jenny on the other end of the line. "Hello."

"What's wrong?" Further evidence that Jenny reads peoples' emotions like other people read books. "Out with it. You don't sound good."

"All I've said is hello." Leaning against the headboard, I try to shake off my dismal mood.

"I know and it's obvious that something's wrong. Was it the meeting with your biological father?"

"No. I haven't spoken to him yet. That's on my To-Do list for today."

"Oh. I thought you were going to try to contact him yesterday. If you need moral support, I can get there in a couple hours. It's not like business is booming right now. After the June weddings and graduations, the need for my services slows down considerably, so say the word and I'm on my way."

"Thank you for the offer." I grab a tissue from the nightstand. "But that won't be necessary. Miguel showed up and, well, we ended up doing the two-step tango."

"*What?*" Jenny releases a piercing shriek before clearing her throat and continuing in a more somber voice. "I can only assume you're speaking in code about getting busy under the sheets—or on *top* of them or on a table—*not* that the two of you recently enrolled in a dance class. Please tell me it was one of the first options and not the last one."

"The first one." I can't contain the bittersweet smile that emerges at the memory of his hands as they caressed my skin. "I kind of forced him to make love to me."

"Good one." She laughs for a good two minutes. "Like you would *need* to force Miguel to make love to you. That man is crazy about you. It's about time you acted on it."

"You've got that wrong." I decide to ignore her laughter. "He is *not* crazy about me. He has a girlfriend."

"Then what was he doing in *your* bed?" Her voice

is smug as if she's just beaten me in a game of cards.

"Well, let's see." Even though she can't see me, I use my fingers to count off how I'd seduced Miguel. "One, I took off my clothes. Two, I removed his pants. Three, I invited him to join me on the bed with the pretense of wanting a massage. No, I take that back—I *did* need a massage."

"Did he say no?" Her tone is light.

"He asked me if I needed anything, and I told him I loved him and, basically, that I needed him to make love to me." I add, "But not necessarily in that order."

"Well, dang, girl!" She releases a long low whistle. "I'm super proud of you. Why so glum? Was he a disappointment?"

"Hardly." Desire stirs in me just thinking about last night. "The man has moves for days. He definitely knows what he's doing."

"I have been waiting for you to see what's been obvious to me for a long time. I'm sure he's relieved to no longer be alone in his feelings."

"That's where you're wrong." Standing up, I make my way to my suitcase. "He never once said, 'I love you.'"

"Ahhh. Just because someone doesn't say they love you, doesn't mean they aren't *in love* with you. He was probably too caught up in the heat of passion to actually say the magic words. It's obvious to everyone else that the man has been in love with you for years." At times, Jenny sounds more like a teacher than me. "People confess their love in their own time and way. Look at you. How long have you known Miguel and you are just *now* realizing how you feel about him? Just because *you* felt like saying it now doesn't mean that *he* has to say it at exactly the same time." She takes a deep breath before continuing, "Let's face it. You are particularly vulnerable right now. But don't let unrealistic expectations ruin what could be a really good thing."

"Isn't it during lovemaking when people typically confess their love? I'm not buying your justification. He was here *all* night, and a good portion of the morning." I rummage through my clothes until I find a long sundress to put on. "I'm over it all ready." I am *so* lying. "I showed him the door."

"*What*?" She gasps. "You *didn't* kick him out."

"Not exactly, but... kind of. He tried to explain, but it didn't make sense. If Miguel has romantic feelings for me, why hasn't he said something? We are together all the time."

"Haven't you ever wondered about that? Like, why he doesn't have a girlfriend in Sunnyville, and why he is always with you? If he was having a relationship with someone in Santa Lorena, why does he almost *never* go there? Think about it. He's only there now because his mother said his father needed him, not because of any woman."

"I have to admit, you present a good case." A twinge of guilt surfaces as I face the fact that I've never asked him about his love life, yet he's always been there to hear me out as I lament my failed relationship. "Let's say he does feel something for me—why hasn't he said anything before now?"

"Really?" She releases a loud exasperated sigh. "Are you *kidding* me? You've been so hung up on Raymond that you never bothered to notice the gorgeous man who's been there for you through all your ups and downs. Didn't you tell me you were sobbing at the wedding about not being the one Raymond picked?"

"Yes, I did." If only I could erase the memory of that wedding day and the ride home afterward. What I'd felt for Raymond wasn't love at all. We'd never had a deep conversation. Everything had been surface level. We'd never connected the way Miguel and I did, which is on a mind, body, and soul level. With him, I feel completely safe and comfortable, able to share the most vulnerable aspects of myself.

"You've been through a lot. Before your breakup with Raymond, you were recovering from your mother's unexpected death. You've had a rough last year, and maybe you've overlooked a few things that have been there all along—like the man who shared your bed last night."

"I don't know. I can't think about it now." I'm unable to process what she's saying, not when I'm about to meet my Bio-Dad.

My body tenses just thinking about coming face-to-face with a man I hadn't known existed a week ago. "Maybe after I get through this meeting with the sperm donor, I can figure out if what you are saying about Miguel can be true. Right now, all I know is that I need to follow my instincts, and they're telling me that if Miguel truly loves me, he would have said something sooner."

\*\*\*\*

On the weekends when I'd visit my father, we'd never ventured out of the Santa Lorena suburbs. We'd never visited the orange groves, but I'm in awe as I take in all of their beauty and the intoxicating scent of citrus.

As far as the eye can see, there are long rows of orange trees with firm, green leaves, small white petals, and unripe fruit. Rolling down the windows, I recall how much I use to savor the simple pleasure of biting into fresh fruit, whether it was tangy, sweet, or tart. The sun breaking through the green foliage brings back the recollection of a time when my life wasn't so complicated.

It's not the penetrating heat that has the sweat dripping down my brow as much as it is the apprehension of what's about to happen. The roads are narrow and winding here, at least until I come to a clearing at the top of a hill. In front of me, is a two-story Spanish-style, colonial home, surrounded by purple and pink bougainvillea trees and neatly trimmed flowerbeds.

But I'm not ready to leave the safety of my rental car nor brave enough to approach the double front doors. My heart beats erratically and the palms of my hands are sweaty as I attempt to regulate my breathing. I lose track of time as I sit in the safety of this car with the windows now closed as I work up the nerve to knock on the door and announce myself. How do you tell someone you're the daughter they never knew they had?

Perhaps driving here has been a monumental mistake. It's not too late to drive back down the road, and resume my normal life. But would that even be possible, now that I know this? I wanted to know why it was that Father #2 and I never got along, and now I know the answer. That old saying of being careful what you wish for certainly applies here. Discovering I have another father is something I'd never expected. It's not until I taste blood on the tip of my tongue that I realize I have been biting down on my bottom lip.

Closing my eyes, I rub my temples and wonder what my mother would say if she were here. Most likely she'd encourage me to turn around and leave things the way they have been my entire life, with me in the dark about my genetic lineage. *Leave well enough alone*. But *well enough* isn't really *well enough* after all. That's what her and Father #2 had done—they'd decided for me and if I hadn't pushed, I'd never have found out the truth. She'd thought it was better for me to believe the man she'd divorced was my father, but I needed to know more.

A knock on the window has me jumping in my seat.

"Hello." Standing by the car is a tall, striking woman with chin-length dark hair. Kind brown eyes filled with concern stare out at me. "Are you lost?"

I'm so jittery I'm not sure I can answer, but I roll down the window anyway. "I don't think so." Between the nervous blinking I can't seem to control, my bleeding bottom lip, and my profusely sweating forehead, I probably look like such a mess that she's wondering if it's safe to talk to me. Taking a deep breath, I nod. "My name is Leah Ann. I'm looking for Mr. Hart."

"Oh." A shadow of sadness passes over her face, and she looks uncomfortable as she steps back from the car while shielding her eyes from the sun. "He's no longer here." Her voice falters before she continues, "He died two years ago."

My mouth opens, but I don't know what to say as a sense of loss surrounds me. My father died two years ago. I'm too late. I feel like a balloon that's been punctured with a sharp needle, as if all the air has gone out of my body, and I slump forward until my head hits the steering wheel.

"Let's get you inside." She opens the car door, and when I get out, she links her arm with mine. "You don't want to get heat stroke." Still holding my arm, she leads me down the long walkway into the house.

"Thank you," I mumble. Inside, the coolness of the terra cotta walls is a stark contrast to the air outside and I immediately feel better. Remembering my manners, I add, "I didn't know he had passed." Heaviness settles in my stomach at the realization that my biological father had been here the entire time. I'd never known he'd been so close and, now, I'll never know him.

"It was sudden." The timbre of her voice reveals that she must have been close to him.

I follow her through a long hallway into an open kitchen with a center island. Colorful potted plants with fresh herbs are spaced along a wide window above the sink.

"Please, sit down. You don't look so good." She indicates a cushioned stool at the counter before she hands me a bottle of water from the refrigerator. "This should help. By the way, my name is Elaine."

"I'm Leah Ann James." The cool water trickling down my throat calms my nerves, but I'm disappointed that I've made the journey two years too late.

Setting the bottle on the speckled granite counter, I say, "I'm sorry to be such a bother." Should I tell her why I came? Did she know Mr. Hart? Is she the new owner? Maybe she can tell me something about him. Even though I never knew him, I still feel a sense of loss for the relationship we might have had. Maybe he wouldn't have found it difficult to love me, but, now, I'll never know.

"Did you know my father?" She's a good four inches taller than me, and she seems to glide as she takes a seat across from mine. "He was involved in several civic and community organizations."

"No. I wasn't acquainted with him through a group." Clutching my hands in my lap, I glance down and my thoughts splinter in several different directions. I wish I'd had the opportunity to meet him. I can't blurt out that I'm a product of a sperm donation he'd made thirty years ago; she'll think the heat has already gotten to me and scrambled my thoughts. "He sounds like he was a good person."

"He was. The best." Her eyes light up as she talks about him. "How did you know him?"

"Actually…" I squirm uncomfortably under her curious gaze. "My father… provided me with Robert Hart's name."

"*Robert* Hart." She places a hand on her chest, and, with a warm smile on her face, leans toward me as if she's known me forever. "I thought you meant *my* father, *Thomas* Hart. This is—*was* his house. I live here now, but my uncle Robert lives nearby, on the other end of the property."

"I have this address." I scrounge around in my purse for the slip of paper father #2, had shoved into my hand. Unfolding it and smoothing the edges, I silently reread the name and address that I now know by heart. I hadn't considered that finding a father might include discovering other relatives. My fingers tremble as I hand her the paper.

"This is my Uncle Robert's address." She raises a perfectly arched eyebrow and looks at me curiously for several seconds before adding, "His house is less than a quarter of a mile up the road. The addresses are almost identical. This is 4300 Bristol Road. My uncle lives at 4300½ Bristol Road." She glances down at my athletic shoes. "You've got on the right shoes for the walk. He splits his time between here and a place in Littleton. If you have time and are feeling better, I can walk you to his place, but I can't promise he'll be home."

"I am feeling better." Hopping off the stool, I add, "The water helped and I'm willing to take a chance to see if he's at his house. I don't mean to interrupt your day. I can make the trek myself."

"It's not a problem. I just set my daughter down for a nap. She'll be out for a while, plus, I have a camera in her room. I'll be able to see and hear her the minute she wakes. The house is not far." Picking up her cell phone off the table, she places it in her pocket. "There are two paths, one leads to the orange groves and the other one goes to Uncle Robert's place. It will be better if I take you there, so you don't go the wrong way."

As I follow Elaine out the door, a surge of excitement—along with some apprehension—shoots through me. Minutes ago, I'd thought I'd missed the chance to meet my biological father, and now I'm heading up a hill for introductions. Elaine must be my cousin if our fathers are brothers. How will she feel about that, considering she'd had no idea I existed until a few moments ago? My parents were only children, so I never had a cousin before, but, now, the possibility of having a relative close to my age has me feeling almost giddy.

After walking for a few minutes, Elaine pauses and, swiveling around, places her hands on her slender hips. "Are you okay? Let me know if I'm walking too fast."

"I'm fine." Emotions make it difficult for me to put together a complex sentence. I don't want to say the wrong thing, like, *did your uncle ever mention he might have children somewhere out in the world.*

Wait—*children?* Didn't some men make it a habit to donate sperm as a source of income?

As I take in the beauty of this property, it's obvious he wasn't poor, so why do it? Maybe I'll soon know the answer to what had motivated him to become a donor.

My pulse quickens and I stumble over a rock at the possibility of *more* siblings.

"We'll stop here for a minute." She reaches out a hand as if to steady me from tumbling down the hill. "I'm so used to the steepness of this area, I forget it can be a challenge. Plus, there is still some debris left over from the last fires."

"At least your property wasn't damaged." Smart move—I can use a distraction from the subject of my conception.

"I wish that were true." Running a hand through her hair, she takes a deep breath. "It *was* significantly damaged. The remodel was completed three months ago."

"I'd never know." As we resume walking, I'm wondering how long it will be before we arrive at our destination. Will his house be as beautiful as hers? "It looks great."

"Thanks, I tried to restore it as much as possible to the way it used to look. I grew up there, so it has a lot of memories."

We walk in silence for another fifteen minutes until the path becomes less visible under a covering of withered leaves and overgrown grass. After Elaine pushes open a rusted wire gate, she lifts her chin and I follow her gaze to a charcoal-gray, single-story home that's surrounded by overgrown weeds and leaning trees that look like they could fall over at any moment. Chipped broken stones lead to a front door that's covered by a security screen. It's jammed full with newspapers and flyers. A For Sale sign, tilting precariously to the side, is staked in the middle of the yard.

"This is it." I'm not sure if it's regret that I hear in her tone and if it's there because the house has so obviously been neglected. "I don't see his car."

"I've missed him, then." I'm stunned by the contrast between the two homes, but she had said that he doesn't live here most of the time. Maybe that's why he's willing to sell this house.

In any case, I'm not sure if I'm relieved or disappointed he's not here. "Well, thanks for bringing me here. I'll have to come back another time."

"Sorry about that." She shrugs. "He's really not here that much, but I thought we'd take a chance and maybe you'd get lucky."

"It's fine." Maybe this is a sign that I'm *not* supposed to meet him. Maybe I should march down that hill with my new cousin—who doesn't have a clue we're related—and resume my life with the people I already know. Will it make any difference if I meet him? Probably not. After all, he may not be any fonder of me than my other father.

Darn. Why hadn't I thought of that before? Well… it doesn't really matter because I still want to meet him. If it's not today, I'll return in the future. Now that I know he exists, I'm willing to take my chances.

"Do you hear that?" Elaine abruptly halts before grasping my arm and pulling me to the side of the rode as a navy sedan screeches to a halt directly in front of us. "Your timing is good. That's him right there."

A gray-haired man of average height with a portly build and a half-buttoned black jacket flapping in the wind emerges from the car. With a wrinkled brow and an angry scowl, he stomps toward us, kicking rocks with each step.

"What are you doing here?" He addresses Elaine without once glancing in my direction.

Straightening her shoulders, she says, "This woman, Leah Ann, wanted to see you."

"I thought she was one of your friends." When he faces me, his frown softens as he pulls a cigar out of his shirt pocket. "You interested in buying my house?" He places the cigar between his lips and struts toward the house before I have a chance to respond. "I'll show you the inside."

"Are you here to look at the house?" Elaine looks at me questioningly. Her voice is different now—with an edge of tension, as if she would prefer not to be here. Maybe it's because her uncle's voice was so curt when he addressed her.

"Well actually—"

"Obviously," Robert Hart says before I can finish my sentence. "What else would she be here for? Good God, I'm surrounded by idiots." As he makes his way toward the door, I turn to Elaine and shrug.

"No. I'm not here about the house." The words come out wobbly. "It's something else." I glance at Elaine, as if she can provide some type of moral support.

"Whatever it is, this is your chance to speak to him. Don't worry—he's gruff but harmless." She brushes her hands against her jeans, swiping off the dust from the road. "I'm headed back home."

"You're leaving?" A part of me wants to beg her to stay, but I don't really know her, and this cantankerous man *is* my father after all.

"I promise he won't bite." She chuckles. "You'll be fine. By the way, it was nice meeting you." She gives my shoulder a friendly pat before turning around and heading back down the road. Obviously, she doesn't want to linger here too long, or maybe she's just trying to give me a private moment with her uncle.

Taking a deep breath, I catch up with my biological father as he opens the front door. One thought keeps racing through my mind, distracting me: *be careful what you ask for, because you might not like what you get.* But then another part of me says, *Focus. This is the father you have wanted to know ever since you learned of his existence.*

"There are three bedrooms and two bathrooms." He opens his arms wide as if he's showing me a palace instead of a dusty living room with cobwebs on the windows and cracks in the ceiling. "What do you think?"

"I'm not sure." I'm not about to tell him I'm thinking he seems worse than Father #2 who, at least, doesn't talk *at* me instead of *to* me.

"If you think I'm going to go down on the price,

you're wrong." He grunts. "That's why I didn't hire a realtor. They cave in too easily, plus, why should I give them any of my hard-earned money? Everyone wants a handout these days." Strutting over to a window, he peers out. "I'm not lowering the price by even one cent, so you can forget that. You're wasting your time if you think you can convince me to change my mind. This is prime California real estate here." Thumping his chest, he adds, "I know the value of my land."

"I'm not here about the property." I've come this far; I should get to the point. He needs to know that I came to see him about something far more important than a plot of land or his neglected house.

"What?" Striding toward me, he takes a deep puff of his cigar before blowing smoke in my face. "Well, what are you here for then? I don't have time to waste. Whatever you are selling—"

"I'm not selling anything. I'm… I'm your daughter." There, I've said it and I don't care if he's looking at me as if I've lost my mind.

"You got the wrong man." He steps back as dark, angry eyes scrutinize my face. "You're lying. I don't have any children." His skin turns purple and his thick bushy brows furrow as he stomps into the kitchen—with me following closely behind him. "You don't know what you're talking about, whoever the hell you are. Go back where you came from, girl."

"Sperm donor." Balling my hands into fists, I glare back at him. "You donated sperm thirty years ago and, guess what? I'm your daughter whether you like it or not. I know I sure don't."

Okay, so this is definitely *not* the father-daughter reunion I had imagined, but he has some nerve implying I concocted a lie to get something out of him. "Sure, it was a long time ago, but I don't believe for a minute that a man can forget something like that."

"You don't know anything. You've come to the wrong place." His nostrils flare. "I hope you find your daddy, but he ain't here."

"I found him all right." My voice rises and my head is pounding, but I won't back down. Father #2 isn't perfect, but he would *never* give me false information, especially with something as important as this. "It's you."

"Bullshit!" He's yelling now, fury and indignation behind each word. "Besides, those records are confidential."

"I'm afraid not." He doesn't have to say anything else; it's as if he's just confessed. "Children who are the offspring of sperm donors have the right to know the identity of their biological father."

"Damn it all to hell." He curses. "So you come sniffing around now that I'm older, thinking you can get this house and whatever else you can get your grubby hands on. Well, you got another thing coming. You ain't gettin' nothin'. I'll donate this to charity before you'll get anything."

"Why'd you do it?" My heart is pounding and my legs are trembling so much that they could give out at any moment, but I can't leave, no matter how much it hurts to have this conversation.

Leaning against the counter, I stare him down. He doesn't frighten me. He's more scared than I am. "Why'd you do it?" I repeat my question even though I know it hardly matters. What little I know about this man is already more than enough.

"That's none of your damn business, but since you asked, I did it for the money. It was a long time ago and they paid pretty well." He shrugs while looking off to the side, a smug look of satisfaction on his face. "It was obvious my brother was getting the big house when our pops died. My parents said I didn't know how to take care of Hartland." He stops long enough to cough and spit into the sink. "So it was easy enough to do. Donate a little sperm and get a little cash. Why the hell *wouldn't* I do it? That's the better question. Hell, it was the easiest money I ever earned."

"Enough." Holding up my hand, I fight the ball of nausea forming in my stomach.

"You wanted answers, you got them." He swipes the back of his hand across his mouth. "Life ain't always pretty."

"No, it isn't." Taking a deep breath, I nod my head. "You're right. I asked why you did it and you told me."

Moving swiftly, I rush through the house, stumbling out the front door, then running down the path, before slipping on a piece of broken cement and falling to the dirt.

Scrambling to my feet, tears streaming down my cheeks, I ignore my aching knees and scraped hands as I strive to escape the father I wish I never knew.

Limping, I finally reach the car, and am about to pull away when Elaine comes rushing out of the door.

"How'd it go?" Glancing at my face, she places a hand on my shoulder. "Oh my God, what happened?"

"I'm fine." The odd part is that it's true. I'm not overjoyed biological father is a jerk, but I'm very glad he didn't raise me.

"No, you aren't." She's obviously concerned.

"Why don't you come inside for a minute? I can see you're upset. Was it something my uncle said?"

"I can't talk about it right now, but thank you for your kindness." Taking a tissue from my purse, I wipe my eyes. "But, in the future, I would like it if we could talk."

Well, at least Elaine is one positive I got out of this day. I now know that I have a cousin and I do want to get to know her, but, at this very moment, I desperately need to be alone, away from the bitter man who'd sold his sperm for profit and couldn't care less about the results of his actions.

Chapter 18

*Miguel*

Now that I'm here, standing outside Leah's hotel room, I have a moment of doubt. It's been two days since the morning she kicked me out, and I've been debating the risks versus the merits of trying to speak to her again.

Raising my fist to knock on the door, I know I don't have an option. I *need* to see her and maybe, now, she'll be ready to listen to what I have to say.

"Miguel." She's wearing a purple blouse and faded blue jeans, and her hair is pulled back from her face. "Come in."

"I missed you." Walking in, I sit at the desk and avoid looking at the bed which will lead me down memory lane to that one unforgettable night when I was finally able to caress Leah's soft skin, to hear her catch her breath as I moved over her, to taste the sweetness of her lips as they pressed against mine.

"I was going to call you." Sitting across from me on the edge of the bed, she folds her hands in her lap. "We need to talk."

"I agree."

When she looks at me skeptically, I wonder if she's remembering how she'd said she loved me and I hadn't returned the sentiment. "I have something I need to

274

say." I know this is not the time or place, because I can see she's distracted. When I tell her that I love her, I want her to be focusing on my words and nothing else.

"I do want to hear what you have to say, but—" she holds a hand up—"not today."

"I can see you have a lot on your mind, so what I have to say can wait." I move to sit beside her.

Her guarded look tells me to proceed with caution, no matter how much I want to hold her in my arms.

"Why do you look stressed? What's happened?"

"I need to follow up on something." She purses her lips before standing up and picking up her purse from the dresser. "There's this place in Dominguez Hills I need to visit."

"I don't want to hold you up." Why hadn't I considered she might have other things to do besides be with me? For all I know, she's on her way to meet Aaron. "I'll let you go." A muscle in my jaw jerks as I move to the door.

"I was going to ask if you wanted to come with me… since you are here." She places a hand on my arm and looks at me with uncertainty. "You're still my friend and I could use your moral support. That is, if you have the time."

"Sure, I've always got time for you." I don't know where she's going and it doesn't matter as long as I'm spending time with her. She needs to know I *do* love her. Nothing has changed that.

On the way to the car she's rented, I'm able to breathe more easily knowing she isn't about to go on a date.

Now that she's had a couple of days to think it over, does she regret that we made love? Because that's what it was. She had to feel it too, didn't she? Can one person feel *that* connected and the other person feel indifferent?

When she'd called out my name while she was in the throes of passion, it *had* to mean something, and I'm not going to believe it didn't, regardless of what she may be telling herself or even what she tells me. There *was* something there; I know it in my heart and soul.

"We can listen to music or," she pauses long enough to slide into the car and fasten her seat belt, "we can talk." Pulling out of the hotel parking lot, Leah drives several blocks before merging onto Highway 10.

"It can wait." I want to make sure she's listening, not concentrating on the road when I tell her that I've been in love with her for years. She needs to be able to look in my eyes and see that I'm being open and honest with her.

"Okay, then I'll fill you in on my crazy life." Sighing, she glances at me out of the corner of her eye before refocusing on the road. "I told you about my father and the whole sperm donation thing, right?"

"I was going to ask you how you were feeling about that," I say, trying to not sound as guilty as I feel. The truth is, I've been so focused on wondering how she feels about *me* that I had shoved the ordeal with her father to the back of my mind.

"Honestly, I was excited at first." Rolling her eyes, she continues, "I thought this would be my big chance to find the man who was my *real* father."

"I get that. You want to know your biological dad." The fact that Leah's father was able to discover the sperm donor's name shows that very few things remain confidential forever. It's strange to refer to her biological father as a sperm donor. It sounds artificial and cold.

"I do." She honks at a car before changing lanes. "Some time ago, the laws were changed so that children whose fathers were sperm donors could find their biological fathers."

"For medical reasons, I can see why that'd be important." Turning to face her, it occurs to me that Leah may be dealing with a situation I don't know anything about. "That's not something you are dealing with, is it?"

"No, nothing like that." She purses her lips. "No health problems here. I'm emotionally stressed, but nothing physical."

"Well, at least you know that." I adjust my seat so I can see her face better. "How do you feel about knowing his identity?"

"A hundred different ways." She doesn't offer clarification and I don't ask for any details, figuring she'll share more when she's ready.

Eventually our exit sign comes into view, and she steers into the left lane. Dominguez Hills is a neighboring college town, slightly bigger than Santa Lorena, but, unlike Santa Lorena, it has two malls, a movie theatre, and a bowling alley, all of which cater to the bustling college student population.

"There's a coffee shop straight ahead. I could use some caffeine about now. I didn't sleep much last night."

"I can see why."

She pulls into a parking space in front of a café called Koffee Klash.

"I can drive the rest of the way, if you want to take a nap."

"I'll be fine as soon as I get something to drink."

I take her hand in mine as we enter the coffee shop. After we've given our orders—a large black coffee with a shot of espresso for her and a cup of green tea for me—we take a seat at a table near the window.

"I was excited about the prospect of meeting him." She grimaces while removing a napkin from its holder and shredding it. "I imagined this heartwarming scenario where we would embrace before he confessed he's always wondered about me." Gathering the scraps of paper, she smirks. "I could see it so clearly in my mind. The reality is a *whole* other story."

"Did you meet him?"

No wonder she wasn't able to hear what I was saying; she had major issues she's struggling with that are as deep as the shock of discovering her father was having a baby with one of his previous students.

"I did." She shivers, as if suddenly cold. "I can tell you this much—it was *nothing* like my fantasy. He was awful."

"When did you meet him?" I place my palm over her hand as the waitress sets our beverages on the table.

"Can I get anything else for you? Cream, sugar?" She frowns at the pile of shredded napkins on the table before moving on. "More napkins?"

"We're fine, thank you." After the waitress leaves, I give Leah's hand a reassuring squeeze. "Go on."

"I went by his house yesterday." She wraps her hands around her mug, peeks at me over the rim. "I was surprised it was so close." She frowns before taking a sip of her coffee. "There is *nothing* sentimental about that man. He basically called me a liar and accused me of claiming to be his daughter because I wanted something from him." Setting her cup down, she takes a deep breath. "It was terrible. *He* was terrible."

"I'm sorry he wasn't the man you wanted him to be." I want to comfort her and tell her the man doesn't know what he's missing out on by not having her in his life.

"He didn't even come close." She takes another sip of her coffee before looking up and shaking her head. "It's funny… compared to him, my *other* father is a saint. He may be stilted and not that easy to connect with, but at least I know he's trying his best."

"That's something." I think of my father and how, recently, we've been able to talk to each other without me feeling like I'm disappointing him. "What are you going to do now?"

"I need him to *know* I'm not lying. That, even if I never have a relationship with him, I *am* telling the truth, and I can't do that with a slip of paper with his name on it that I got from my father, who got it from an anonymous source, who got it from another anonymous source."

There's fight and determination in her voice as she draws her shoulders up.

"He won't be able to deny the evidence I'm going to give him. After I show him the documents from Biotech, he won't be able to accuse me of being deceitful. He and I will both know he's the one who's living a lie."

"So they'll just give you his name?" I ask cautiously, not wanting her to get her hopes up only to be disappointed once again. "Confirm he was the person who donated the sperm?"

"Basically yes, although I have to present my identification, and I have a picture of my birth certificate." She pats her purse. "I don't want anything from that man, but he *will* know the truth."

"What's the next step?" I ask, ready to support her any way I can. Maybe when she has this part of her life resolved, she can focus on the man sitting across from her who wants nothing more than to have her in his life forever.

"We finish our drinks and then I drive to Biotech and get the confirmation I need to prove to 'Mr. I'm-Not-A-Father' that he is, indeed, a father whether he likes it or not."

"You need to do this for yourself as much as him," I say as we head out the door.

"You're right." She drives past the various brick buildings that compromise Dominguez College. Summer school must be in session, judging by the number of students milling about the sprawling campus. Stopping at a red light, she turns toward me. "Who does he think he is to question my motives?"

I decide it's best not to answer. The real question is not who he thinks he is as much as who he swears he isn't—her father. I have no doubt the information Leah has is correct, but it's not me she's trying to convince.

An hour later, she turns onto a tree-lined street cluttered with a series of nondescript small stores. It's a quiet block, which is probably an ideal location for a man to discreetly come and make a "deposit" without drawing attention to himself.

"It's on this block." Turning off the ignition, she peers at me, steely-eyed. "If he wants confirmation, I'll give him confirmation." She doesn't move for several seconds before slowly opening the door and getting out of the car. "This is it." She indicates a storefront wedged between a florist and bakery.

The windows are darkened and it's unclear if it's opened or closed until we are close enough to read the sign on the door. There's a green cross and a drawing of what's obviously a marijuana plant with the store's hours etched in white below.

"Do you think this is a cover for Biotech?" She's obviously grasping for something that will allow her to believe this trip wasn't a waste of time. "I'm going inside. Biotech is probably in the back."

"Excuse me." As soon as we walk in the door, a young woman with short-cropped blonde hair, tattoos on the side of her neck, and wearing a navy-blue security guard uniform approaches us. "Do you have your prescription with you today?"

"No." Leah's eyebrows rise as she scans the room, taking in the glass shelves containing various medicinal cannabis products. "We aren't here for marijuana."

"Then we can't help you." The guard takes a pair of ear buds out of her pocket. "If you want more traditional medicine, there's a pharmacy about five blocks from here."

"Thanks, but we aren't looking for a drug store." There's a twinge of desperation in her voice. "By any chance, is there another business in the back?"

"Huh?" the security guard asks as she jams her ear pods back into her pocket. "There's no other business here."

"The company's name is Biotech," Leah continues, as if the guard hasn't already answered her question.

"Never heard of it." The guard heads back to her post near the door.

Leah doesn't say another word as we leave and head back to the car, but the slump of her shoulders says it all.

"I'll drive back."

Without looking at me, she hands me the keys and lets herself in the passenger door. This was not the proof she was hoping to find and it's obvious she's too distracted to drive. How many disappointments can she take before the pressure is too much? Maybe when she realizes I truly do love her, she'll know that she doesn't have to bear her burdens alone.

"I can't believe Biotech isn't there anymore."

"It *was* thirty years ago." Rolling the windows up, I turn on the air-conditioner and glance at her. "Maybe they moved to a new location… somewhere else in town."

"I don't think so." She takes her cell phone out of her purse. "This was the name my father gave me, and when I searched for the address, it's the only Biotech company that came up." Still, she methodically scrolls through her phone before piercing me with a dismal expression on her face. "Nope, there's no other address."

"You'd think they would leave some kind of forwarding location." I drive slower as we approach the bustling college campus. "I'm sure you aren't the only person who's tried to find records or legal documents verifying the name of your biological father."

"Exactly." Closing her eyes, she massages her temples. "I believe father #2 gave me the correct information. It's not like he would make that up. Who knew my biological father would be such a horrible person?"

"The thing is, your, uh… biological father didn't deny he donated sperm, so—"

"Exactly!" She snaps her fingers. "That's evidence right there. I should just leave it alone, but I can't. Even though the man is virtually a stranger to me, I don't appreciate the fact that he's, basically, calling me a conniving liar who's out to get some kind of inheritance."

"He doesn't even *know* you." Any man would be lucky to have Leah as his daughter. The guy must be some kind of idiot. "If he knew you, he'd love you." I stop myself from adding that I'm speaking from my own personal experience.

"Hah, that's a good one."

She places a hand on my thigh, and absently rubs it as I try not to drive onto the sidewalk.

"You're forgetting my track record of men finding it a challenge—if not impossible—to love me." She holds a palm up. "My father who raised me is number one. Raymond is number two, and, now, my biological father is number three. I'm not feeling sorry for myself, but if my life was a baseball game, I would have had my three strikes and would have been tossed out of the game."

I've exhausted my options for consoling her as she leans back against the headrest with her eyes closed for the rest of the way back to her hotel. I don't know where she can go from here, except to take comfort in the fact she knows she has another father, even if he's a disappointment.

Twenty-five minutes later, I pull into the hotel's

parking lot and face her. "You awake?" It's hard to tell with her eyes still closed.

"I am." Slowly, her eyes flutter open and she focuses her gaze on me. "I could use some company." She gives me a weak smile, but something about her expression reveals the stress she's trying to hide. "I'll treat you to room service if you want to hang out and watch a movie with me. I'll even let you pick the movie, although I may regret it later."

"That's an offer I can't refuse." I place a hand on top of hers. "I have to warn you, I'm ravenous. I want a steak and baked potato." *And to hold you in my arms after we've made love until the sun comes up.*

"You aren't exaggerating, you *are* hungry." This time, the smile reaches her eyes. "You must have had a long walk this morning."

"I did." We step out of the car and head toward the hotel. "I might want apple pie for dessert."

"Mr. Montoya." She points an accusatory finger in my direction. "I can see you are going to be an expensive dinner and movie date."

It's good to know she's pushing through her disappointment. Hearing her chuckle as we walk through the lobby and enter the elevator lifts my spirits.

"Exercise tends to increase my appetite. I went for a long run after I finished with the walking group."

"Don't overdo it." She pushes the button for her floor before turning to look at me. "I like you just the way you are."

Is she flirting? I hope so. It's hard to tell with Leah. Little does she know that the night we spent together fulfilled one of my fantasies. Surpassed it, really. Before we return to Sunnyville, she'll know the truth about how deeply my feelings run for her and that Taylor may work wonders for the inn, but she doesn't do a thing for me.

Chapter 19

*Leah*

I'm shameless, but I vow *not* to seduce my best friend tonight, no matter how much I'm tempted. No use drowning my frustrations with mind-blowing sex with Miguel—again. Who knew he would be that stellar in bed? I should have known the man doesn't know how to give less than a hundred percent in anything he does. I've accepted the fact that settling for friendship with Miguel is a great gift all by itself. I'm not going to repeat past mistakes of expecting more than what's there.

Stepping off the elevator, we take just a few steps down the long hallway when Miguel abruptly halts, a bewildered expression clouding his handsome features.

"That's odd." Rubbing his jaw, he raises his brows. "What are *they* doing here?"

"Who?" Following his shocked gaze, I see Elaine and another woman, who resembles a shorter version of her, standing in front of my room door. "Oh, that's Elaine. I met her yesterday." Apprehension and dread settle in the pit of my stomach.

She'd been kind and helpful yesterday, but, now, she's probably come to confront me about whatever horrible things my biological father told her about me. Of course, she'd take his word over that of a complete stranger.

She's brought someone else with her, possibly a sister, or cousin. On the other hand, the other woman could be a friend that Elaine brought along for moral support. Are they here to identify me as the imposter who has the audacity to try to force herself on their family? They'll be surprised to discover I'm not going to back down with or without Biotech documents as confirmation.

"I don't know why she's here and I don't know who the other women is." I stand frozen in place, unable to take a step forward. The last thing I want after my heated discussion with my biological father is to argue with his niece. Does she hate me now, thinking that I'm some kind of money-grubbing charlatan?

"*I* know who they are." Taking my hand in his, he squeezes it, and I hold on as if it's a lifeline. He pulls me with him toward the two waiting ladies. "The question is, what are they doing *here*?"

Before I can ask for clarification, we're standing outside of my room, and my legs feel weak as I reach for the keycard in my back pocket. If I'm going to be cursed out, I'd rather it not be in a public place.

"Elaine and Morgan, two of my favorite people," Miguel says warmly as he embraces each of them. "I've been meaning to come by, but I've been so busy at the inn that I haven't gotten around to it."

He focuses his attention on the shorter woman who looks vaguely familiar, with dark, shoulder-length, curly hair and a voluptuous figure.

"Morgan, I didn't know you were back in town."

"We flew in last night." Her response is directed at Miguel, but she never stops openly appraising me.

"Can we take this inside?" Why is he consorting with the enemy? Obviously, he knows them and hopefully they won't try to persuade him that I'm not to be trusted.

I nervously open the door as Miguel, Elaine, and the woman named Morgan follow close behind. I'm glad I've straightened the room earlier this morning. My clothes are in the closet and housekeeping made the bed. Apprehension and dread have me releasing a loud sigh.

"We're sorry about barging in on you like this, but I didn't have your phone number or any other way to reach you," Elaine says as she and Morgan take a seat on the edge of the bed.

I warily sink into the chair at the desk. Miguel stands behind me, his strong hands lending support as they rest on my shoulders. Strangely enough, Elaine and Morgan don't look upset. If anything, they look at me with a mixture of curiosity and compassion.

"I'm not sure why you would be looking for me." My voice is defensive as I wonder about the identity of the other woman, why she's with Elaine, and how they happen to be friends with Miguel.

"We checked at Aunt Lucia's inn first and when you weren't there, we knew you must have checked in here." She glances at the woman I am assuming is her friend. "There aren't any other options in town."

"So, I know you are related to my—I mean, Robert Hart—and you are also cousins with Miguel." None of this is making any sense, but since they referred to Miguel's mother as an aunt, they must be first cousins—

*Oh God no. Please don't let me be related to*

*Miguel.* A knot forms in my stomach. "You're here for a reason."

If Elaine wants me to back off of the truth as I know it, she's going to be disappointed. The father who raised me is many things, but he is not a liar. "You might as well get to the point." I nervously shove my hair away from my face and, feeling agitated, stare expectantly at both women.

"Morgan and Elaine are my god-sisters."

Miguel squeezes my shoulders and I release a breath I didn't know I was holding. Okay. I can handle the fact that they aren't blood relatives. The knot in my stomach disappears. So they're sisters, which means I am related to both of them. This is a lot for one day.

"We're sorry for popping up like this, but we really wanted to speak with you, didn't we, Morgan?" Elaine smiles warmly and gives me a reassuring look.

Yes, my first impression of her had been accurate. She's not angry at all. No, her eyes hold a hint of mystery and what appears to be joy.

"Absolutely." The shorter woman rubs her hands together. "I'm sorry for not introducing myself." Her eyes light up as she leans forward. "I'm Morgan, Elaine's younger sister. She told me you were at the house talking to our Uncle Robert yesterday." She chuckles, before adding, "I understand you had him all riled up. What I wouldn't have given to see the look on his face when you introduced yourself. He was probably ready to blow a gasket."

"You're not upset?" Baffled by her response, I raise my brows and wonder what's going on. "That's not the response I was expecting."

"Leah, Morgan and I came here to speak to you

289

about your meeting with our uncle." Elaine eyes Miguel, before continuing, "We love our god-brother, but what we have to say is private. Maybe we should talk *without* him here. Do you mind, Miguel?"

"I need to get going anyway." Miguel releases my shoulders. "I understand. Leah, I'll take a rain check on our date."

"No," Grasping his arm, I hope he can read the desperate plea in my eyes. I *don't* want him to leave. I don't know Elaine and Morgan, and whatever they have to say, I want Miguel here—with me. "Miguel is one of my very best friends." I swallow so loudly, the people in the next room probably hear it. "I don't have any secrets from him. He knows I approached your uncle yesterday and that I told him that I believe he is my biological father. My parents were unable to conceive and eventually they went to a sperm bank. It's called Biotech and it's not far from here."

"Hmmm." Elaine's eyes widen in shock as she stands up straighter before looking at Morgan. "We didn't know anything about Uncle Robert donating sperm, but I'm not completely surprised."

"The way he thinks is unpredictable." Morgan snorts before folding her hands across her middle. "We never know what he might have been up to or why he even decided to donate his sperm. It's not like he needed the money."

"In any case..." Elaine shifts her attention back to me, "we didn't know how you were related, but there was no doubt in my mind that you are somehow kin folk."

Miguel loudly clears his throat, as if to remind us that he's still in the room. "Leah, you never told me your biological father's name." He runs his hand across his jaw and shifts his position. "I had no idea that Robert Hart was the name your father gave you." Eyeing the door, he takes a cautious step toward it. "This is family stuff. I don't need to be here."

"Please. I want you to stay. I wasn't keeping the name a secret. It never occurred to me that you might know him, but, of course, it makes sense. Everyone in town knows about Hartland Orchards."

There it is, the truth sparkling like a piece of cut glass with multiple prisms. The brief time I spent with Robert Hart made it abundantly clear that, other than biology, Robert Hart and I have no connection. The man my mother married, who raised me the best way he knew how, *is* my real father—flawed relationship and all. *Not* the sperm donor.

"The Harts and Montoyas go back a long way. Elaine and Morgan's father was my father's best friend. The two also worked closely together." A frown appears between his brows. "Thomas Hart was my godfather and like a second father to me, which is how Morgan and Elaine are my god-sisters."

"And Miguel's parents are my godparents." Morgan chuckles and rolls her eyes. "I know it's a lot to process, but, as you can see, our families are extremely close."

"I think I got all of that." My thoughts struggle to keep up with this new revelation. "I know your uncle called me a liar and I don't care if you choose to believe him. The man who raised me is honest, almost to a fault, but he's no liar. He would never say I was conceived with the help of a sperm donor if it wasn't the truth." Springing up from my chair, I pace in front of them. "I need to make something clear. I don't want anything from him or you." Throwing my hands up, I add, "I only wanted to meet him, not have a relationship with him." Glancing away from them and biting my bottom lip, I add, "Okay, maybe *some* part of me hoped he would have been thrilled to meet me and to have the opportunity to get to know me—maybe even be a part of my life." My voice trembles and I force back the tears that are threatening to spill. "My relationship with my other father isn't that great, so I thought just maybe—"

"We believe you." Morgan abruptly stands and wraps her arms around me. Stepping away, she continues. "We came here to say welcome to the family."

"What?" I pause, not sure if I heard her correctly. "You actually *believe* me?'

"Yes, completely." Elaine says warmly as she joins Morgan in embracing me.

Relief sweeps through me as I glance at Miguel, who has a huge grin on his face.

"This is a lot to take in." I step out of Elaine's and Morgan's welcoming hugs. "You don't understand. I don't have concrete proof." Pulling away, I return to my chair. "Biotech, the company where your uncle donated the sperm, is no longer there, and I don't know how to contact them. I don't want anything except to be believed, but, with no way of contacting Biotech, I'll never be able to prove to him I'm not lying."

"Don't worry about him and whatever he's saying." Morgan waves her hand dismissively as she sits back on the edge of the bed. "When Elaine first told me about you, I couldn't believe it." Her joyous laughter fills the room. "Sure, if we wanted to, we could always do a blood test, but, honestly, that's not necessary. Now that I've seen you, I *know* you are one hundred percent correct. We *are* related."

"How can you be so sure?" I have to ask the question even as warmth and a feeling of belonging spreads through my chest. Why is this woman I just met so trusting?

"I think we all need to go to the bathroom." Elaine heads into the other room, glancing back once. "Follow me."

"Uh, this sounds a little too kinky for me." Miguel exclaims, as he backs away. "I'm staying here."

"Get your head out of the gutter." Morgan shakes her finger at Miguel before facing me. "I believe you and trust that you're telling the truth. Now, I'm asking you to trust Elaine and me." Reaching out, she takes my hand in hers and smiles encouragingly.

I hesitate only seconds before I allow Morgan to lead me into the bathroom.

The three of us stand side-by-side in front of the large rectangular mirror above the circular sink. My make-up is spread across the white porcelain counter, but my eyes are focused on the reflection staring back at me.

Uncertain about what Elaine is seeing, I search the mirror for signs of a unique dimple or birthmark that perhaps we all share, knowing full well that my birthmark is behind my right knee.

"Look." Elaine's voice rises in excitement as she steps back from the mirror and nudges Morgan closer to me so that our shoulders are touching. "What do *you* see?"

"What do you mean? I'm looking in a mirror." Baffled by the question, I shake my head. "I see your sister standing beside me."

"Look closer." Elaine's voice is low and encouraging as she raises a hand toward the glass.

"Elaine, I confess, I'm not sure what we are doing here." Morgan's voice carries a hint of confusion as she places her hands on her hips. "What's the point?"

"Keep looking, both of you, and you'll see what I see." Elaine's voice is calm and confident as she smooths back dark bangs, revealing a small z-shaped scar above her left eye.

"Oh my God!" Morgan brings both hands to her mouth while her eyes look like they are ready to pop out of her head. "I don't believe this. I knew it! We *are* related."

"What are you two *talking* about?" Initially, I don't notice anything unusual or unique as I scrutinize Morgan's stunning features—although I *do* still wonder why she looks so familiar and then, like a bolt of lightning, it hits me.

Gasping, I slowly process that looking at Morgan is like looking at a mirror image of me, with only slight color variations. I've inherited my mother's hazel eyes and paler complexion, but everything else, including the shape of our eyes, nose, mouth, and even our cheekbones, are identical. "I see it." I try to keep my voice steady as I face Morgan, who is even the same height as me. "We're first cousins who look enough alike to be sisters."

"Everything okay in there?" Miguel calls from the other room.

"We're good!" Elaine responds before facing

Morgan and me. "I think we should return to the other room and sit down before we say anything else." A mysterious glance passes between the two sisters.

Walking into the next room, I stand excitedly in front of Miguel. My striking resemblance to my cousin confirms what I already know. "Miguel, did you notice how much I resemble Morgan?"

"Couldn't miss it." He caresses my cheek. "Your complexions are obviously different, but, besides that, you two look damn near identical."

"Why didn't you say anything?" I search his face, wondering when he noticed the similarities.

"I figured it wasn't my place to point out the obvious." He says it so matter-of-factly it occurs to me he's right. He's here, but it's not his place to interject as he observes my family drama unfolding.

"Fair enough." Even though I've just met Morgan, I automatically feel a kinship to her, and it's not just about our shared features. Does she feel it, too? "I now have another father and two cousins." Regardless of how I feel about Robert Hart, I like the two women sitting across from me and would love to get to know them better.

"There's more." Elaine takes one of my hands in hers.

"Such as?" My breath catches in my throat. What if they don't want anything to do with me? They're happy with each other and what if they don't want to interact with their uncle's unknown offspring who has just sprung up out of the blue. "Are you saying you don't want anything to do with me?" My voice cracks with pain. Family found and family lost. It was a mistake to assume they would automatically open their arms and accept me as part of the clan.

"No!" Morgan holds her hands up. "I speak for both of us when I say that we are thrilled to meet you, but you've got it all wrong."

"So, you *are* calling me a liar, just like your uncle did." Anger, frustration, and disappointment have me shouting back. "I don't lie!"

"Of course not. We believe you."

Morgan's laughter startles me. I don't know how she can find humor in this situation.

"But you aren't my cousin; you are my *sister*."

"What? I don't understand." Thoroughly confused, I stand near the window, and look out at the cars parked below. "How can that be when you two are sisters? You aren't making any sense."

"I can leave any time now," Miguel says, clearly wanting to escape.

"Miguel." I look at him pleadingly. "No secrets between us ever, remember?"

"Okay, then." He shrugs, appearing uncomfortable, but resigned to stay the course.

"Several years ago, when our wonderful father, Thomas Hart, was still alive, the family decided to do one of those ancestry tests." Morgan sighs and fidgets with her hands before continuing, "I thought we might meet some new family members and was excited. Our father liked the idea, too. Uncle Robert also agreed to provide a saliva sample even though he complained it was a stupid idea." Morgan crosses her legs at the ankles while folding her hands in her lap. "Thomas Hart was married to my mother and I'd assumed he was my father until the DNA test came back and showed that Uncle *Robert* was actually my biological father. No, need to upset my sister and father or say anything to Uncle Robert. So, I told them the DNA company had lost our samples." Her large eyes, shaped so similarly to mine, pierce me with a penetrating stare.

"I had no idea that my mother and uncle were in a relationship," Elaine chimes in, "until our father died. Per a stipulation of my father's will, I went to see our mother, who I was shocked to discover was living in another town with Uncle Robert."

"After Elaine told me what she found out, I shared the DNA results with her." Morgan rolls her eyes, but there is no bitterness in her voice. "We learned that we are half sisters. Same mother. Different fathers. It's not pretty, but it *is* the truth."

"A least our father died never knowing the depth of his wife's and brother's betrayals." Elaine brushes her hand across mine. "We are sorry that this isn't a nice, neat family lineage story."

"No, it isn't." I release a shaky breath, knowing that I hadn't considered that finding my biological father, would entail unveiling other family members and their complex relationships with me and each other. "Thank you for sharing this information with me."

"It's been our family secret." Morgan stretches her legs in front of her. "Not because we are ashamed, but because it's complicated."

Elaine glances at Miguel. "We *never* told anyone this information."

Morgan points a finger at Miguel. "We trust you to keep our family secrets."

"What family secrets?" He pulls a pair of white ear buds from his shirt pocket and places one of them in each ear.

"Very funny," Morgan smirks. "It's a little late to put them in *now*."

"I'm sorry," Miquel taps the ear buds while shaking his head. "I can't hear a thing you're saying."

"I'm attempting to keep up with what you're telling me." I hesitate, unsure if I should ask my next question. This is all unchartered territory and the last thing I want to do is offend them. "I think I understand, but I'm not clear about one detail."

"What?" Morgan and Elaine say in unison.

"Does my… uh… your Uncle Robert *know* you're his daughter?" The question is directed at Morgan.

"No." Her answer is as swift as her gaze is steady. "I didn't see the need. Never considered mentioning it to him. The man who raised Elaine and I was a terrific human being. I'll always consider Thomas Hart as my father, not my uncle."

"We're sorry to dump all of this on you, but we felt you had the right to know the facts, both the good and the ugly." When Elaine smiles, her face lights up. "The minute I saw you, I *knew* you were family. The resemblance between you and Morgan is incredible." Elaine smooths down her dark fringe of bangs. "I wonder why Uncle Robert decided to be a sperm donor."

"That's the million-dollar question," Morgan says. "You never know what to expect from that man."

"Except…" Elaine looks reflective, "Uncle Robert always felt like he was entitled to more of everything— the bigger house, a bigger portion of our grandfather's and father's will, and, apparently, his brother's wife. He even manipulated my ex-boyfriend, who was our family attorney, to try to get more money and control of my father's estate. Our uncle has always been about the money, and if I understand what I've previously read about payment for sperm donations, our uncle probably felt that he could always use more cash."

"Plus," Morgan sits up straighter, "he undoubtedly believed that he was making a positive contribution to the world by donating his sperm. In your case, Leah Ann, I'd have to say he was correct."

Once everyone has left my hotel room, I collapse on the bed, emotionally drained, but clear about what actions I need to take in order to have scientific evidence of my connection to Robert Hart. The good part is that it doesn't involve locating Biotech.

After a few minutes, I take several deep breaths, silence my racing thoughts, and pick up my cell phone. I search for the DNA website Elaine and Morgan used to trace their lineage. For an extra thirty dollars, the test kit can be delivered via overnight express. For another thirty dollars, the results can be expedited within a week after the company receives the sample.

Twenty minutes later, it's done. I'll have my vial tomorrow and the results shortly thereafter. At this point, irrefutably confirming my paternal connection no longer has anything to do with needing anyone's approval; I need to do this for myself.

Tension dissipates as I lean back in the deep tub, surrounded by the scent of lavender bubble bath. There's no way I'll be able to get any sleep tonight, not with all the thoughts swirling through my head. My mother used to say that, sometimes, it's better to leave well enough alone, but is it?

When the tips of my fingers are nothing but squiggly lines and the water is lukewarm, I step out of the tub.

I've opened a Pandora's box by coming here expecting to get closer to father #1. That was a bust. Instead, I'm about to have a stepmother who's younger than me, a baby brother or sister in the making, a cantankerous biological father, and a lovely accepting new cousin and sister. I've finally learned to trust my genuine feelings and instincts. And those feelings tell me that Miguel is the man for me. There's no use denying that I'm in love with him, even if his feelings for me remain platonic.

As soon as my head sinks into the pillow, the cell phone rings. Maybe that's him trying to reach me. He's probably relieved to *not* be in love with someone who has such a complicated family. I hope he appreciates how fortunate he is to have grown up with two parents who love him, despite any differences he and his father have endured in the past. It was pure selfishness on my part to want him with me for support when all the sordid details of my dysfunctional family drama were being played out. It's time for me to stop leaning on Miguel so much. Although, I will never regret the night we spent together. That night was the best night of my life.

"Hello." Looking at the screen, I see Jenny's picture, long flowing braids, eyes lined with jet-black kohl, and vivid red lipstick outlining her perfectly formed lips.

"I hope it's not too late to call. I've been thinking about you."

I imagine her sitting in her living room, looking concerned, possibly sorting through her deck of tarot cards, trying to figure out my future.

"How's everything?"

"It's not too late to call. I'm happy to hear your voice." Sitting up in bed, I pull the covers under my chin before turning on the lamp. "I can't begin to tell you what's been happening. It's way too much."

"I knew it. My telepathy was telling me something was troubling you." She makes a loud humph sound. "Are you okay?"

"I am… good." I hesitate, uncertain about how I am at this moment… until it dawns on me that I *am* fine, *regardless* of what comes out of the DNA test and despite the fact that my world has been flipped upside down. "Just trying to sort out a few things, that's all. As soon as I get back, I'll fill you in on all of the sordid details."

"I'm going to hold you to that." She yawns loudly. "Until then, take care of yourself. Remember, the goddess is always with you."

"I know." Chuckling, I disconnect the phone, grateful for Jenny's unconditional support and love. There's nothing like best friends to get us through the tough times.

By two a.m., I abandon all efforts to fall sleep. Instead, I pull a romance novel out of my suitcase and read a story where life isn't filled with messy family dramas. Thirty minutes later, unable to concentrate, I set the book down, wondering how long it took Morgan to be comfortable knowing that Robert Hart was her biological father. Finally, exhaustion has me falling into a deep sleep.

Some time later, sharp hunger pangs have me waking up with a jolt. Looking at the clock on the nightstand, I'm surprised to see it's already after 10:00

and bright sunlight is streaming through the window. I order room service before calling downstairs.

"What time does the mail carrier usually deliver mail?" Anticipation has me antsy. "I'm expecting a delivery."

"It's usually delivered by three," the front desk clerk says, before adding, "We notify guests as soon as we receive a package. Have a good—"

"I'll be here." I don't let her finish her sentence. I'm anxious to have the vial so I can collect my saliva sample and return it. Potentially having a new sister and cousin is strange, but exciting, too. Granted, my resemblance to Morgan is uncanny, but, still, a part of me doesn't want to get *too* emotionally invested before I have the verifiable, scientific truth. I've come too far to not go all the way to find out as much as I can. I've been an only child my entire life, and, now, new possibilities are everywhere.

I'm halfway through the first of many movies I'll be watching today, knowing I'm too distracted to drive anywhere when a loud knock on the door has me jumping off the bed and running to open it. "Oh, it's just you." Stepping aside, I indicate the dresser space I've cleared for my food.

"I'm sorry." The room service attendant sets the large circular tray down on the table along with a large carafe of coffee, and some cream and sugar. "Were you expecting someone else?"

"No, not really."

"Oh." She wrinkles her brow, looking at me strangely before lifting the metal cover off the plate. "You have sausage, bacon, two scrambled eggs, waffles, maple syrup, and coffee."

"Thank you," I mumble before handing her a tip. My current level of stress requires a heavy dose of comfort and, right now, it will have to be in the form of food.

Five minutes later, just as I've finished cutting my waffles into bite-sized pieces, there's another knock on the door. Opening the door, I say, "Hopefully you're bringing extra maple syrup and possibly another waffle?"

"Pardon?" It's not room service bringing me more syrup; it's a hotel clerk from downstairs bringing me my package. "I believe this is for you."

"Thank you," I force myself to inhale as I begin to close the door.

"I need your signature." He holds out a clipboard and pen.

"Of course." I scribble my name on the confirmation form and, once he's gone, I sigh with relief.

After tearing open the box, I read the instructions four times. I need to get this right. The last thing I need is an email saying I did not provide enough saliva to fill the vial, which, according to the directions, is a common occurrence. To be on the safe side, I add slightly more than requested, before securing the top back on the vial, placing it in the self-addressed, stamped envelope. Foregoing makeup and combing my hair, I change out of my pajamas into shorts and a T-shirt then head to the nearest post office.

Once the package is mailed, the rest of the day passes in a blur of film and snacks. Both father #2 and Miguel call, but, not in the mood to speak to anyone, I let the calls go to voicemail. I'm not sure how I now feel about my father and our awkward relationship, and I need to distance myself from Miguel—pull back from the intimacy and enjoy the friendship. Plus, he could probably use some breathing room after the earful he got yesterday.

Morgan and Elaine have been fine all this time without me adding complications to their lives. What will they tell people if a cousin-slash-sister suddenly emerges from out of nowhere? Their carefully concealed family secrets will be on display for the world to view and all because of me. The smartest thing I can do is wait for my results and then bow out gracefully, while I still have some remaining dignity. I'll exit everyone's lives: my father's so he can start fresh with Melissa, Miguel's so he can be with Taylor, and Elaine's and Morgan's so they can maintain their lives without interruption.

Chapter 20

*Leah*

Four days later, I'm folding my clothes and placing them in my suitcase when I hear someone pounding on the door. I've sworn off room service food for the rest of my life, so I'm not expecting anyone.

Opening the door, I see Miguel and I'm not surprised he appears upset—probably because I haven't been answering his calls.

"Are you going to let me in?" He runs a hand through his hair and cautiously peers at me as if I'll close the door on him at any moment.

"Of course." I pause long enough to wish I had bothered to comb my hair and put on something other than the same wrinkled pink pajamas with dancing green elephants on them I've worn for the last couple of days.

"I've been trying to reach you." Miguel takes in my disheveled appearance but is too much of a gentleman to comment. He looks good, with his black jeans and a midnight blue shirt. "What's going on?"

"Have a seat." Indicating the bed, I look down, avoiding his piercing gaze. So much for being able to quietly escape. "I'm great." The quiver in my voice betrays the mixed emotions swirling inside.

"What's this?" Nodding toward the open suitcase,

he continues, "Are you getting ready to leave without answering my phone calls or saying goodbye?"

Anger, I can deal with, but he sounds more hurt than anything else, which makes me feel like crap. "I'm sorry." Sighing heavily, I stand stiffly by the window. "I… didn't want to bother you. I know you have one or two more hikes to take the ladies on this week." I don't mention his relationship with Taylor. I'm certain she hasn't appreciated me consuming so much of his time—time he could be spending with her.

"That's bullshit. I'm finally done with the morning hikes."

His voice is gruff, and his dark brows come together in a scowl. I've never seen Miguel this angry. "This is *not* how friends treat each other."

"You're right." Heat infuses my cheeks as I acknowledge my mistake. It's cowardly not to speak to him directly, but I've been protecting my heart more than anything else. I've hated the thought of saying goodbye to the man who's been in my heart all along. "I'm sorry, but I… need to get back."

"For what?" He joins me near the window and forces me to face him. "School won't start for another five weeks."

"True." Lifting my chin, I add, "However, a lot of preparation goes into being ready for the first day of school."

"Yeah, right." He eyes me with an expression of steely determination. "You owe me."

"I do?" Now I'm confused. "I said I'm sorry. What more do you want?"

"You'll find out in due time, but, for now, it'd be nice if you put on some clothes for a start."

"There's no reason for me to get dressed." I tug the bottom of my pajama top. "I'm not going anywhere." Wiggling my nose, I add, "Besides, I'd need to shower first."

"Good idea," he says with a smirk as he picks up the remote control before turning on the television. "You've been in this room too long. I'm taking you out."

"You're being bossy," I say defensively even though I know he's right. I *have* been in this room too long, ruminating on the turn my life has taken. I now have two fathers I'm not close to. I can live with that, but to know that Miguel doesn't share my feelings is breaking my heart. I said I love you and he never said he loves me back. Now that hurts, more than I could have imagined.

"You're right." He chuckles before adding, "And I'm not taking *no* for an answer, so don't take too long. Let's get out of here."

"All right." No need to deny myself a little more time with him before I return the rental car and go back to my life in Sunnyville. Making my way to the bathroom, a part of me wishes he would join me under the cascading warm water so we can make love one more time. As I remove my clothes and step into the shower, I know *that* will never happen, except in my dreams.

Forty minutes later, I'm riding beside him in his car, unsure of our destination. Rays of bright sunlight stream through the open window. After staying huddled in my room for the last few days, everything looks startling bright, and I'm reminded that, no matter what I'm going through, the world continues as if nothing

---

has changed.

"I like that dress." Miguel gives me an appreciative perusal while waiting for a light to change. "You look especially beautiful in red."

"It's the only thing that isn't already in my suitcase or dirty." The bright red dress with a scooped neckline is one of the last gifts my mother bought me before she died and, when I wear it, I always feel close to her. I'd brought it on this trip thinking that maybe my father and I might try the new French restaurant in town—yet another failed plan.

"Are you going to tell me why you ignored my calls?" His angry tone has been replaced with curiosity.

"I did the DNA test." I know that's *not* the answer he was expecting, but I'm not about to confess my love for him *again*. I've got to start protecting my heart, and creating distance between us seems like a good beginning.

"Why?" It's clear that he can't possibly understand my need to have proof of who I am. "There's *no* mistaking that you and Morgan are sisters."

"For my own knowledge." My chest constricts as I review my decision to leave my newly discovered family.

"Yeah, but who you are is obvious."

We drive by the newly renovated trailer park and toward the foothills before he says anything else.

"Is this about Robert Hart accusing you of being a liar?"

"Let's just say, I feel better having scientific evidence to back-up the truth."

"I don't have to ask about the results." Smiling, he rolls down the windows and the scent of fresh citrus fills the car as he slowly approaches the two-lane road leading to his mother's inn.

I think he's about to pull into the parking lot, but he continues driving up the winding road. So much for one of her delicious meals.

As we pass the inn, a rush of memories surfaces, mostly of me wanting him so badly that it hurts like a knife piercing my heart, and the anguish of knowing the feeling isn't mutual.

Taking a deep breath, I refocus on the present. "It was all there." I had eagerly opened and read the contents of the email that would forever alter my life. "I couldn't stop staring at the bold lines genetically connecting me to a string of new relatives, including Elaine and Morgan—clear evidence that I *am* a Hart."

"How do you feel about that?" Finally, he stops along the side of a road. After putting the car in PARK, he drapes an arm across the back of the seat and faces me. "Tell me what you're thinking."

"Honestly, I don't know." I swallow the ache in my throat, fight the mixed emotions, making it difficult for me to formulate my thoughts.

"Fair enough." Unbuckling his seat belt, he steps out of the car and walks around to open my door. "It would be a lot for anyone to process."

"Take a walk with me." Grasping my hand in his, he leads me up a slope, and the sound of soft jazz fills the air.

"Wait." I tug his arm, bringing him to an abrupt halt. "Isn't this near Elaine's house?"

"It could be." With a mysterious smile on his face, he pulls me closer, encouraging me to keep walking.

"Hold on a minute." In the distance, the stucco roof

and jutting chimney of Elaine's home is visible. Panic surges through me. This is going to be awkward; it'd be so much easier if I never see her or Morgan again. But, of course, Miguel doesn't know anything about my plan to slip out of town quietly. "This *is* Elaine's house."

"You're no dummy." He chuckles and, with the long strides of a man who exercises daily, he increases his pace, leaving me behind.

Rushing to join him, I catch up and yank his arm. "We can't barge in on them." Apprehension has me wanting to run back to the safety of his car. Why didn't Miguel tell me he wanted to come here? Seeing Elaine again and knowing it will be the second and last time I'll ever see my sister, Morgan, will be painful. "I'll wait in the car," I say hastily. Relief washes over me as I think of my escape.

"We're here now," he says, as if leaving isn't an option. "Please."

And, with that one simple word and his encouraging nod, I reluctantly give in. "Okay, but this better be quick."

From the outside, it looks as if every light in the house is on, and several cars are parked along the rustic road.

"They obviously have company."

"Obviously."

Disregarding me, he continues until we are standing in the bright light of the front porch. What sounds like live music streams from several open windows.

"You okay?" He lifts a brow before brushing his lips against my cheek.

Hesitating, I look at the rows of orange groves off

in the distance. Conflicting emotions surface, making my heart beat faster and my palms sweat. "Sure," I say shakily, while smoothing the front of my dress. "I don't want to stay long. Let's just say hello and then get out of here."

"All right." He smooths a curl off of my cheek. "Whatever you want."

Clearly, we both know that's not true or I wouldn't be standing in front of Elaine's door, listening to the buzz of voices inside as Miguel rings the doorbell.

"I'm so glad you could make it." Elaine opens the door, and she looks stunning with her shoulder length hair swept back and wearing a red jumpsuit that outlines her svelte figure. A tall man with golden brown skin stands by her side. "This is David, my husband."

"Welcome to the family." David wraps me in a warm embrace, before tilting his head toward Miguel. "Hey, man." The two men engage in a complicated handshake that ends in the tapping of each other's fist. David indicates a wine bar in the corner of a spacious room with a high-beamed ceiling. "What can I get you to drink?" He's completely relaxed, the consummate host.

I take in the people clustered in small groups chatting with each other and laughing. "I uh…" Fumbling with my hands, I glance to the side, uncertain if I'd heard him correctly. Did he say *family*? Of course, it makes sense Elaine would tell her husband about me, which means that I've misjudged her. Perhaps her and Morgan aren't trying to hide my existence after all. "Whatever you have will be fine."

"Surprise her." Elaine looks lovingly at her husband.

"Good idea. I think I know something she may like." Facing Miquel, he adds, "I'll let you get your own drink." David chuckles, as he heads toward the bar.

"I am a bit thirsty and since I have to serve myself, I'll leave you two ladies alone." Miquel brushes a curl off my forehead before leaving us.

"Don't worry, David makes great drinks." Elaine winks and takes my arm. "I promise you won't be disappointed."

"Okay." I'm still having difficulty piecing together a complete sentence as I absorb the fact that Elaine and David greeted me with genuine warmth.

"Slow down." Elaine's voice is firm as she halts two teenage girls, one white, and one black, who pick that moment to rush past us. But they aren't quick enough to avoid Elaine's outstretched arm. "No running in the house. Meet your Aunt Leah Ann."

"Hello, Auntie Leah Ann," they murmur in unison before surprising me with perfunctory hugs then dashing off.

"Your daughters?" I mumble as strange new feelings bubble up inside me. Is this what it means to be surrounded by family—people automatically accepting you and giving you hugs?

"No, I have one daughter, at least so far." Her smile widens as she mentions her child. "Twyla is upstairs with the nanny right now. Those are *Morgan's* daughters, Trisha and Bailey."

"Did someone say my name?" Morgan appears, looking sexy in a chartreuse mini skirt and matching silk blouse with a plunging neckline. "I saw my girls dash by and knew I better check to make certain they didn't cause any damage."

"They are lovely." It was obvious the two teenagers are having fun as they navigate their way around the adults. It's good to see Morgan again, even if it makes my leaving more difficult.

"I think so too—most of the time." Chuckling, she links her arm with mine. "Sorry that Dakar—that's my husband—couldn't make it. He's been deluged with work at the hospital and won't be able to join us until the end of summer. I didn't want to wait for him to fly out from South Africa to have our welcome party."

"South Africa?" I push down the disappointment that rises up in my chest. Is that where Morgan lives? I didn't want to say good-bye, but I liked knowing she lived in the same state.

"I know it sounds crazy, but we live there most of the year. I do some grant writing on the side, but I'm also a teacher, so I bring the girls back to California each summer. They have family connections in both places that we don't want them to lose."

"That makes sense." I have to mention the fact that we happen to be in the same profession. "By the way, I'm a teacher, too."

Morgan's eyes widen and she gasps as she brings a hand to her chest. "We have a lot in common, don't we? Later, we'll have to get together and have a nice long talk where we can take our time and really get to know each other." Her eyes mist up before she adds, "I can't think of anything better than finding out I have another sister to love. But, for now, we've decided to not be selfish, so we'll share you with our friends and other family members."

"We hope that's okay." Elaine peers at me from

under her long lashes.

"We wanted you to know how happy we are to have you in our lives," Morgan says as David walks up with two glasses in his hands. "Plus, people want to get to know you as much as we do."

"Wine coolers for the lovely ladies." David hands one glass to Elaine and the other to me. "This wine is from the Montoya's vineyard." He notices Morgan. "Can I get you anything?"

"Nope, I'm fine. Someone is headed this way, who, no doubt, wants to speak to you, Leah Ann. Meanwhile, I'm going to mingle." She gives me a genuine smile. "Let's not forget to exchange numbers before you leave."

"Sounds good." And it does. The prospect of having all these new people—new *family*—is a little daunting, but mostly exciting. It's always been my mother and me with the occasional visits with my father.

"Leah Ann."

Recognizing the familiar deep voice, I spot my father making his way in my direction. Has it only been several days since I last saw him and Melissa? It feels like it was a lifetime ago. So much has happened since I left their house.

I hide a small smile. He's wearing an emerald green shirt with beige slacks. Melissa has been a good influence on him in terms of getting him to agree to wear something besides brown every day.

"Excuse me. I have to talk to my father."

We meet in the middle of the living room and the tension dissipates after I embrace him. We move to the sofa by a large fireplace.

"I've missed you." Clearing his throat and taking a deep breath, he continues, "After I left you, I regretted sharing so much information. It was probably too much."

"It was quite a bit to take in." I pause as I struggle to put my thoughts into words. "I'm glad you told me. It explained a lot of things about our relationship and why it always felt, well… not quite right."

"You can say it. At times, I wasn't the *best* father. I regret that now. Hope to do better the second time around. My father was never around, so I didn't have a clue as to how to be a dad, and then, with the situation, I'm afraid I got worse." Pursing his lips and with a heavy sigh, he takes my hand in his. "I'm sorry. Just know that I *do* love you very much, and if you are willing to give it a chance, I'd like it if we could start over. After all, you're going to have a little brother."

"You know it's a boy already?" Something inside me melts at his heartfelt words and at the prospect of having a baby brother. "I'm excited at the thought of being a big sister, and yes, I'd love it if we can start fresh." I blink back a tear. "I'm grateful you told me, otherwise, I wouldn't have met more of my family. And, honestly, I am happy to consider *you* my one and only true father." Leaning forward, I kiss his cheek. "I love you, Dad, and always have. Honestly, I'm happy for you and Melissa. She's great and you two are obviously good together."

"That means the world to me." His glistening eyes and quick sniffle let me know he's feeling as moved as I am. "Through everything, I have *always* loved you. You need to know that. I'm not sure if I said it before, but I'm saying it now." He gives me a rare embrace before clearing his throat. "Melissa wants to say hello, too, but I can't get her to leave the buffet table. At this point, her appetite has more than doubled."

"Well, she *is* eating for two now!" Our laughter clears the air and lightens the mood.

"Leah." It's Miguel and he's headed in our direction. Earlier, I saw him chatting with Taylor and Aaron, but he's returned now and stands by my side after shaking my father's hand. "Hello, Mr. James. Sorry to interrupt, but do you mind if I borrow your daughter?"

As Miguel joins us, holding his arm toward me, the impact of his use of the word *daughter* solidifies the truth of who has been my father all along— imperfect relationship and all.

"By all means," my father says. I finally understand that this man will *always* be my father, regardless of the results of any genetics test, just like Morgan and Elaine will always be my family because of the genes we share.

My father nods as he heads toward Melissa, who's standing at the table, but not before, he gives Miguel a quick wink.

"Did my father just wink at you?" I ask Miguel. "You saw it, right?"

"Yes, I did." He says casually. "I don't have any idea what that was about. However, I hope you don't feel that I deceived you by not telling you where we were going."

"You actually did bring me here on false premises, but I can't really complain, not when I'm having such a nice time. The truth is I'm grateful and more than a little overwhelmed."

Soft Lies and Hard Truths

"Would food help? Miquel says.

"Most definitely." With an ache in my chest, I face that I'm falling more in love with Miquel by the minute and there's nothing I can do about it.

"We will eat. I promise, but first let me show you one more thing." He leads me out, beyond the dinette, and through a sliding door leading to a spacious tree lined backyard, toward a white wooden fence. The scent of jasmine is everywhere, and I see that several jasmine shrubs border the yard.

"If you insists, but I warn you, I'm not up to talking to anyone else right now. I need a minute to catch my breath."

"That's completely understandable." When he takes my hand in his, I cling to it, and recall the night we shared knowing that it was a once in a lifetime experience that I will always cherish.

"How did it go with Taylor?" I sound as nonchalant as I can, as if it doesn't pain me to know that he's in a relationship with another woman.

"I'm not sure what you're talking about." Bewildered, he rubs his jaw. "If you are still imagining that Taylor and I are an item, you are wrong. She's aggressive and I admit she tried, but you need to trust me, she and I were never a couple. I have always been honest with you."

"I do believe you." I peer into his eyes and can finally see that he *is* telling the truth about not being involved with Taylor. "I owe you an apology. My own insecurities have prevented me from being able to take you at your word and you deserve better."

"Apology accepted." He pulls me to him, holding me so close that I feel his heart beat. "I want the best

317

for you."

"I know and appreciate it." I could stay nestled against his chest like this forever, but he releases me from his embrace and nudges me forward.

"Let's continue our walk." He leads me down a narrow, stone-lined path.

"I don't have the right shoes on for one of your long hikes." Glancing back at the house, I add, "Plus, Elaine and Morgan went through a lot of trouble to throw this party, so I don't want them to think I left without saying goodbye."

"Don't worry, I told them we were stepping out and that we'd be back."

We continue in silence for several minutes before I stop in my tracks. "What are we doing *here*?" There's no disguising the irritation in my voice. Miguel has led me to Robert Hart's house. I'm not ready to see my biological father again—if ever. It's been a perfect evening—until now.

"Don't worry. I promise you that Robert Hart is nowhere in the vicinity." Miguel's grin is wide as he steps closer to the house. "Do you notice *anything* different?"

"No." The grass is still overgrown with sprigs of flowers emerging through the cracked cement leading to the faded front door. The garage leans to one side, as if it could fall over at any moment. "It's the same as when I saw it the other day."

"Look closer." His brown eyes focus on the neglected lawn. "What do you see?"

"Nothing." I say slowly... but then... I *do* notice what's different.

Actually, it's not *what* I see, but what I *don't* see—

the For Sale sign is gone.

"Good for him. He sold the house. Hopefully that means, I won't run into him when I visit Morgan and Elaine."

"*I* bought the house," Miguel says triumphantly as he wraps his arm around my shoulder.

"*You* bought the house?" Baffled, I stare at him. "For God's sake, *why*?" Was this his way of telling me he's not ever going back to Sunnyville? A sense of loss engulfs me, as I imagine not seeing his gorgeous face every day.

Love lost.

But a love I never really had.

"Robert moved to Littleton, and I don't think any of us will be seeing much of him. I've been saving to buy a house."

"I see." The thought of living away from Miguel fills me with sadness—though, it's probably for the best. It's time to move on with my life. After all, not everyone has a happily-ever-after ending unless they're a character in a fairy tale. "I'm sure you'll be able to fix it to your liking."

"I was hoping you'd help." Pulling me closer, he frames my face with his hands. Brushing my hair back from my face, his lips explore mine, kissing me deeply until my legs feel weak.

Bringing my arms around his neck, I return his kisses with all the passion I feel for this man, before pausing long enough to say, "Of course, I'll help you decorate, but it's not like I live here."

"Leah, I have been in love with you since the day we met when you saved me from failing fourth-grade math."

His voice is filled with desire and longing, has me numb with shock and disbelief.

"Miguel, how could I have been so blind to what I now see so clearly?" I murmur, standing back and searching the face I know so well. Gazing at his dark eyes, I feel the unmistakable passion that matches what I feel for him. *Did* I know but hadn't been able to believe it? Is *this* what my mother was hinting at when she stated that Raymond was not the man for me? She'd known all along that it was Miguel.

Always Miguel.

"I've loved you from afar, even when you were in love with someone else." There's no anger in his words, but the disappointment comes through.

"I love you so much, that my heart has been aching thinking that the feeling wasn't mutual. I'll always be grateful for this trip. This is where I faced the fact that you are the person that makes me smile, laugh, and feel completely secure." Shaking my head, it's hard to acknowledge that I almost missed out on this once in a lifetime type of love. "I only thought I was in love before, but now I *know* that what we have is the real thing."

"My love for you has grown throughout all these years. It's never going anywhere. You've had *so* much going on in your life that I was willing to wait until things settled down. And now that they have, I don't want to wait anymore. I want to make this *our* home, and you, *my* woman."

"I like the sound of that." Placing my hand on his chest, I say, "I'll be your woman as long as you'll promise to be my man."

"Consider it already done." Sweeping me up in his

arms, he swirls me around in a circle before setting me down again. "I'm glad I never gave up on you."

"Me too." I glance out of the corner of my eye at the neglected house. "I can't believe you really bought this house."

"This house should rightfully be yours by inheritance, and, now, it is. Yours and mine, my dear sweet Leah—the woman of my dreams."

"A healed relationship with my father—Elaine, Morgan, you, and now *this* house…" I move toward the house and throw my hands in the air. My breath comes out jagged and uneven, and because my legs are too wobbly to support me, I sit on the ground, head bent as tears of joy stream down my face. I choke out, "My whole world has turned right side up."

"I'm here." Miguel sits beside me, wrapping his arms around my waist.

"I'd planned to leave today—to go back to Sunnyville and resume my life without…" I wave my arms, "… you."

"That would have broken a lot of people's hearts, including mine." He caresses my back.

"I wanted what I thought was best for everybody." I snuggle closer to him, feeling the warmth of his body near mine, the tenderness of his touch, the sincerity of his words. "But, what I really wanted, but feared I could never have is you in my life." I fling my arms wide smiling so hard it hurts. "You and me together. Always. Your family and mine nearby." A feeling of deep joy flows over me as the truth of the statement sinks in. "My vote would be building bonds that last forever, making a life with the man I love."

"Is it too soon to tell you I informed your father I

plan to share my home and my life with you by my side?"

"Ahhh, so that's what the wink was about." I never would have envisioned my father and Miguel having a heart-to-heart talk.

"I wanted him to know I was serious about you." He trails tender kisses along my neck. "Together, we'll erase all signs of the last owner and create our own bright new future. You should also know that the next time we stay in the honeymoon cottage it will be for real. As in will you be my wife, Ms. Leah Ann James?"

"The answer, Mr. Miguel Montoya is yes—a thousand times yes. I will be your wife, for always and forever. I'm ready for this new chapter with you."

"You have made me one happy man." His next kiss is so long and deep that it leaves me lightheaded.

When we finally come up for air, I add, "There's one thing that I have to mention."

"Yes?" He asks cautiously. "What is it?"

"Jenny's going to insist that before we move in here, we'll need to burn sage to get rid of all the bad energy from the previous owner."

"That's fine with me. She's welcome anytime. I know how much she means to you. She can light candles, burn incense, and even place crystals on all the counters."

"Be careful what you say; that sounds exactly like what she'll want to do."

Holding hands, the light and the laughter envelop us as we head back inside.

Engrossed in our own thoughts, we walk across the patio and through the open double doors.

"Stay right there." He stops me before I can take

another step. "I'll be right back, my love."

"I won't move." While waiting for him, I take in all the people who are here to welcome me, and my soul is bursting with indescribable joy and a sense of belonging.

The pianist is playing a whimsical song while Elaine and David dance together, and Morgan holds hands with her two daughters, twirling them around the room.

Miguel returns with a champagne flute for each of us. "To our love." His voice brims with the promise of new beginnings, and he's never looked more handsome and desirable than he does right now.

Basking in the glow of being cherished and loved by the man I adore, I'm filled with an exhilaration I could never have imagined. Only a month ago, I'd thought I'd had the worst luck in love and with family, and, now, I have an abundance of people who are eager to know me and welcome me with genuinely open arms.

"To never giving up on love." Raising my glass in a toast, I silently vow to always push through the dark days until the sun comes shining through.

## A word about the author...

Dalia Dupris has been a bibliophile as long as she can remember. She's always excited about the prospect of opening the pages of a new novel and becoming immersed in a well-told story. She has won two EMMA awards and is a Romance Writers of America Spectrum Grant recipient. Dalia's degree in English Literature from UCLA and a Masters Degree in Social Work from the University of Southern California, in addition to many years of experience as a licensed psychotherapist, contribute to her relatable characters and her ability to create multicultural, emotion-driven novels with complex plots. In her spare time, she enjoys bike riding along California beaches with her husband, and hiking with her daughter. She loves hearing from her readers. To learn more about Dalia and her books check out www.daliadupris.com and https://linktr.ee/DaliasBooks. http://daliadupris.com